REAL LOVE

Natasha watched him swallow a moan and open his eyes, his palms again finding her arms, the edges of his thumbs moving over her breasts till her head dropped back. The pull against him was instant. The palm at the small of her back was a heated flat grip that soon covered her backside while his mouth sought hers. The kiss produced delirium, a level of insanity that she hadn't expected or experienced. The soft wetness of his mouth made her pelvis fuse to his. The hardness against her belly nearly made her cry out, but his deepening kiss smothered it. She broke away from his mouth needing air, only to find her breath halted by the long, wet, burning kisses he landed upon the swell of her breasts. The sensation he created made her turn into the attention, lift herself, panting, edging her breasts up to the low-cut top of her dress if he would just take the sting away with his lips.

KEEPIN' IT REAL

Leslie Esdaile

Kensington Publishing Corp.
http://www.kensingtonbooks.com

DAFINA BOOKS are published by

Kensington Publishing Corp.
850 Third Avenue
New York, NY 10022

All Kensington titles, imprints and distributed lines are available at special quantity discounts for bulk purchases for sales promotion, premiums, fund-raising, educational or institutional use.

Special book excerpts or customized printings can also be created to fit specific needs. For details, write or phone the office of the Kensington Special Sales Manager: Kensington Publishing Corp., 850 Third Avenue, New York, NY 10022. Attn. Special Sales Department. Phone: 1-800-221-2647.

Dafina and the Dafina logo Reg. U.S. Pat. & TM Off.

First Printing: May 2005
10 9 8 7 6 5 4 3 2 1

Printed in the United States of America

This story is for all of us who have secret gifts and talents but may not have realized them yet—simply because the way others have defined us has made us absorb misinformation about ourselves. But if we look deeply and allow our hearts to see our own profound inner beauty, we can "keep it real." Be encouraged, for you are special and have value, so share that unique light!

Special acknowledgment goes to my agent, Manie Barron, who always sees something special inside me; to my editor, Karen Thomas, who allows my voice to be heard in its own timbre; to my daughter, Helena, who I knew from the moment I conceived, was a very special gift from God . . . and to two other very special people in my life— my stepmother, Pat, who sees so much and who provides constant encouragement and love, and to Zulma Gonzalez, an angel, a sister–friend, somebody with a unique brand of caring that is so real. Bless you!

Chapter 1

Miami, Present day . . .

In just the short walk from her air-conditioned Lexus across the parking lot to the frigid television studio, Natasha could feel the humidity climb up her back, matt her jewel green blouse to her spine, and threaten perspiration exposure on her electric blue crepe suit.

"Not today," she breathed quietly. She could feel the insufferable morning heat opening her pores and siphoning out an oily t-zone on her face. But she dared not attempt to blot it away without a mirror. Thank God she wore her hair in short natural twists, anything else under Miami's sweltering, liquid heat would have rendered her head a disaster. That was all she'd need. Image was everything.

Today, *everything* had to be perfect. She had to look the part, play the role, and go into that meeting with authority to face a bunch of old fart television executives from the network.

Never let 'em see you sweat. She said the TV commercial phrase over and over again like a mantra as she smiled tensely, flashed her ID to the security desk, and offered a quick morning greeting.

Her pace quickened as a coworker passed her and stated flatly, "Another hot one, huh, 'Tash."

Oh, yeah, she was on a mission. The ladies' room was in sight, and she needed to get in there to repair Mother Nature's damage before anyone else saw her, especially one of the bigwigs.

As Natasha pushed through the door, she began to relax—that is, until she stood in front of the mirror. Her face looked like an oil slick. Mascara was beginning to smudge at the corners of her eyes. Now, with beads of perspiration on her brow and her face brandishing a high sheen under the glaring fluorescent lights, her lipstick seemed just a little too shiny against her dark, ebony skin. She sighed loudly, and glanced at herself in profile, then shivered as much from the freezing temperature inside the building as she did from a case of raw nerves. Yes, the suit was fly, but if she'd just gone to the gym a few more times to possibly reduce the shelf her backside created in it . . .

Suddenly, she felt paralyzed as she looked at her reflection. Every flaw, real or imagined, came to light in the huge, unforgiving bathroom mirror. Every hurt that had been slung at her, every time she'd been teased for being the tall, skinny, dark-skinned girl with the big butt and knobby knees and knotty hair came back to haunt her. She could feel her heart racing, each heavy, erratic thud straining against her breastbone. All the hard work she'd invested to improve her self-esteem, all the studying, all the career achievements, truncated into a single mental whisper: What if you're not good enough? What if they'd been right?

Setting down her portfolio with care, she began to dig in her purse to find her makeup to repair the external damage. She blotted away oil with pressed powder, refusing to allow the demons of the past to steal her confidence. No. She would not be moved. It didn't matter that her mother said she was in a whore's industry and needed to go to church, settle down, come home, and get married.

Natasha snatched a tissue off the counter and pressed it between her lips to tone down her lip gloss. Yeah, right. Come home to the backwoods of Florida and do what? Marry who? At twenty-eight, with two degrees, some common sense, and an unwillingness to share her man were a marital liabilities, in this day and age. The pickings were slim. What was she supposed to do, have five children and raise them alone, like her momma did, with the church as her husband? Not. What was the point of going to college, then? Shoot, she was still paying off student loans!

Adjusting each twist, she worked with her semi-damp hair, trying to get each spiral to sit just right. She needed a funky-urban-cosmopolitan look to go with her slammin' presentation. A sister usually only got one shot at the title, and this morning was her big chance. The thing that was scaring the bejeebers out of her was the fact that, she'd proposed her concept offhandedly in a meeting with the boss. It had been a lark, a quick answer to make it seem like she was really paying attention in the boring brainstorming session. It had only been meant as something witty to say when she'd been zoning out. But the man had stood up, applauded her for a fresh idea, and had called in the big dawgs. Oh, Lord . . . *what had she done?*

Immediately, she pushed everything else from her mind and began rehearsing her pitch for the umpteenth time. Okay, she had the credentials—Florida A&M undergrad, NYU Communications program for graduate studies. She could do this. She'd lived in the Big Apple, where these old boys were probably from. She was a top-notch TV producer in her own right, and the industry was kind to young, fresh ideas. So what that her concept had been formulated during a male bashing session with her girlfriends on a bar stool?

Natasha froze. This was the craziest, most off the hook, ridiculous risk of her career. She was gonna go into a boardroom meeting and tell a bunch of sixty-year-old white men about the troubles young, upwardly mobile, educated, single African-American women had in finding a life partner—and these old guys were going to just nod, empathize, and agree to drop goo-gobs of money on a hip, urban-targeted, singles-mating-game reality television show? Oh, my God!

She began packing her makeup away with a vengeance, instant defeat claiming her. Maybe it wasn't too late to go back home and live with Momma and whoever else had crash-landed back at the old homestead. As the middle child and the ugly duckling in the Ward clan, she was used to being overlooked and ignored. Maybe she could just disappear and not be seen in the meeting, or at her mother's home. She was the conservative one; the one who'd played by all the rules and had never shamed her mother's name. Momma *had* to let her come home and heal after she humiliated herself and lost her job.

Maybe she could just find a job at a convenience

store. As long as she worked hard, her mother would have her back, right? Hard work had been her watchword, and her mother could use someone around the house to help out, any ole way. If she lost her job, that would be the only reasonable option. There was no way she could keep up her apartment, pay utilities, and the rest of her bills, not without a good job, so it was about scaling down—fast. Panic began to set in and Natasha dropped her makeup bag twice before she managed to get it back into her purse.

Plus, it wasn't like she would be dragging kids and a man back home with her. The last relationship she had with a philandering fool ended in three months, and that was over a year ago. She could even sleep on her mother's couch, if there was no room at the inn. Momma would let her come home to recover after they laughed her out of the boardroom this morning and then told her like Sir Donald had told so many, *You're fired.*

"Yo, man, I told you, we cannot book this event without a heavy deposit to secure the venue."

Tyrell listened to the litany of expenses that the booking agent for the Coliseum rattled off, his patience wearing thin. "Look, I know that we're a new label, but my artists are—"

"Brand new, haven't built a real following, and we are not booking any performances on spec. Got that? Now I suggest that you get your money together, and then you call us. Have a nice day, Mr. Ramsey."

Tyrell listened to the telephone abruptly disconnect in his ear and hurled his cell phone across the living room. This was complete bull. True, he wasn't P. Diddy, or Russell Simmons, but his artists had taken Hotlanta by storm. They'd done the chitterlin' circuit, and had served the crowds dirty south with cuts that were mad-crazy. His boyz could spit like nobody's business, and his crooners . . . sheeit. So why was he trapped in a day gig, selling insurance, while trying to also handle his business? It just wasn't right. And, he was trying his best not to go out like so many of his boys, running a little illegal product to build up his cash flow situation only to reinvest it in his dream enterprise.

Sure there were plenty of thug brothers with extra cash willing to invest, but that would mean being tied into something he'd never get out of. Silent partners weren't always silent, and once the cash started rolling, it would get stupid. However, it was becoming crystal clear that the sales commissions he'd used to start Off Da Meter Records would not be enough to sustain it, promote it, and make it pop like it needed to. Maybe they were right?

He stood and began pacing. But how right could they have been? He only had to think about his two older brothers who had done bids for getting caught up in the street game. No. He wasn't going out like that. He had to come up with twenty-five Gs, do a huge gig with a lot of PR hype, and make his money at the door through ticket sales. Then, he could roll that over to help get his CDs distributed properly, get enough to have the big chain stores stock his merchandise, and get the mega radio networks to give his artists airtime.

Tyrell put on his suit jacket and glanced at his briefcase with disinterest. If he'd just been a little taller . . . Being six-four with a wicked jump shot had gotten him into college and had paid for his business degree at North Carolina A&T, but it was too short for the NBA . . . just like his pockets were just a little too short to afford grad school. Now, at thirty-two, his pockets were too short to follow his dream, and all the wonderful plans he'd laid out on paper in a business plan weren't worth the toner that his laser printer had spit on the page.

Nobody legit wanted to give a young brother with no real collateral any small business loan to finance an entertainment business, not in this economic climate. All of his street smarts and blacktop ball-playing, junk-talking savvy had drawn artists looking for a shot to him, but he knew in his heart that another dry year without a big deal for at least one of them would start a mutiny. One by one they'd defect to larger labels, and before long his entire investment would have been for naught.

It wasn't about going back to his momma's crib as a failure, to sleep in his old bedroom in Roswell, to fight for the bathroom or the last of the Kool-Aid with his ex-felon brothers and their kids, when they fell by with their babies' mommas. His mother didn't deserve to have the one son who had made good, her baby boy, come home to leech off of her at her age. If anything, he should have been sending her money, not trying to get some crazy dream off the ground.

Slowly advancing toward his briefcase, Tyrell picked it up, straightened his tie, and grabbed his Honda keys. He had to get his head right. It was time to go to work.

* * *

"Good morning," Natasha said as professionally as possible. "Thank you all for coming." She glanced around the table, monitoring the tension in her boss's expression. If Nathan Greenberg was unnerved, that was not a good sign.

Perhaps what was worse was the fact that the VIPs she'd addressed from the network had only nodded and returned a curt, "Good morning," then had opened their folders in a silent signal for her to get to the point.

"We wanted to bring you gentlemen here to Miami to see our facility and to show you the terrain, a bit of the flavor of the—"

"Nate," a suit from the far end of the table said with impatience. "We're busy men, we've seen the Miami scene before, and only agreed to come down here because the golf is good." A round of gruff chuckles followed his comment, and he pushed back from the table and stared at Natasha hard. "We had other meetings nearby with our newest, Spanish-speaking acquisition—so we made time on our morning docket to hear your pitch for a new show concept. Miss Ward, talk to us."

Natasha nodded and picked up her laser pointer, working the laptop PowerPoint presentation as she began showing viewership statistics.

"We know, we know," another suit grumbled. "The American television market is going ethnic. That's not news. But we agree that reality television shows are hot—if you've got the right mix of pathos, drama, insanity, and the bizarre. What do you have? Get to the meat of the presentation. Skip the MBA preamble."

She could feel her armpits getting damp. But it was something in the arrogance of their tone that struck a nerve in her. If she was gonna lose her job, then she'd go out with a bang. Natasha straightened her spine the way she'd seen her mother who scrubbed floors do when a person thought he or she was better and addressed her mother in that same patronizing voice.

"You know what?" Natasha stated, trying to keep her tone icy-professional. "You don't have a clue about how to enter the so-called ethnic market, because you don't know what the people who click on the tube and surf the channels are interested in."

She walked away from the desk, and tossed the laser pointer on it with flare, enjoying the shocked expressions on their faces. The only person she felt sorry for was Nathan. He looked like he was about to have a coronary.

"What do young urbanites discuss at the clubs?" she asked, folding her arms over her chest. "Do you know?" It was a rhetorical question, and she loved every minute of watching the old boys squirm. "I didn't think so."

Emboldened by their obvious lack of knowledge she began slowly walking behind each chair, circling the table like a shark. "Young women, my age, want it all—a great career, a comfortable lifestyle, a great lover, who will ultimately turn into a great husband and father. We want the same things other women do, and would love to be Cinderella, just like other women do, whether they'll openly admit it or not. The fallacy of perception is that African-American women don't care about those things. That's what will make this proposed show more than leading edge—it'll be cutting edge."

Pausing for emphasis, Natasha stopped at the head of the table. "Believe it or not, it's about three times as hard for a young African-American female to find all of the above, because of the statistics that you interrupted me from showing you. But let me recap quickly."

Counting off the issues on her fingers, she spoke from the heart. "A large population of African-American baby boomers took advantage of the Civil Rights reforms and sent their kids to college. Only problem is that more young women than men actually made it out of the urban morass to go to college and finish, and then onward to find decent jobs. That, coupled with rising minority male incarceration rates, and a perilous drug culture, has created a significant imbalance. So, do you want to have the major ethnic purchasers within the urban market—ethnic women—with disposable income, watch your show, and be glued to their television sets and locked on your channel? Then give black women an opportunity, through a reality show, to find a black prince charming. Very simple."

Natasha held her breath as she watched the concept take root and transfix the old men around the table.

"That is absolute genius," one suit whispered, raking his manicured fingers through his blonde and silver hair.

"The buzz that would create," another said, sitting forward and making a tent with his hands before his mouth.

"The hair salons and churches will be on fire with show buzz," Natasha said without blinking, her idea stoking inner embers of conviction within her. "Imagine it, gentlemen." She held their steely gazes, unwavering. "You have these young, gorgeous sisters, who look like they've stepped out of the Miss Black U.S.A. contest, with long paper and hot degrees from the nation's best schools—five of them picked from thousands—on a yacht for ten episodes with ten fine, credit-checked, drug-free, baby-free, never-been-to-jail, eligible bachelors."

She could feel a smile tugging at her mouth as she began gesturing with her hands. "Latino men, to get the hottest, new crossover market, African-American men, Italian men, whatever, a mix, to ensure that the other markets also watch the show just to see if the sisters will go past race and culture to pick the best guy, or if they'll limit their options and go for the top candidate just because he's a brother. The talk radio shows will keep the issue at fever pitch. Let's put the theory to the test and let the best man win."

"Revolutionary," the lead executive exclaimed, closing his folder and pushing it away from him. "How will this all work?"

Nathan Greenberg cast a nervous glance around the group. "Ten weeks for the ten episodes. Every contestant would get twenty-five thousand for participating, with a waiver on the money if they just up and walk. That will be enough to encourage someone to give up their solid day job for two months with a cushion to find new employment, if they can't get a leave of absence."

"Yes," Natasha added. "The rules are simple. We have them all on a yacht to create tight living confines. We set up and coordinate five beautiful women and ten male studs on a chartered yacht originating out of Miami, for ten weeks. Right there, having a two-to-one ratio will be drama in and of itself, because currently, for a woman of color to find a single man of her same social-economic and educational status is normally a ten-to-one scenario not in her favor. It's like finding a needle in a haystack. And, once she finds him, getting him to be monogamous is a whole other can of worms. Most of the top-notch eligible men in her sphere, at that level, think they're God's gift to women. So, gentlemen, we're going to flip the script and make this an old-fashioned Sadie Hawkins dance." She sighed and sat down, knowing the odds all too well from a very personal perspective. If they couldn't grasp that sad reality, what more could she tell them?

"Natasha, is it *that* bad?" the lead executive asked, his gray eyes holding her line of vision, seeking answers.

For a moment, she didn't respond. The senior executive had a truly puzzled look on his face and he'd called her by her first name. Within the depth of his gaze she saw a true quest for understanding. The man really had no clue. Interesting.

"Ted, it's *that* bad," Natasha confirmed, taking the risk to use his first name and level the playing field within their interaction. "But during that live-in-close-quarters set up, each contestant will receive twenty-five thousand dollars just for being on the show, each having the chance of winning ten thousand each round, unless they are eliminated one by one, with a grand prize to the final pair standing of two hundred fifty thousand dollars. All our team has to do is come up with crazy assignment challenges for the group to test their mettle, and coordinate the film crew to follow the contestants day and night."

"Where will the yacht go?" the suit from the far end of the table asked, leaning forward again with interest.

"The venue is the Caribbean," Natasha said with a wry grin. "The yacht will stop at points along the way, and with each stop comes a daring challenge. The objective of the game is simple: each of the guys must win the hearts of *all* the ladies on the boat. To that end, sleeping with any of them during the competition would give one of the female contestants an unfair advantage. Therefore, if fraternizing is discovered, the female group can meet as a whole to vote the entangled pair off the boat. Conversely, just to keep it interesting and to create a reverse elimination process, each of the female contestants has to win the hearts of *all* the men onboard, because the final male standing will be given the choice of which female contestant he'd most like to be with—hence, determining the winner."

The senior executive threw his head back and laughed. "Natasha Ward, this is so outrageously insane, I think it just might be television history in the making. We will make a mint off this program, gentlemen." He glanced at the others who were also nodding, their once grim expressions giving way to broad smiles. "Our Latino affiliate will eat this up—this thing could go into syndication in foreign markets!"

"That's right, Ted," she said with conviction, keeping her focus on the decision maker in the room. "I've given this a lot of thought, and some old-fashioned graduate school research, too," she added, casually redressing the earlier dig. "For the first challenge, we'll take the contestants to the sumptuous Atlantis Hotel and Casino in the Bahamas, giving each male two thousand dollars to gamble with or to use in any way he feels best—the goal being to let the women see how each man handles his money and his business." Her gaze swept the men seated at the table. "You can tell a lot about a man by the way he makes financial decisions."

Satisfied when all heads nodded, Natasha pressed on, electricity of a near victory coursing through her. "After each round, the five women will caucus, will discuss the merits of each male contestant, then vote on who stays and who leaves. From there, we'll take the group to Jamaica for a hard-down physical endurance test to select the most physically fit specimen. It will be the male version of a t & a display of steel buns and rippling chests, six-pack abdominals, you know, a high ratings spike thing."

"That's awesome," Nathan said, his color much improved, along with his breathing. "People watch gambling, and love the physical-primal-sexual element spiced up with catfight type bickering."

Natasha nodded, although Nathan's comment was getting on her last nerve. "I did my homework," she said, issuing a sly wink at her boss to keep him pacified and silent. "Remember, the tension point is the fact that these young, attractive, athletic, and very stimulated contestants, who are living together in tight quarters and experiencing romantic Caribbean environs, are to remain civil with each other, *and* celibate, for *ten weeks*." She paused for dramatic effect and smiled broadly as the senior exec blew out a long whistle. "They'll have ten chances to make it or break it, and each challenge is designed to demonstrate the personal character and integrity of each man on that boat. Of course, St. Lucia is on the agenda to explore each man's romantic streak, with plenty of other exotic locales and challenges along the way."

"What could go wrong?" Nathan asked, now standing and talking with his hands. "This is genius.

Brilliant. 'Tash is on the cutting edge and the ratings will go through the roof! She's got a combination of *The Bachelor, Fear Factor,* scaled-down *Millionaire Celebrity Poker* . . . I don't know what all this young woman, who is obviously my best producer, has rolled into a very messy and very saleable ball of yarn. The human dynamics, the drama—"

The senior executive held up his hand and his tone took a dangerously serious turn. "Ms. Ward, what's the proposed name of the show?"

Natasha hesitated. This was the moment of truth. "Keepin' It Real," she said, forcing her voice to remain steady as her gaze locked with the senior executive's.

He nodded. "Keepin' It Real." He rubbed his jaw and stood up, making the others stand with him. "This was definitely worth a delay on the green. Sold. Make it happen."

Chapter 2

As soon as Natasha entered the club, she spotted her best friends Camille and Jorgette. She could instantly feel the fused reggae, Latin, and Caribbean music pulsing within Mango's Tropical Café. She rushed toward them as they stood up and squealed, the triumvirate laughing and hugging.

"You did it," Camille said, laughing, while spinning Natasha around. "We're so proud of you, lady!"

"Tell all," Jorgette demanded through hearty laughter. "Tell us how you slayed 'em at the boardroom table."

"Order the chile a drink," Camille chided, hailing a waitress. "Champagne for our sister-girl, and nothing but the best."

Pure excitement rippled through Natasha as she laughed and sat down. "I love you guys," she said, nearly tearing from the overwhelming emotions. "But I'm so scared."

"Scared?" Camille said, indignant, flipping her shoulder-length braids over her shoulder. She smiled at Natasha and peered over the top of her glasses, leaning in. "As your attorney, I forbid you to take a defensive posture. You've got this locked, hands down."

"That's right," Jorgette quipped, taking a liberal sip of her martini. "You ain't got nuthin' to be scairt of. We got'chure back. Told you that you could do it. So give up the tapes."

Natasha let her breath out slowly as she accepted her champagne flute from the waitress, all three women clinking their glasses in celebration. She was surrounded by love, her best girlfriends in the whole wide world, the only people who'd gone the distance from junior high school with her, through high school, and had remained fast friends even through their various college experiences.

As she sipped her champagne and gabbed about all the details of the board meeting, a certain peace settled into her bones. Maybe they were right. Maybe this was her time to shine. She studied her friends as they whooped and shared in her success.

Camille was the brilliant one, and now tall and sexy and beautiful. Her clothes were immaculate, always doing a fierce power suit, Prada shoes, newest Beamer, and top-of-the-line designer bags and accessories to match her pretty caramel skin, in a way that Natasha could never afford—but still, no steady man. It was unfathomable to Natasha. Camille was the sweetest, most sensible, smartest woman she knew. Her girlfriend had literally transformed into a butterfly, having lost the coke bottle glasses. With corrective dental surgery and a good weave, girlfriend was now da bomb.

Then there was Jorgette, the creative force of nature, who looked like an African goddess. Jorgette was a deep, rich shade of chocolate, and she wore beautiful, handcrafted art pieces—to call her necklaces, earrings, and bangles jewelry was an understatement. She had big, pretty eyes surrounded by lush lashes, a behind that made men turn around in the streets, and she swathed her gym-fit body in the most sumptuous fabric and colors from the motherland. She'd always admired Jorgette's carefree, graphics artist existence. She seemed in balance with the universe, but still had no steady man. Why?

Natasha could understand why she didn't cut the grade. She wasn't as pretty, or as witty, or as anything that her best friends were. She'd always gauged her ability to attract a mate by them, with the notion that if they couldn't find anyone, surely she was out of luck. But it was with that same sense of hopelessness bordering a tad on desperation that she'd come up with her brilliantly wacky concept for the show. Surely she and her girlfriends weren't the only sisters in America who were approaching thirty, were tired of the dating scene meat market, and wanted to be in a committed relationship, a marriage, where they could feel safe to begin families. Why was that basic human right so hard to come by these days?

"You're talking to us, but you're a million miles away, girlfriend," Camille said, laughing.

"Yeah, where's that big brain of yours off to now?" Jorgette asked, a little tipsy from her third martini.

"I was just thinking that none of this made any sense," Natasha replied, hailing the waitress for another champagne. "The fact that I can do a show about this whole man issue is absurd."

All three women raised their glasses, clinking them loudly.

"I mean, when's the last time a beautiful woman like you has gone out, Camille?"

Camille stared at Natasha, her smile fading a bit, and then falsely brightening. "Months," she stated flatly. "But, hey. I've got my condo, my hot wheels, my wardrobe, a solid 401K, and investments, plus a dynamite career, my freedom, and *no babies* or man telling me what to do."

"But are you happy?" Natasha asked, her tone quiet and gentle.

For a moment, no one spoke. Jorgette sipped her drink carefully and glanced at Camille.

"Well, you can't have it all," Jorgette finally said while Camille was formulating a witty comeback that never came. "See, me, I know that I'm way too eclectic for most brothers. Who's gonna deal with an artist who keeps wild hours and must have her space to be inspired by the Muse?"

"It's not right," Natasha said, taking a liberal sip from her glass. The champagne was going to her head as the bubbles tickled her nose, and the combination was making her morose. "I can understand why I couldn't pull one. My job keeps me under the gun, running all over the place, plus, with these teeth that are still too big for my face, and my big behind and—"

"Stop it," Camille said, her voice firm but her tone gentle. "You are perfect."

Jorgette nodded and covered Natasha's hand with hers. "Don't you go back to that old mess from yesteryear. You're tall, gorgeous, have a drop-dead Nubian figure and—"

"Oh, figures the artist in our crew would see some semblance to four-thousand-year-old wall carvings. But, I hate to tell you, Jorgette, these new millennium brothers are not feeling a sister with a B-cup and high behind." She forced herself to laugh and was dismayed when her girlfriends only joined in with weak titters.

"It's their problem, not yours. Besides, how did we get on this sour turn of conversation?" Camille asked, shaking her head. "Tonight is about what we have, not what we don't have."

"We're supposed to be celebrating your achievement, girl. What's wrong with you?" Jorgette added in, her tone becoming annoyed.

"I'm sorry," Natasha said, looking away at the dance floor. "You guys are right. I just don't know if I can handle this assignment."

"Oh, pullease," Camille said, ordering another round of drinks. "You are Miss Efficiency."

"Girl, you need to stop," Jorgette fussed. "You are the one who keeps everything straight."

Natasha looked at them both and then glanced down at her drink. "You know what bothers me the most?" She waited before continuing to be sure they wouldn't cut off her confession. She had to get this out, had to explain it to somebody who would listen and understand. "When I told that old geezer the premise of the show, he looked at me with pity, actual pity, in his eyes and said, 'Natasha, is it *that* bad?'" She let her line of vision settle on her stunned girlfriends. "I might have gotten this assignment because those old dudes really want to know one of our community's deepest schisms . . . not because I'm good, not because the whole thing makes sense, but because they know if they've tapped a misery vein, they can exploit it and get paid. And what hurts my soul is that I've contributed to this madness."

Camille sighed and squeezed Natasha's hand. "You, too, are about to get paid." She chuckled and downed her margarita. "Face it, this whole issue is a problem. You're simply bringing a national spotlight to it. If anything, you're reopening a dialogue that was once a hot topic and then it was like people forgot about it. A whole lot of sisters will thank you for making their pain known."

Natasha smiled. "Leave it to my attorney girlfriend to twist it around to make a compelling closing argument."

They all laughed.

"But think of the benefits," Jorgette said, her voice excited and conspiratorial. "You will have access to thousands of eligible men's records. You'll know where they live, if they have kids or not, their credit history—chile, when this is all said and done you will have the little black book of life!"

Natasha opened her mouth and closed it as Camille and Jorgette laughed hard and slapped high fives.

"Information is power, girlfriend," Camille stated flatly. "I want all eligible brothers who make over six figures on your list, fine or not, just pass them my way and let me sift for myself."

"That's a breach of confidentiality," Natasha said, shocked. "I can't just—"

"No," Jorgette interrupted, "what you can't do is let all that U.S. Grade A beef on the hoof go to waste." She pressed her point as they all laughed harder. "Girl, Camille is right. Just because they don't make the television-level-fine cut, doesn't mean they ain't fine. My biggest question is, how are you going to keep yourself together to sort through all those fine brothers without messing up?"

"That's right," Camille said, merriment making her hazel eyes sparkle before her lids slid closed. "I couldn't handle that—being on a yacht, in the Caribbean, watching all that buffness just romping in the sunlight . . . mmm, mmm, mmm. I'ma watch your show every episode, girl. Believe that!" Camille opened her eyes and polished off her drink and ordered another one. "If you're like me, you haven't had any in a couple of years."

Jorgette and Natasha's eyes opened wide. Jorgette mouthed the words, *two years.* Natasha's voice caught in her throat. It had been so long since Natasha had made love that she couldn't even estimate when it had been, if ever. Sure, she'd had sex before, but she knew they were all talking about more than that. What each of them was secretly seeking was the real, committed, caring experience where the person who was with you was solely with you, flaws and all . . . loving, kind, good.

"What?" Natasha finally whispered. "*You?*"

Camille smiled and nodded, and accepted her drink. Once the waitress had gone, she leaned in closely, making the others lean in to hear her whisper. "Y'all, there are days I'm so horny, I'm about to lose my mind, but I refuse to accept less than I deserve." She sat back, gathered her composure, brushed invisible lint off her chartreuse Ellen Tracy raw silk suit, and sipped her drink, stone-faced, fondling her freshwater pearls. "It's the price of success, I suppose."

"Dayum . . ." Jorgette murmured. She looked down her tied-dyed bright yellow mini wrap dress and at her cowry shell necklace, and then back up at the group. "And I thought it was just me. I wasn't about to risk my life with some fool who might be living on the DL or who had five chicks on the side. But a year and a half dry spell had me acquiring some mail order, battery-operated yang. Oh, close your mouth before you catch flies. Fantasy works. It beats a blank."

Natasha covered her mouth and laughed hard as Camille joined in.

"Shut up, girl. Don't even tell your attorney no mess like that!" Camille squealed through her giggles.

"Jorgette, you're such a trip," Natasha said, still giggling.

"A girl has to do what a girl has to do, and STDs these days will kill a sister, feel me?"

Camille clinked Jorgette's glass. "Exactly my point. And I want more than sex, because that's what I bring to the table. If the brother can't give me the full monte, then he's history—and no booty to go along with it."

"Yeah," Jorgette agreed with authority, sloshing her fourth martini as she slurped it. "These hoochies out here are making it hard to hold the line, girl. So, do your show, 'Tash, and give us all some hope that there's a nice guy out there *some-dag-gone-where!*"

"Okay, Ty, I hear you," Bernard said. "But maybe it's time to pull up out of Atlanta? Maybe we should try to get this thing off the ground on the West Coast, or go up to New York or something? We've been hitting our heads against a brick wall for three years now, just grinding. I mean, pretty soon we'll look up and be forty, with nothing to show for it but a failed record label and a bunch of drama."

Tyrell kept his focus on his beer. This was a conversation to be had in the living room, not within Club Vision's twenty-five thousand square feet—where everyone and their mother came to see, be seen, and floss. The last thing he needed was for his best friend to get shaky on him. He knew what Bernard was saying was true, but it didn't take the sting out of the accusation.

"Look, Bernie . . . man," Tyrell said slowly, sipping his beer in the process. "We've already invested how much in this thing?"

"Yeah," his friend said, glancing around the club, "but it doesn't take an MBA to figure out that you can't keep throwing good money after bad. We're undercapitalized. Period."

Tyrell studied his homeboy. "If this falls through, you still have your good marketing job at Coca-Cola. You've got an MBA and have options. Me, I'm an insurance salesman with a bachelor's degree. If this falls through, where am I going to go?"

Bernard looked down at his Chivas and rolled the glass around between his palms. "I hear you, but I can't keep dropping nearly my whole paycheck into studio time for CDs that never get airtime, or promoting chitterlin' circuit gigs. My 401K is bled out, I'm in a condo, whereas I should have a house by now. My Beamer is four years old—"

"I drive a Honda, man, live in an apartment with no equity, and don't have a 401K to bleed out—feel me?"

"That was your choice," Bernard said, downing his drink. "In a few years I'll be ready to settle down, maybe start a family, and a man needs a level of stability to be able to pull more than one of these club hoochies." He looked at Tyrell hard. "Time is marching on, brother. I'm not living like this for the rest of my days, scrambling. The only reason I got into this with you was because you were my homeboy, we go way back, and you had the vision. I agreed to invest with you, keep your books straight through the other brothers I knew who are on the up and up, and I agreed to use my contacts from my day gig to help leverage some promotions. But at the end of the day . . ."

"Yeah, I know," Tyrell said, growing weary, "we're undercapitalized."

For a moment, neither man spoke. It was as though a very sad and silent understanding had bonded them, yet disconnected them at once. In truth, Tyrell had to admit that this whole adventure was his dream, not Bernard's. He couldn't fault the man. Even growing up, Bernard had always been the cautious one, the conservative one, where he'd been the risk taker.

"I understand," Tyrell finally said, his voice mellow as he sipped the remainder of his beer. "You've gotta make some decisions. So do I. A man has to do what a man has to do." He pushed back from the bar and turned to look at Bernard, and then extended his hand. "You'll always be my boy, though. No matter how this goes down."

Bernard held onto the handshake and pulled Tyrell into a male friendship embrace and then released him.

"Sit down, man," Bernard said. "Let me order you another round—on the corporate card."

Tyrell smiled sadly. "Naw, I'm aw'ight. One day I wanna be able to put down the plastic for you with my own corporate card from Off Da Meter. Platinum version."

Bernard sighed. "That's why I said sit down and talk to me, man. I haven't gone anywhere yet. I'm just . . . you know. Trying to see where we're headed."

Begrudgingly, Tyrell sat down and hailed the bartender. He glanced around the club, noting the outrageously dressed women and the way no one really interacted with anyone there, except for what appeared to be on a surface level.

"Be honest," Tyrell said after the bartender slid a beer in front of him. "This ain't you, man. Never was."

Bernard chuckled and sipped his fresh Chivas. "This is your world, I'm just the guy who keeps the engine room going."

Both men laughed.

"Bernie, you're supposed to be in the suburbs by now with two-point-five kids, a wife who plays tennis and does the soccer mom thing, with you riding a John Deere mower around your two-acre spread."

Bernard smiled and cast his gaze out across the writhing bodies dancing at the club. "She ain't in here, man. That's no lie."

"Hell, even *I'm* half scared of what's in here, man," Tyrell said, laughing and clinking his beer bottle against his best friend's rocks glass.

"You mess with some of this stuff in here," Bernard said, his gaze riveted to the dance floor, "you might come away a dead man walking, or worse."

They both looked at each other and spoke in unison.

"A baby's daddy."

They gave each other a fist pound and shook their heads.

"I ain't trying to go out like that, man," Tyrell said, setting his beer down hard.

"Brother . . ." Bernard said, blowing his breath out hard. "But you think it's bad now, what do you think is gonna happen if you make some serious dollars?"

"I might have to beat J. Lo off me with a stick, but I could stand it," Tyrell said, laughing hard.

"I might be conservative," Bernard said, laughing with his friend, "but even I could stand *that*. Shoot, after this recent dry spell, I might take my chances out here tonight."

"Brother, sit your rusty butt on the stool and keep it there," Tyrell said with a wide grin. "You'll wake up in the morning with your BMW gone, your wallet missing, and having to explain to the boss about how all your credit cards got jacked with Louis Vuitton bags showing up on the receipts. A dry spell will pass; mess around and lose your job and you'll be all turned out."

"This is why I've been on my P's and Q's for over a year, man," Bernard said, his gaze taking in a group of beautiful women who passed by them with smiles.

Stunned, Tyrell just looked at his friend, slack jawed.

"Hey, man," Bernard said, growing defensive. "I've been focused on the business."

Tyrell just smiled and twirled his beer bottle on the bar. "You'd better be careful, man, before you develop a nervous twitch, or before Homeland Security seizes your computer and telephone records. That ain't healthy, brother."

"I do not indulge in cable or telephone fantasy—that's a waste of money," Bernard said, growing testy. "I've got discipline."

Tyrell chuckled. "Yeah, brother, and in a minute, if you don't stop watching the floor like a hungry buzzard, you might have more than that."

"Shut up, man, and get off my case," Bernard said, chuckling and slurping his drink. "I'm just here to indulge in a little spectator sport, try to have a business conversation with my boy, and enjoy a little eye candy. Can't a man do that in peace? Besides, I haven't seen you out there, either."

"I'm handling my bizness, as you say. I'm focused," Tyrell said, tapping his temple with one finger. "Using my brain to bring home the bling bling and can't worry about distractions right through here."

"Be honest, man," Bernard argued, baiting his friend. "How long have you been focused, as you call it?"

"Don't worry about my focus. It's laser sharp." Tyrell polished off his beer and ignored his friend's probing question. There was no way in the world that he was going to admit that he, *the Tyrell Ramsey*, confirmed player, had been on an eighteen-month dry spell. Never happen.

"That long, huh," Bernard said, his grin wide as he lifted his tumbler to his lips.

"We ain't all that different, man. I want the same things, long run, that you do. But I'm willing to make the sacrifice, short term, to come away holding so that my family, whenever I start one, has everything I didn't have growing up." He paused when Bernard's face became solemn, suddenly feeling vulnerable by the admission. "No woman or wife, before I get my thing straight. No babies before then. No drama. I've lived that all my life, saw my brothers give my mother the blues, and jack their lives up before they even got out of the starting gate. I vowed I'd never go out like that. So, my singular goal is to put my thing down, hard, and then proceed with authority." He glanced around the club, growing disgusted. "They'll always be fine women out there."

Bernard nodded and set his drink down with care. "I'm in with you, man, for at least another six months. I'll try to stay focused in the interim." He smiled and cast a wistful glance at the dance floor one last time. "But after that, I may have to break camp and go find me somebody to settle down with. Damn, they fine."

Chapter 3

Three months later . . .

Miami, Chicago, Detroit, New York, Philly, D.C., L.A., Houston, St. Louis, and finally Atlanta. They'd gone to the top ten major cities where there was a heavy concentration of African-American singles, and as expected, the women came out full force. Fine women, homely women, crazy women, old women, widows, women with nine children, drug-addicted women, four-hundred-pound women, anorexic women, high school drop-outs, women with Ph.D.s, recently incarcerated women; they were all standing in line, hoping to get picked.

Finding men who passed muster was just as hard a task. Everyone was fronting, both males and females, alike. Brothers had come in with child support judgments and outstanding warrants against them, claiming to be childless. Brothers with valid marriage certificates on record, claimed not to be married. And the credit reports made her dizzy.

Her boss, Nathan Greenberg, thought they'd hit Lotto. All he could see was the frenetic response to the ads and the way the hype was crackling in the industry as droves of lonely people and fame-seekers came out. What he couldn't see, because he didn't have to deal with it, was the long nights and the painstaking sifting process.

Fatigue had become the marrow in Natasha's bones. She and her crew had scoured the nation, doing endless auditions, background checks, and research. She'd seen enough insanity to make her wanna holla. She'd also seen enough buff, athletic bodies to make her want to go into permanent hiding. She worked in the industry, and knew people had cosmetic work done, but dang!

She knew some folks had their thing together, but she still wasn't prepared for some of the salaries that some applications legitimately displayed. Her crew would simply look at each other hang-jawed at times. There were some sisters that made them all just want to forget even trying to find a mate. They were wealthy, by her standards, had it all going on, and yet stood before the interview team nearly in tears confessing their inability to find someone solid to build a life with. Then there were those who flossed into the room with such arrogance that she just wanted to slap them. A debate about whether to pick those always ensued with half the team wanting to select a witch just for the drama she'd bring, with the others outright hating. The compromise was a mix between the sweet victim type and the Elvira's of the world. The black love boat was gonna be a trip!

And the men . . . they blew her mind. Some were so arrogant that she almost had to stand up and walk out of the interviews to keep from leaping across the table to strangle a fool. Others were so wimpy that she was nearly gagging. Then, there were some who were so outright fine that she had to remember that they had to pass all the background check hurdles. And sometimes what the detectives found was not only shocking, it was scary. People were crazy!

By the time she and her crew had reached Atlanta, she was numb. Pretty faces, long stories, sad sagas, buff bodies, sumptuous hotel environs, none of it impressed her. She didn't give a hoot about any of it. She just wanted to get the show going, rake in the ratings, and be done with the whole project. Three months of hard touring had made her mean. The fact that her mother didn't approve of the whole concept got on her last nerve. Why couldn't her mother just, for once, be happy that she'd landed a coveted position to do a groundbreaking show?

Her sisters and brothers and tertiary friends had worn on her spirit—none of them could pass muster, all of them were begging for a spot on the show, and that wasn't even allowed. But did they care? No. They were all not speaking to her because she wouldn't risk her job to let them parade their tired behinds on her show. Good riddance. She didn't need that drama right through here anyway. If they didn't talk to her, whateva. She was functioning on four to five hours of sleep a night, working seven days a week, and didn't have time for their issues.

She now understood the nasty responses the *American Idol* judges gave. After you'd seen so much insanity, and heard so many long stories, patience was at a premium.

Sitting in the Doubletree Hotel, she had no patience, no nerves, no civility, and no humor left at all. Natasha sighed and flipped through the stack of applications, bracing herself for the next onslaught of potential contestants. She tried to remember what her best friends had told her; pick a wide range of women from various backgrounds. Be sure to choose women who adhere to multiple cultural standards of beauty, not all Mariah Carey types. Beauty came in all shades and hair types. Okay, she'd done that, despite having to, at times, hotly educate her all-white staff on that point.

All she needed was one last male to fit the bill.

"Tell me you're lying!" Bernard said, laughing out loud.

Tyrell pulled his cell away from his ear to shield his hearing from Bernard's sonic boom. "It's twenty-five Gs, man," he said quickly, as he circled the lot again looking for parking. "You said you'd give me six months, three are gone. What's the worst that could happen? If I don't make it, then I have three more months to come up with financing alternatives. For every round I hang in there, if I make the cut, it's ten grand to the good. My job sucks, and I ain't got nothin' to lose. Besides, if I get on the show, I can hype the label, use it to get us exposure we couldn't buy with our pockets."

"You know," Bernard said, still laughing. "This is the craziest, most off da hook scheme you've come up with yet. But from a promotions standpoint, it's brilliant. If you make it on there, man, even if you can only hang for one round before they boot your butt off the boat, the amount of exposure for the business will be incredible!"

"That's what I'm saying, man," Tyrell said, his confidence growing as he pulled his car into a hard turn to find empty space. "I'm gonna go into the interview, serve those stodgy old judges my best drama, and keep hope alive."

"Man," Bernard said, laughing, "if you make the cut and get on that show, I'll give you another six months, even if you get booted after round one."

"Get booted after round one?" Tyrell laughed. "Me? *The* playa, player? Never happen. I will wrap those babes around my pinky finger. I'll have 'em eating out of the palm of my hand, brother. I'll have them begging me to pick them, throwing panties on the star berth bow when I walk across the deck. You *know* who you talkin' to, right?"

"What I know," Bernard said, laughing harder, "is that you have to get past probably some old white ladies and crotchety old white men who ain't hearing your drama, no matter how you serve it. So just go in there and do your best. Good luck, man."

Tyrell chuckled and shook his head as he turned off his ignition. "I don't need luck, my brother. Tyrell Ramsey's got skillz."

The wait was interminable. He sat in the hotel lobby with his number, rehearsing his most dashing smile, his best lines, and rethinking his entire life. Every so often, he smoothed the front of his Armani suit and double-checked is Cole Haan slip-ons to be sure the shine hadn't dimmed. Occasionally he would stand and adjust the French cuffs on his shirt, ensuring that the French blue fabric showed at just the right length beneath his jacket sleeve, and then would straighten his silk tie, adjusting the solid gold collar bar beneath it. He peeped down at the crisply pressed handkerchief in his breast pocket to be sure that the exact quarter inch was showing.

Yeah, he was ready. He could do this. His life dream was just a little bit of drama away. He didn't have to be nervous. There was no such thing as fear. It didn't matter that there were brothers in there with him who looked like supermodels. So what. Forget the Italian boys and the Greek guys who looked like they could be young JFK's twin. He wasn't worried about the Nordic-looking blonde dudes who looked rich as dirt and like they skied in Vale all winter. They couldn't bring game to no sisters like he could. He just wished he'd been able to add a Rolex to his whole outfit, but that was beyond the budget. Whatever. It was about charisma, anyhow. He would just go in there and kick serious game.

Natasha stretched and yawned. "We need to take a break before this last group of knuckleheads comes in here."

One of the junior producers glanced at her nervously and then at the rest of the group. "We only have a few more, 'Tash. If we can get through these, we can all go home."

Rumblings of dissent ran down the long table and Natasha sighed hard.

"I know. I want to go home and sleep in my own bed tonight, too. But right now, if I don't take a break, I'm going to be really mean."

Stephanie Michaels, her assistant, laughed. "Oh, and you haven't been mean, yet?"

Natasha had to smile. "No, I was just warming up."

Devon slapped his forehead. "Heaven help us, then," he said, shaking his head. "Feed this woman. Let her go take a potty break. Get her out of here for five minutes. But don't let her decimate another group of hopefuls, or we'll have to start all over and stay another day."

Natasha held up her hand. "Okay, okay, I'll behave and give them a chance. But have you heard some of the responses. Where do these people come from?"

"The world is simply twisted," Devon said with a weary sigh. "These people are tragic, but beautiful and will make for good ratings. So, Miss Thang, will you please try to contain yourself from reducing them to puddles of anxiety during their interviews? At least on this round?"

"I will try," Natasha said, chuckling at her own bad behavior. "No promises. Because if one more man comes in here and flexes—"

"But that's what they're supposed to do," Stephanie countered. "They have to—"

"That fool made his crotch flex!' Natasha said, her voice rising with both gall and laughter.

"And you didn't pick him," Devon said, becoming morose. "Hand me his application, he was all that."

"Stop. TMI, too much information," Natasha said, holding her head in her hands. "Send in the next victims. I can't take it any more. God as my witness, I can't stand anymore."

* * *

He was already standing when they called his number. He'd previously witnessed the most confident men in the world walk out of the room with their tails between their legs. The sight of grown men with tears in their eyes, hopes dashed, and spirits broken was enough to give him pause. So he took his time as he followed the burly security team to the dreaded double doors of fate. Who was this panel? Most of the guys came out of the room, passed everyone without a word, and simply left defeated. One guy had simply shook his head and told them all, "Good luck, but she's a real bitch." Okay. He had to regulate his breathing, be cool. Had to keep his palms from getting damp—not a chance.

He entered the ballroom and stood before a long table, sizing up the judges. They were all young. Shocker. Which one was the dangerous one with the razor tongue, he wondered? There was one sister in the middle with her head down, reading his file. There was a guy to her left, who smiled brightly at him. There was a young blonde chick on her right who offered a business-only smile. There were two more young kids, probably studio interns, off to the side doing the administrative background work, apparently, since they only glanced up, nodded, and went back to their paperwork. But the sister hadn't looked up. What was that about?

"All right, Mr. Tyrell Ramsey. You have ten minutes to impress me."

He got it—she was the dangerous one.

The sister still hadn't looked up as she'd spoken. All he could see was a thicket of jet-back, natural twists that shone like velvet under the big ballroom chandelier.

It took a moment for him to react; her comment had been so sharp within her silky toned voice that it was disorienting. Trying to get himself together with a smooth answer, he paced his response as he watched her slowly raise her head.

But his one-line rebuttal caught in his throat as he saw her pretty, oval face. It was her eyes. Huge, dark, intensely beautiful, blazing with impatience and determination and rimmed with thick, jet-black lashes. Gorgeous ebony skin, flawless, not a mark on it, with features so striking that she seemed like a piece of rare art. For a moment, he couldn't take his eyes off her full, lush mouth. He didn't catch himself before his gaze trailed down her long, delicate throat to take in her perfect, palm-sized breasts that strained, unencumbered, under a hot pink tank top. The color of the fabric seemed to make her beautiful skin glow, and it barely concealed her tiny, pebbled nipples. He glanced at her hands . . . long, slender, natural nails, graceful . . . like her toned arms. This was no old lady he was dealing with.

"I don't know if I can impress you in ten minutes, ma'am," he said in the deepest baritone he could muster. "I'll do my best, but I'm used to a lot more time than that."

She cocked her head to the side and raised one eyebrow as her table erupted in laughter. Then she shook her head and flashed him a brilliant smile that seemed to light up the room. He couldn't take his eyes off her mouth, and knew he was wasting precious interview time. But this woman had blown him away.

She sat back in her chair and folded her arms over her chest. "Mr. Ramsey, we've all had a long day. Please. Dispense with the drama, and tell us why you should be selected for the show."

He smiled a half smile, encouraged that although her tone was testy, her smile was still bright and her eyes contained an easy to read curiosity.

Natasha sipped in a shallow breath. Sure, she'd seen more fine men than most women had a chance to see in a lifetime, but this one had an edge to him. It was in the way he looked at her. He didn't come in the room running his mouth. He'd assessed her with such unabashed desire that she had to cross her arms. It had been a long time since a man looked at her like that, and yet, she had to drive his arresting image out of her mind. But, Lord have mercy, this man was awesome.

"Well?" she said, determined to stay in character.

He nodded and came closer to the table, trailing an earthy cologne that produced mild delirium. She'd meant to cut him down to size with a hard grit as she allowed her gaze to travel up his six feet four, chocolate brown frame and over his solid chest and built shoulders, up to his clean-shaven, handsome face to challenge his stare. God, this man was fine, she could tell he had the body of life, the way the designer suit hung so perfectly on his frame. He was basketball player lean and wasn't too muscle bound . . . in a way that made her wonder what he'd look like in Speedo trunks on the beach. She kept her gaze on his face, but his smoldering, intense gaze almost made her look away from his dark brown eyes and those thick curly lashes. His mouth was so full and sexy, moist, it made her almost want to lean up and brush his lips with her own—but this was about business.

"My story is very short, and won't take ten minutes,"

Tyrell finally said, leaning forward with both hands on the desk, and staring at her without blinking. "I'm the last of four brothers. My mother worked like a dog to keep us fed. I'm the only one in the bunch who went to school and did something with his life. They've all gone down the slippery slope of street life and have crash-landed back on her sofa. I have too much respect for her and myself to go there at thirty-two years old. She deserves better and did the best she could with what she had to work with. It's my job to go to the next level and build on the foundation she gave me—which was working hard and knowing right from wrong."

He pushed away from the table and folded his arms over his chest, his gaze raking the group. "I'm a working man, never miss a day. But I also have entrepreneurial dreams and want to at least give it a shot to be able to say, I tried. I would hate to wake up and be seventy, just retiring from a nine-to-five, and wishing I had, once in my life, tried to go for broke. However," he added, unfolding his arms and slowly walking before the length of the table while pointing at his temple, "my momma didn't raise no fool. While I'm getting my business off the ground, I'm working a normal nine-to-five to finance my goals. A lot of people gamble, go in debt up to their eyeballs, or get their start from nefarious sources. Not me. Coming out to this show contest is about the craziest stunt I've ever pulled."

He shook his head and chuckled and stood before the table front and center, offering the panel a shrug. "Pick me or not. I am what I am, a fairly simple guy. To me, this isn't about fame and fortune or being seen on some show. For me, my goals are straightforward. The prize money from this show will allow me to one day own my own business. I wasn't born with a silver spoon in my mouth, I'm not a hotshot computer wizard or stockbroker with long paper. My credit is average, and I don't have a lot of assets—I sunk everything into the business venture. My partner is about to walk, but I'm focused on making my business plan work. I don't have any babies or baby momma drama, because I've been working too hard to get involved with all of that nonsense. If this pans out, fine. If not, whatever. I'm a regular guy with regular dreams, and enough discipline to put some backbone work ethic behind what I want to achieve in life."

With his closing statement, Tyrell Ramsey folded his arms. He watched her watching him. Her study of him was electrifying, yet, unreadable.

"Well, that was definitely keepin' it real," she said with a slight tremor in her voice. "Do you have any questions, panel?"

Devon shook his head and closed his folder. "I like his style. Refreshingly honest. Blue-collar vibes in a white-collar profession. Very cool addition to the boat, I'd think."

"Stephanie? Your take and comments . . . questions?"

"I agree with Devon. This gentleman came in here and gave it to us straight, no chaser, and isn't a fame seeker, a wannabe model/actor, and didn't give us a load of crap." She ruffled her fingers through her short, blonde hair and closed her eyes. "Thank God. The others made me so weary!"

"Well, Mr. Ramsey, do you have any questions for this panel—since you have about three minutes left?"

She watched a half smile tug at his mouth until it

gave way to the most dashing, megawatt brilliance that lit up his entire face. She noticed that he had a very slight gap between his front teeth; the perfect imperfection of it was totally mesmerizing.

"Yeah. I have two," he said in a deep, slow rolling thunder that vibrated all through her. "Am I in or out?"

She laughed. He was outrageous. "We have to caucus and review all the candidates. So, what's the second question?" she hedged, thoroughly enjoying sparring with him.

"*What*—is your name?"

Shocked, she blinked twice, unable to immediately answer as her fellow panelists erupted again in a gale of laughter. "My name?" she finally stammered, "Mr. Ramsey—"

"I figured I'm out. There are better candidates with more education, money, and looks. I'm a reasonable man. But I'm also a man who hates to blow an opportunity, rare as those are these days. So, I'm asking you your name because, if I'm not a show contestant, I can't see where there's a conflict of interest . . . and I have to tell you, sister, I walked into this room and got messed up. All my lines and rehearsed rhetoric was blown when I saw you. So, since you messed up my chances for getting on the boat, the least you can do is tell me your name . . . maybe slide me your digits in my last three minutes on the clock."

"Oh, Christ," Devon exclaimed, slapping his forehead. "This man is in. Done." He stood up and leaned across the table and shook Tyrell's hand. "Let's stop screwing around and go home."

Stephanie nodded and stood, slapping Devon on the back as the interns joined in the celebration.

"Face it, honey, the camera loves him, he's got chutzpah, and is the ground wire we need on that yacht. The viewers will go crazy when he flashes that Colgate smile. Welcome aboard, Mr. Ramsey."

Although Natasha was laughing her face was burning hot. Tyrell Ramsey was sharing in the congratulations with the others, but still kept his gaze locked on her.

"We still have ten more men out there in the lobby to interview," Natasha said, trying to stay professionally distanced from the premature celebration.

The commotion in the room stopped, but Tyrell Ramsey seemed pleasantly amused.

"Okay, then," he said casually. "That's cool. So, what's your name and number?"

For a moment, no one spoke. Natasha smiled and pushed away from the table, but refused to stand. "We will give these other candidates the same courtesy we gave you," she warned, casting a firm glare at her fellow panelists. "That's only fair."

He nodded. "Yep. That's only right. They got all dressed up, came all this way, even if it's a formality, they still should have their chance to be heard. But you still haven't answered my second question."

"It is only a formality at this point, 'Tash. Come on," Devon pleaded. "I am so tired and a rag."

"We should hear them out, though," Stephanie said, flopping into her chair with an exhausted sigh. She glanced at the college interns who had slumped their shoulders as they trudged back to their worktable that was filled with papers. "So close and yet so far."

"Okay. I'm out," Tyrell said, appearing unfazed. "Y'all have a good, long evening. May the best man ultimately win. Thanks for the opportunity to give it my best shot—on both counts." He winked at Natasha. "Even if you won't give me your number, you have all of mine and all my business, verified, in your hands . . . no wife, no woman, no kids, no momma at my crib. Call me anytime, pretty sister."

Natasha watched his tall carriage, and the way he so graciously took the disappointing news. Her eyes scanned his broad shoulders, followed the path down his spine, noticed the slight dip at the base of it as his perfectly chiseled behind worked beneath the expensive fabric, his long, thick thighs taking panther graceful strides toward the door. She knew she was crazy, but her mouth opened and her vocal cords engaged without consulting her brain. "Only out of mercy on my staff and so that I don't have to answer the second out of order question, Mr. Ramsey, you're in."

Chapter 4

Tyrell sat at the traffic light for a moment just staring straight ahead. He'd turned off the radio in the car, the sound of silence cloaking him. A rush of media had greeted him as he'd left the hotel ballroom, but he'd been instructed to keep his responses obtuse until the other candidates had completed their pro forma interviews. It was deep. It was Hollywood. He'd gotten in!

Almost in a dreamlike state, he navigated to his apartment, his fingers resting on his hands-free cell phone unit. He had to tell Bernard, but if Bernard slipped up and told all of creation—which his friend would—before the final word came out, then that could possibly jeopardize the pretty sister's job.

As he pulled into a parking space at his apartment complex, Tyrell allowed the Honda engine to idle, the cool flow from the air conditioner wafting over him as he closed his eyes. They'd called her 'Tash. Was her name Tosha, Natasha, LaTosha . . . ? She had to be tough, no doubt, to make it that far that fast within an industry that took no prisoners. But she'd smiled at him, had laughed with him, had issued him a private, knowing glance that told him they'd come from the same place in life. Within her eyes was almost a plea that said don't out me brother, I'm just doing my job in front of them.

And why he was so focused on this gorgeous woman with the knowing eyes, he wasn't sure. He should have been jumping for joy that his major dream was about to come true. He'd just scored a winning shot. He'd just landed twenty-five grand with a chance at the championship title. With this money he'd be able to launch his enterprise with full authority. He could quit his day job. Maybe it was the fact that none of it was official until the FedEx came tomorrow. Maybe it wouldn't hit him until media showed up at his door, and until he would have a frenetic few days to handle his business, pack, and tell his job, "It's been real."

But one thing was for sure. No matter what happened on that boat, and no matter how many rounds of the show he'd make, that gorgeous sister with a half name that he'd just met would remain on his mind.

It all seemed like a blur to Natasha as they suffered through the remaining interviews. As each candidate presented his case, she held her breath, hoping that none of them would give a better story than Tyrell Ramsey. While she knew judges were supposed to be impartial, simply making decisions based on just the facts, that was impossible. It was a ridiculous concept. Judges were human; each had their preferences and prejudices going in. All she could hope for was that as the comparisons were made, her colleagues would also continue to find Mr. Tyrell Ramsey as charismatic as she had.

She nearly held her breath as the last candidate slipped from the room with nervous anticipation. Part of her felt bad as she watched Devon issue a silent thumbs-down behind the exiting man's back. And she stood on wobbly legs as the room erupted into cheerful high fives, hugs, and pandemonium. He'd passed. Tyrell Ramsey was still in. Why that was so important to her, she couldn't fathom.

What did that mean, anyway? He'd made it on the boat, would be surrounded by a bevy of stop-your-heart beauties. The goal of the show was to pair him up with some lucky lady—not her. It was a bittersweet victory, one so hollow that she couldn't muster real joy. Yet she knew this brother deserved a chance . . . some lucky sister out there did too. So, maybe that was her role in the universe, to give other people a chance at some happiness while waiting in vain for that elusive thing herself.

She numbly gave her team instructions as they gathered their files and papers and prepared to leave the hotel. "Alert the media channels. I'll call Nathan. Send Tyrell Ramsey his packet by same day courier. Don't make the man wait until tomorrow to hear his good news."

Tyrell sat on the sofa, smooth jazz filtering through his apartment. He'd abandoned his suit the moment he got in, donning his favorite gear: a pair of gray, raggedy, comfortable cutoff sweat shorts. He'd reached for the telephone a hundred times, if once. He'd composed his resignation letter on his laptop computer, but didn't want to jinx his chances by even printing it out. He was going to call home to his mom and brothers, but thought better of that. Bernard's number was making his fingers itch, but his boy had to wait. The doorbell sounded and made him nearly jump out of his skin. If it was Bernard, it was all over. He'd have to spill the beans.

Instead of Bernard, it was a courier standing in the lobby when he bounded down the stairs, not waiting for the elevator. His heart was beating out of his chest. This thing could go either way. They might have found somebody better, and were kind enough to let him off the hook with the immediate news.

He didn't even wait for the courier to leave, nor did he go back up to his apartment as he tore into the thin, letter-size packet. He held it for a moment. The courier didn't move but stood in the lobby area, curious, and all in his business.

A jolt of electricity shot through him as he suddenly hugged the dumbfounded courier and his voice thundered through the small confines. "I won, man! I won!"

Nathan's voice boomed through Natasha's cell phone as she quickly paced through the airport with her crew in tow.

"Yes, yes, yes," she muttered. "We've got it covered. They each have two weeks to get ready, so they can serve notice to their employers and pack under duress."

She nodded as Nathan's excited voice reached a pitch that felt like it shattered her eardrum. "Yes, a weekly call-in and Internet poll will keep audiences involved. Yeah, Nate, I told you, we just have to get back their signatures on all the disclaimers before we can send our camera crews to each of their homes." She sighed. "*I know* it's important to get their background stories and bios for the first episode. Yeah, I got that. We'll show them packing; do little segments on their histories. Relax." She could feel her blood pressure rising as she spotted news cameras in the offing. "Nathan, our team is about to be mobbed again by *Evening Magazine* and *Access Hollywood* reporters. I'll talk to you when I get back to Miami."

"Man, stop playing!" Bernard shouted and laughed as his voice filled the telephone receiver.

"I've got the papers right here, brother," Tyrell said, laughing. "I worked it like a pro, man. I told you I'd come out holding!"

"And I told you that I'd hang for six more months if you did. Congrats, man, but now what? You need a strategy to win this show. You can't go in there without a game plan, and I'm your coach. We need a signal, or something, since they're taking all your credit cards and resources . . . you're gonna be totally dependent on them for the duration—but a brother needs to have an edge. So, whatcha gonna do?"

Tyrell shook his head. "I honestly don't know. I hadn't though about it that far. But you have a serious point."

A hearty laugh filled the cell phone. "You didn't think you'd make it, did you? Tell the truth."

Tyrell flopped down on his sofa. "In all honesty, man, I didn't think I would."

* * *

She didn't have time to think, much less breathe, and she couldn't wait to get into the sanctuary of her apartment. She *had* to call Jorgette and Camille. Her girls would flip when she gave them the rundown on the whirlwind of insanity she'd just been on. Together they would savor every bit of gossip, and could laugh until they cried. She'd missed them so much, but her body was so weary that all she could do was drag her carcass into her empty apartment and drop to the sofa.

After a half hour of lying prone, she sat up and peered at the telephone, then punched in the code to retrieve her voice mail messages. She buzzed past her mother's entreaties not to tangle with the devil, and erased her sisters' and cousins' jealousy-filled, weak congratulatory blurbs. Her boss, Nathan, had blown up her cell phone, and she was thankful that he hadn't also left a list of to-dos on her personal home telephone. But there were no messages from Jorgette and Camille. That was odd.

Sitting up straighter, Natasha called Jorgette first. She waited impatiently for the call to connect. When it did, Jorgette's upbeat voice filled the telephone and Natasha relaxed.

"We did it, gurl," Natasha said, brightly. "Phase one, is over."

"Cool," Jorgette said, casually. "Glad you got all that squared away. So, when do you leave for the islands?"

For a moment, Natasha just stared at the telephone in her hand. "In two weeks," she said, carefully choosing her words. "You okay, lady?"

"Yeah, just busy. You caught me working on a project. Can I call you later? I'm on deadline, 'Tash, and really have to bang out this storyboard."

"No problem," Natasha said, as a swirl of emotions she couldn't describe began to enter her. "Girl, listen, I'm sorry that I didn't call from the road . . . everything was so frenetic and crazy . . . and I had to keep the process confidential. I told you guys that was how it was gonna go down, right?"

"Hey, it's your job. We know you had to focus. That's all I'm trying to do right now, 'Tash, is focus on my job. Okay?"

The saltiness in Jorgette's tone cut her to the quick. But what could she really say? Her girl was obviously hurt by the lack of communication, no matter what the circumstances. For the first time in her life, the rift was paralyzing. This was not the homecoming she'd expected, nor the response. Natasha sighed quietly and willed her voice to remain gentle. "I'll call you when I can, lady. That's a promise. And I'm sorry, okay?"

"Yeah, girl," Jorgette said curtly. "No problem. Go handle your business and we'll just watch it on TV."

Natasha said a quiet good-bye, hoping that it wasn't a final one. She disconnected the call but hesitated before calling Camille. What was happening to her life? Where were her roadies? They were supposed to barge into her apartment with bottles of champagne and laughter, or be dragging her out to a club against her protests. A deep sadness claimed her as she called Camille's line and got her voice mail. Part of her was glad that she didn't have to possibly hear attitude in her other best friend's tone.

Leaving a brief, upbeat message with a promise to call, Natasha quickly got off the phone. Loneliness propelled her from the sofa toward her bedroom closet. Right now, she had too much to do, too much to worry about, and too many variables hinging on her success to deal with Camille and Jorgette's momentary crisis. Sadness began to give way to anger. This was the first time in her entire life that things were going her way. This was the first time that she had some real positive news to share, and really needed them to celebrate with her. And this was the first time that she could actually bring herself to acknowledge that her friends just might have a twinge of jealousy regarding her career . . . when all this time she'd been the one hovering in the background, cheering them on, being there for all of their accolades and accomplishments.

Hot tears of anger and disappointment filled her eyes as she surveyed her choices. Natasha sniffed hard and blinked back the moisture in her eyes. She didn't have time for that. She had to pack.

"I want you on the set at all times," Nathan said quickly, walking around the conference room like an elf on steroids. His semi-bald head gleamed under the fluorescent lights as he strutted his short, pudgy form to and fro.

"But I thought I was just going in on the advance team to get the various port venues ready?" Natasha hedged. "When we conceived this, only the camera crew, Stephanie, and Devon would be on the boat. I was to work the hotels, make sure—"

"No, no, no, no, no," Nathan fussed. "We were shortsighted. Nothing can go wrong and we need you to draw the drama out of the contestants." He threw up his hands and allowed them to land with a loud slap on his bald head. "Have you seen the bios?"

Natasha, Stephanie, and Devon glanced at each other and nodded.

"Well?" Nathan shouted.

Devon sighed. "Boring."

"Exactly," Nathan said, beginning to pace again. "What was that crap? The camera guys have footage that drones on and on about my momma this, my high school buddy that . . . my job as an engineer, a pilot, a computer nerd, what the hell eva!" He opened his arms and leaned forward. "Where's the drama, people? Where's the excitement? Where's the flava, as they say?"

She had to agree; the early footage was dismal. "Nathan, I hear you. Okay, look, we can—"

"No, you look, 'Tash," he exclaimed. "When you were doing the interviews, the barbs, the one-liners, the attitude you served drew out the contestants' personalities. This is *supposed* to be a *hot* show with tensions running high. I need a catalyst behind the scenes to spike emotions, get the group at each other's throats. I can't work with this drivel. They'll cancel us on the second episode! As it is, I can only use, *maybe*, ten to fifteen minutes of the bios— which was supposed to take up a full half hour."

"Nathan, calm down," Stephanie said with caution. "We'll use edited footage of the interviews to burn the first fifteen minutes, then cut to the bios, from there we can get each judge's take on each contestant, maybe clue in the audience about the first challenge, and then show the arrival on the boat, the contestants settling in, etcetera."

"That could work," Nathan said, letting out a deep breath as he found the chair at the head of the table and flopped down into it. "All right, people, think.

Gimme an angle to make the boat boarding scenes pop."

"Match up contestants that we can pretty much tell will be oil and water," Natasha said, her thoughts a million miles away. "Put the around-the-way-girl salon owner who has money in the same room with the broke psychologist chick from Harvard, and then squeeze the real estate saleswoman in with the computer equipment telemarketer and the wannabe actress into the same room. You want drama, Nathan, put three strong personalities in the same quarters fighting over the dresser and mirror space. Do the same thing with the guys." She let her breath out hard, thinking of her now fragile triumvirate. "You don't need me on that boat for ten weeks."

"Oh, no," Devon argued. "If we have to be trapped on there with those crazy people, you do too."

Nathan smiled. "Think of it as a paid vacation, 'Tash."

She stared at the man. "It will hardly be a vacation, Nathan," she said almost through her teeth. "That was not a part of the original concept. I need space to think, time to get the logistics squared away, and—"

"It's not negotiable, 'Tash. Be a sport," Nathan said, chuckling. "Now I know none of us wants to be trapped on the yacht with all those personalities. Everyone's nerves will be frayed by the end of this show, including the crews'. But that's the beauty of the concept. But, 'Tash, this was your brainstorm, and just in the very simple basics you laid out just now, you have to orchestrate every step."

Did the man say, us? Nathan knew good and well he wasn't about to set foot on the yacht, much less be inconvenienced by tight confines, whining, nervous breakdown—readied contestants. Nor was he about to subject himself to ever present cameras that were even installed in the bathroom stalls. Natasha wanted to scream.

"He may have a point, 'Tash," Stephanie said gently. "I mean, me and Devon were going to allow the contestants to pick their own rooms to see what the natural pairings would be, if any. But it is a far more tension-creating scenario to assign the rooms and to make them have to deal with whom they'd rather not."

Although Natasha knew Stephanie was trying to be helpful, the fact that she'd just sealed her fate made her eyes narrow. "Thanks, Steph," she muttered.

"Oh, it'll be fun, 'Tash," Devon said, trying to soothe her as he covered her hand with his. "We'll get some great footage, have us some true laughs, and we'll have mad-crazy stories to tell about the behind-the-scenes on this adventure when we come home." He grinned a wide smile when she simply looked at him stone-faced. "And the eye candy won't be bad either, *chica*."

Natasha refused to laugh as chuckles filled the room. She was a totally private person, liked working behind the scenes, and was not trying to be anywhere near a camera or be seen in a bathing suit around the five, hot female contestants who were chosen.

It didn't matter that she was to stay in the background while on the boat. They'd see her morning, noon, and night, and she couldn't wear jeans or cover-ups the whole time while there. If she left it up to Nathan, he'd no doubt use footage of the weary show crew to draw a haunting parallel between how exhausting it was for the show staff, thus the contestants had to be on their last leg. She knew the man that well. Nathan Greenberg was shameless.

Defeat entered her as the conversation went on without her input. The decision had been made; she'd been drafted. The contestants would be banging on her door, complaining, whining, crying, arguing, and relentlessly bugging the doo-doo out of her. She'd get no sleep, would be forced to let people see what the wind and surf and sun did to a sister's hair and makeup. She'd be exposed, even though off camera—instead of the way she'd planned it, which was to show up, full face makeup, hair coiffed, donning a power suit, to deliver the challenges as the yacht pulled into each port.

Plus, something that Devon had said stilled her. *We'll have mad-crazy stories to tell about the behind-the-scenes on this adventure when we come home.* Yeah, right. Who would be her confidantes? Where were her girls? There was no one in her life who she could really share this stuff with and know that they'd hang on her every word, savoring each juicy detail with laughter. There was no one to be truly happy for her; there was no safe harbor for her innermost thoughts. It had finally been shown to her that as long as she was telling hard luck stories or had a problem, her best friends would listen intently—but that was no longer what she had to share with them.

Although she refused to, Natasha wanted to cry.

Chapter 5

"You ready, man?" Bernard asked, peering around the harbor.

Tyrell allowed his line of vision to rove the crowd of glory-seekers held behind the security barricade and then scour the hubbub of media that was descending upon each contestant who made his or her way through the VIP area. "As ready as I'm gonna be," he finally replied, taking in a deep breath to steady his nerves. It had finally hit him; his life was going to be under a microscope for ten weeks.

"Check it out," Bernard said, his voice tinged with awe. "Would you look at that beauty."

Tyrell chuckled and hoisted up his luggage. "Which one?"

"The yacht, man," Bernard said, laughing as they began to walk. "Now *that's* living."

"Yeah, and all that glitters ain't gold, brother. We're talking tight confines, having to share a room with some knucklehead I ain't down with, plus people in my business twenty-four seven." He shook his head. "Now, if that baby was mine, and I was out on the water with my own crew on my own terms, yeah, I'd say she was spectacular."

Bernard cuffed Tyrell's shoulder. "But that's why you're making the supreme sacrifice, brother." He beamed at Tyrell. "And had I known your rusty behind coulda made it on the show, I would have thrown my hat in the ring, too. Dang, the women on there are fine."

There was nothing to say to his partner at this juncture. Tyrell simply kept walking forward, hoping that his media interview would be short. It was all planned; if he needed reinforcement, a few resources to tip the scales, he had to find a way to call Bernard collect with the code. They had developed ten SOS signals that could pass as normal conversation, and since each contestant was allowed to phone home a couple of times during the journey, albeit with monitored calls, his boy had to be on point.

"Just look at 'em," Bernard said in a conspiratorial tone. He motioned with his chin in the direction of the outer edges of the VIP area. "Check out that tall, caramel beauty with the Beyoncé mane . . . dang, baby got back." His eyes searched Tyrell's for answers. "If she doesn't make the cut, you *have got* to give her my business card."

Tyrell heard his partner speak, but had stopped walking. There she was, standing with two other pretty women—but they didn't hold a candle to her.

"Talk to me, man," Bernard said, still ribbing him. "You gotta hook a brother up. I don't mind leftovers."

"She ain't on the show, Bernie. The pretty chocolate one in the middle is the producer, and—"

"Hold up," Bernard said, grabbing Tyrell's shoulder. "You didn't describe the producer. You just said some whack sister grilled you with questions, and—"

"I know, I know," Tyrell muttered, suddenly becoming defensive. His friend was getting on his last nerve. "It wasn't important."

"Wasn't important?" Bernard opened his mouth and then closed it. "That was not some minor detail, bro." His gaze traveled over to the threesome and then back to Tyrell. "She's drop dead fine. Her, and what must be her girls, are all off da meter, man . . . especially the real tall one with the hazel eyes."

For a moment, neither man spoke.

"Look, Ty, since they aren't on the show, and you know the producer, why don't you introduce me?"

"No, man. Chill." Annoyance threaded through Tyrell's system. This was exactly why he didn't go into acute details with his homeboy. It wasn't about all of that. He had to play this real cool and be strategic. But his boy was about to do something stupid that might get him labeled as a dog.

"Why not, man. We're supposed to be partners and supposed to share. Right now, you can't talk to anybody, and have just sold yourself into the priesthood for at least ten more weeks . . . but her girlfriend is *all* that."

Before Tyrell could open his mouth, the media had spotted him.

"Tyrell Ramsey, what's it feel like to be among the few eligible bachelors who were selected for *Keepin' It Real*?"

Tyrell gave them all the dashing, politically correct sound bites he'd rehearsed in the bathroom mirror, and tried to keep from panicking as he watched Bernard smoothly slide away from his side and stroll over to where the woman he knew as 'Tash was standing. This whole thing was about to unravel and he hadn't even gotten on the boat!

There were so many people around and so much activity that she could barely take it all in. Nathan was in his glory, and she spied studio execs over-seeing the operation with pleased expressions. Indeed, the buzz was buzzing. The only thing that abated the tension was the fact that her girls had come.

When she'd sent them VIP passes by courier with a little personal note enclosed, all she could hope was that they'd squash whatever issues they were having about her AWOL status, and would just go back to being her homegirls. She loved them too much to dwell on their potential jealousy. That they'd shown up, with champagne bottles in tow, wide smiles, and hugs made the whole fiasco of having to get on the yacht tolerable.

"Oh, y'all . . . I have so much to tell you," Natasha said, her eyes brimming. "I've missed you so much!"

Camille gave her a warm hug and the two clung to each other as though Natasha were going off to war. "I'm so sorry, girl. I don't know what got into me. It's just that you didn't have time for us, we wanted to . . . oh, 'Tash, we're sorry."

Jorgette joined in the huddle. "I am so sorry, 'Tash. For real. When you get back, we want to hear every single detail," she said, sniffing and laughing and wiping her big, brown eyes. "Me and Camille just had to stop hating. But we thought you'd gotten new on us for a minute." She motioned toward the crystal blue sky. "You just up and left us, are blowing up, got all this going on, about to get on a yacht with all these fine men—"

"None of whom I can even think about, or I lose my job, remember," Natasha said, shaking her head with a wide smile. "You oughta know me better than that."

Camille just nodded, but then froze, making the others become still with her. "Girl, seven o'clock to your left. Who is that tall, fine, chocolate brown specimen headed our way?"

Natasha and Jorgette glanced in the direction of the man who was walking toward their threesome with purpose.

"If he's one of your contestants and gets the boot, can I have him?" Jorgette asked, desire and mischief flickering in her eyes.

"He's not one of the contestants," Natasha said, puzzled.

"Media, maybe?" Camille offered, her eyes now riveted to the approaching male. "He definitely has that corporate carriage . . . most assuredly."

Natasha riffled through her mental database of the who's who in the industry. The man was walking toward them like he knew them, and if she was supposed to know him, but didn't, that could create a social faux pas that could have career impact. But oddly, his gaze was on Camille, not her, and Camille clearly didn't know the man. Confusion made her take an observer's position, and she pasted on her best businesslike smile and waited to be clued in.

The man neared them with a warm, bright smile, and extended his hand to Natasha first. "Hello, ladies. My name is Bernard Epps."

Okay . . . Natasha thought. *And?* Nothing rang a bell.

"I'm best friends with the contestant who's going to win the show," he said, smiling wider as he shook Jorgette's hand quickly and then held Camille's.

Natasha relaxed. Whew! Only a friend trying to get his fifteen minutes of fame. However, instant annoyance coursed through her. The man had strolled over here, with his fine self, sporting his navy Polo shirt and khakis, blown her girls' minds, and eaten into her precious few minutes of bonding time with her girlfriends over some yang. "Mr. Epps, it's a pleasure," she said grudgingly. "I'm glad one of our contestants has the support of good friends. He'll need it."

Bernard Epps smiled, his gaze locked on Camille, and he hadn't dropped her hand. "And you are?" he said seductively, allowing Camille to extract her hand as she began to blush.

"I'm Camille Johnson, and this is Jorgette Graves, and the show's illustrious producer, our best friend, Natasha Ward."

"Ladies," he said, nodding, but still gazing at Camille. "My pleasure. I know the time is short before the contestants will be saying bon voyage, but I told my man that I had to come over here and meet the classiest women in this media mêlée."

"Who's your friend?" Jorgette said, her tone eager as she stood on tiptoes to see over the crowd.

"Tyrell Ramsey," Bernard said, stepping closer to Camille. "He's the CEO of Off Da Meter Records, and as his vice president, I'd put my money on him, hands down."

"Well, if he wins, you'll need an attorney to help you navigate all the contracts and endorsements that are sure to follow camera-worthy gentlemen, such as yourselves," Camille said, her voice sultry as she fished a business card from her purse and coolly slid it into Bernard's hand. "Since you're not on the show . . . perhaps we can do lunch one day?"

"Name the day, and it's done." Bernard used two fingers to glide Camille's card into his pocket, and quickly produced one for her.

This could not be happening! Natasha didn't move a muscle. She refused to glance around the dock to spy Tyrell Ramsey. Her nerves couldn't take the jolt, but her peripheral vision betrayed her. The brother was doing all white Polo, his dark walnut complexion set off like polished stone in the sun beneath his collar shirt and shorts. She had to stop glimpsing the way the bricks in his torso moved beneath the fabric as he tried to get to the registration table . . . and his legs, heaven help her. Each stride was a graceful ripple of sinew that seemed as though it were made of steel cable connected to a greased pulley. When he turned around and bent down to sign his paperwork, she held her breath. She would not stare at that man's marble-carved behind. She had to get it together!

Looking down at her clipboard quickly, she mouthed a lame reply. "Oh, yes, uh . . . a Mr. Ramsey . . . from Atlanta." She glanced up, her expression one of forced calm. Her best girlfriend could not be fraternizing with the best friend of a contestant. If the media got hold of that . . . if Nathan Greenberg heard about it, the man would have a heart attack! There'd be investigations about favoritism. Oh, Lawd!

"*Hot*lanta, GA," Bernard corrected with a smile

and a sexy southern drawl that gave his statement emphasis.

"He has about as good a chance as any to win," Natasha hedged, her mouth going dry as she tried to extract her and her friends from the precarious conversation. "I wish all the contestants well. Now, Mr. Epps, is it? You will excuse us; we have a million details to attend to before boarding. Why not enjoy some of the refreshments provided over *there* for friends and family?"

She waved her arm as casually as possible to motion where he could go, half as an offer, half as a dismissal. The problem was that her girlfriend Camille was smiling, had become flushed and rosy, and was bashfully looking down at her fawn Coach bag as she smoothed the front of her raw silk, pale pink pants suit.

"My apologies," Bernard crooned, his gaze raking Camille. "I didn't mean to intrude on your conversation . . . it was just that I was moved to come over and speak before the opportunity passed."

"Uh, I have a question," Jorgette said, her eyes glittering with mischief.

Bernard's smile widened and he cocked his head to the side waiting for Jorgette to speak.

Tension knotted every muscle in Natasha's back. *Not now, girl . . .*

"Do either of you have any brothers?" Jorgette asked, giggling.

"None that lovely ladies like you would like to meet . . . but we do have some very cool artists signed to our label that we'd be happy to introduce you to."

"Artists?" Jorgette said, her voice a raspy whisper as she toyed with the tie of her lime green sarong halter dress at the nape of her neck. "Any tall, handsome, dreadlock-sporting, creative types who might be interested in *moi*?"

"Since Ms. Ward is obviously very busy, why don't you, Camille, and I discuss how that might be arranged over at the feeding trough?"

Camille and Jorgette's laughter joined in with Bernard's, and to Natasha's horror, her girlfriends air-kissed her quickly, said good-bye, and left her standing alone on the dock. This was definitely not supposed to go down like this! And this was exactly why she hadn't asked the rest of her family to come out to the going away event. But she'd thought *her girls* would have more couth! There were simply no words. Who was this Tyrell Ramsey who obviously ran with wolves?

See, this was why he didn't tell his other buddies or his brothers about the event. He had one VIP pass and thought his boy, Bernard, could handle the whole glitz and glamour thing. But no, his boy had actually walked up to the woman and walked away with not one, but two, of her girls! And he had to get on a yacht, with her, and try to navigate a game show with that fine sister glowering at him and thinking he was a true dawg the whole time.

If it wasn't such a bad predicament, he might have laughed out loud. His homeboy was supposed to be the conservative one, the cool one, the one with the level head. Obviously the abstinence Bernard had dealt with was making the brother foolish. This was business, not a pleasure junket. This wasn't the danged *Love Boat*!

Frustrated, Tyrell made his way beyond the

media huddle to report in at the contestant registration booth. There, he tried to concentrate on the information that was quickly rattled off to him before he signed his life away for the second time. But his focus was splintered between the heavy hitting contenders who gathered around the table with him, and the fine producer who appeared to be as peeved with Bernard as he was at the moment.

Tyrell cautiously sized up the group of male contestants, noting that the women had not yet arrived. Each man offered the next a very careful handshake and a sportsmanlike, rehearsed, "Good luck," none of them meaning it. But none of them cared or took offense. It was all a part of the game. Each was on guard; no one revealing any information about himself that could give a competitor the potential advantage. Only when he saw her come toward the group with a clipboard, did Tyrell's palms begin to get moist.

"Good morning, gentlemen. How is everyone today?"

Murmured greetings rippled through the group. Tyrell only nodded as he stared at the dark goddess on the dock. With the crystal-blue sky framing her, cameras trailing her every graceful move, and the breeze blowing her bright orange wrap dress away from her long, shapely legs so the sun could gleam against them, his voice failed him. A bland good morning didn't cut it. He could practically see her petite breasts through the sheer fabric, and the color of it against her ebony skin was mesmerizing. The way her tiny waist drew in tightly only to swell to her sensuously padded hips, he could only pray that she didn't turn around. If she had a dip in her lovely lower back that gave rise to a wondrous, sister-girl shelf of backside, he might make a fool of himself out there.

He thought that staring at her face would be the most prudent course of action, given that seeing her had burned the saliva away from his mouth. But that was becoming problematic, too. Her smile dimmed the sun. Her mouth was so ripe and full and moist that it seemed like a piece of ripe fruit he was hankering to taste. Her big, dark brown eyes appeared to smolder within her pretty, oval face . . . but her husky voice destroyed him as much as the apparition of her did.

"Well, since everyone is so serious this morning," she said brightly, "let me dispense with the introductions and the shipboard room assignments."

Girlfriend messed up and turned around. Tyrell planted his stance more firmly to keep from weaving as she walked to the table, bent, and gathered up a stack of papers, then returned to stand before the group. Just as he'd suspected, 'Tash had it going on from the rear. He couldn't help himself. He had to scan down her toned back and follow the trail down her spine, his gaze dipping into the swaying valley that rose with two thick mounds of pure carved righteousness. As she spoke, he forced himself to shake the image from his mind, just so he could concentrate. He reminded himself again: this was a business venture, not a pleasure junket.

"Okay. We have Anthony Adams from the Big Apple, who is a publishing executive. You'll be in room number one with Jason Fulbright, a native of D.C., who is a legal fellow on Capitol Hill."

Tyrell studied the two contestants as they stepped forward and sized each other up, and then extended their palms for a quick handshake. Two executives in the same room? Two guys who were both the same tone of caramel, one with a cosmopolitan, wavy curl thing happening, and the other with a conservative, near military haircut—both pretty boys. Tyrell smiled as he mentally placed bets on how long the two pretty boy sharks would take before stabbing each other in the back corporate style.

"Then we have Nelson Carter, a CEO of his own construction firm from Philadelphia, in room number two with Michael Quazar, a software firm CEO from Palo Alto, California—by way of Boston."

Tyrell rubbed his jaw. Yeah, he'd heard about the tall Greek guy from Cali who had pulled a huge media coup by flying into Boston and taking the contest out there by storm. But rooming him in with the hard-hat brother from Philly was gonna be interesting. Tyrell watched the way the two contestants sized each other up. Both were huge, physically, each casually flexing and showing off body builder's physiques, as they accepted their room keys. Two entrepreneurs who think they run the world, one using a computer, the other using a construction crew? Oh, this sister, 'Tash, had a wicked sense of humor.

"Next, Antonio Rodriguez, our telecommunications sales executive from L.A., will be Joseph Scott's roommate, who owns an auto dealership in St. Louis. Gentlemen, you are in room number three."

Two salesmen in the same room? Tyrell almost laughed out loud, but checked himself. West coast meets dirty South. The fly-gear-wearing Latino brother from L.A. probably had a short fuse and was used to pulling all the honeys with his toothpaste commercial smile, and the tall, dark-skinned brother from St. Louis looked like he was pure black prima donna pimp. He knew it in his soul, those two would be talking enough trash to make either one of them snap, lose it, and start a fight onboard. He could feel it in his bones. But as the room numbers were getting higher, and the choices of roommates were thinning out, Tyrell began to worry. Who were they gonna force him to have to deal with?

"Okay." Tash sighed. "Let me see. We'll have Floyd Jackson, an engineer within the auto industry from Detroit, room with Samuel Hartman, an aviation engineer from New Orleans. Gentlemen, you'll be in room number four."

Tyrell couldn't believe it. He could just imagine the tense-looking, light-skinned brother with glasses arguing about who was smarter and who had more opportunities with the tall, blonde, athletic guy who seemed like he was mixed with Creole. Oh, yeah, the contestants in that room would be basket cases before it was all over. Then he stopped as he realized that he'd be walled up in a room with an arrogant Italian guy. She didn't . . .

"And that leaves our final pair. Tyrell Ramsey, an insurance salesman by day, record label owner by night, from Atlanta, to room with Mario Campanelli, who owns a string of clubs throughout Chicago."

It took a moment for Tyrell to step forward. The woman *did not* room him with a Sly Stallone–looking, probably Italian mob-backed club owner from Chi-town! How could she? If dude was in the club business, then Campanelli was most likely as street as he was. Plus, women liked that Italian, foreign language talking bull . . . and he had to hand it to 'em, they could wear the gear, listened to the same music—especially if he was in the hot club scene, and might even be able to dance. Damn! More than likely the arrogant SOB would talk much trash, which meant they might have to come to blows to squash whatever . . . and after the whole show debacle was over, a guy like Campanelli might have him seen.

Begrudgingly, Tyrell stepped forward, shook Campanelli's hand, hard, returning the iron grip that spoke volumes between men—don't start none, won't be none.

Okay, now it was on.

"The ladies will be joining the ship later, and will be sequestered until dinner, where they will each be brought out, formally, and introduced to the group. We will be serving a sumptuous shipboard meal, five courses, and each lady will join the table of pairs, switching tables during each course change so you can have intimate groupings where everyone can better get to know each other. We will not be introducing you gentlemen, that part is up to you. So pull out your best gear, kick your best game, rehearse your best lines, as first impressions set the tone for most interactions. I suggest that you go to your rooms, unpack, and relax until dinner."

Natasha smiled. Tyrell ignored her, having become too ornery about the situation to be moved.

Chapter 6

Tyrell kept his gaze roving as he made his way up the gangplank and followed the others across the hardwood, highly polished deck, down a narrow hall, and then down a flight of metal steps. The vessel was truly magnificent, and he wondered if the other contestants knew about yachts, sailing, and the whole nautical world. He sure didn't. That concerned him.

It was a vast oversight; he should have boned up on boating terms and vocabulary before he climbed aboard. He'd be out of his element, and that wouldn't be good. The other guys could use their knowledge to impress the ladies and show him up. Somehow the process of induction felt like he'd just signed up to be in the navy, rather than a game show.

He stood in the narrow doorway of room five, watching his roommate and competitor lay first claim to the bed he wanted, and then begin to stow his gear as though he didn't have a roommate, taking up more available space than was warranted. Tyrell said nothing, although it grated him as he muttered a hello that was barely returned, and put a stake in his claim for his half of the room.

But as he watched Mario Campanelli function, a slow awareness came over him. This guy wasn't used to sharing; it was obvious in the way his whole body language went rigid as Tyrell calmly plopped his luggage on the adjacent bed and picked up the little note card that was on the pillow. Instantly Tyrell knew that, being a kid from around the way, with a lot of brothers and limited home space, all of that would help him keep his head.

"So, you're from Chi-town?" Tyrell said in a pleasant tone, addressing Mario's back as he opened the small card.

"Yeah," Mario said curtly. "Heard you were from Atlanta."

"Hotlanta, GA, it is," Tyrell said, smiling as he watched Mario neatly arrange his toothbrush and deodorant on the single dresser that contained four drawers. In that instant he decided not to unpack. He'd leave his belongings in a ready-to-roll status. The less any of them knew about him, the better. "We have to go to the main dining room in a few minutes to get our safety training."

"I know," Mario said, sounding annoyed. He glanced at his watch. "We have ten more minutes before we have to be down there."

Tyrell nodded. Oh, so it was like that. But, then, how else was it supposed to be? Tyrell kept his gaze even as he studied Mario. The guy knew something that basic and didn't even say anything to his cellmate? Okay, competition was one thing, but what about a little common courtesy in the mix? Tyrell just smiled, and it turned into a chuckle as he left Mario to arrange his stash of expensive colognes.

The tone had been set. Tyrell walked the halls, exploring, getting a quick feel for the terrain. Notwithstanding the upcoming ship tour, it was important for him to learn where every room was, every bathroom, every closet, and every porthole on his own. During the tour, he'd be watching the competition, studying them, not the fine points of the ship.

As he passed the open doors of male show contestants, bustling crew members, camera jockeys, and show staff, for a moment he paused, wondering if Natasha Ward would be coming along for the ride. He shook the errant thought and regained his focus. He'd tried to start off with a baseline level of cool. But it was obvious that it was every man for himself on every level. There would be no downtime, where he could at least be halfway chill with anybody. However, if one knew going in that they were jumping into a pool of sharks, then forewarned was forearmed. The key was, never allowing the competition to make him blow his cool.

Natasha dropped her bags beside the bed and sighed. This was definitely not what she'd signed up for—but what was done was done.

"Hey, boss, it's not so bad," Stephanie said brightly. "Think of it as an adventure."

"Yes, Steph, it will be an adventure, all right," Natasha replied, her focus on unpacking the basics and arranging them for quick access.

"I went to see this lady—who is very intuitive, before we got this under way, and she said that what is going to happen will change our careers forever."

Natasha groaned as she yanked open the zipper

of her suitcase. Just what she needed; advice from Stephanie's psychic. "You know how this business goes, lady. It's on or off, hot or cold. This will either make our careers or kill them. You could have given me the fifty bucks to tell you that."

"Stop being such a worrywart, 'Tash. This lady is awesome, and she said huge things are going to happen."

All Natasha could do was chuckle. "Okay, kiddo. If it makes you feel better, then we'll stay in the positive cosmic flow of the universe."

Stephanie laughed, flopped on the bed adjacent to Natasha, and sat with her legs folded in a yoga position. "Oh, come on, 'Tash. Where's your sense of adventure? We could have a worse gig, ya know. So, even if this fails, and the ratings suck, we will have had a once in a lifetime chance to do something most people never get to do."

"All right, all right," Natasha fussed, her tone cheerful. "Now you sound, ironically, like my mother. She'd say count my blessings, even though I've been drinking Maalox for the last week leading up to this madness—if I wasn't doing, what she calls, a shameless parade of flesh across the television for all the world to see."

This time, they both laughed.

"It's not all that bad," Stephanie soothed, once her giggles subsided.

Natasha leaned on the door frame. "It better be, or you know Nathan will have a coronary."

Again, both women laughed and the discordant sound of relief combined with nervous hysteria wafted out into the hall.

* * *

Tyrell stopped walking. He'd know her voice any-where. She was on the boat and she was laughing. But the tone within it sounded as scared and strained as he felt. Oddly, that relaxed him, and it also made him bold because it made so much sense. *This was her job.* For her, it wasn't a game. If she didn't do well, then most likely they'd replace her. The entertainment business took no prisoners. That much he was sure of.

He resumed walking, this time with purpose, and rounded the corner to find the source of the fe-male laughter. If a little luck was on his side, maybe she wasn't just giving her team last minute instruc-tions before she debarked. Maybe she'd stay to oversee all the operations? Maybe he might just have one friendly face and set of eyes to glance at from time to time, even if she did have to do her job and boot him off the ship, if he lost a round. But it still made a difference that she was there now, even though she'd sorta set him up with that Mario character.

As soon as he spotted her leaning on the door frame, he smiled. It truly tickled him that her eyes widened for a second before her professional façade tried to freeze him out.

"Hey, ladies. You all going to the safety meeting?"

Natasha watched Tyrell mentally absorb the room at a distance. She could practically see the wheels turning in his head as he glanced at her suit-case, then Stephanie's, before his sheepish grin went megawatt.

"Aren't you supposed to be settling in and get-ting to know your roommate?" Natasha replied, sounding as casual as possible.

"I am settling in," Tyrell said, issuing Stephanie a

wink that made her blush. "Plus, I already know my roommate."

"What!" Natasha and Stephanie said in unison.

"This cannot happen," Natasha said quickly.

"You're not supposed to be onboard with a friend," Stephanie gasped as she shot up from the bed. "Oh, my God, this cannot be happening! We have to call Nathan. We'll have to stop the shoot and—"

"Relax," Tyrell said, thoroughly amused. "There's no scandal. I know his type, not him personally. He isn't all that interested in getting to know me, so my idea of settling in is to walk around and figure out this floating tank I'll be living on for ten weeks."

"Oh," both women said together, placing their palms over their hearts.

Natasha closed her eyes for a moment and inhaled to slow her heart rate. Stephanie weaved and found the side of the bed to sit down before she fell down.

Tyrell shook his head and chuckled as he looked at his watch. Timing was indeed everything, and the brief exchange had confirmed his every hunch. "The safety class, ladies—unless you've already taken it, begins in three minutes."

She sat there at a dining room table listening to Captain Russell give the VIP overview of boating safety, while his crew demonstrated life jacket use, pointed out emergency exits, lifeboats, and how to use a shipboard fire extinguisher. And even though the captain's voice was of the smoothest Caribbean silk tenor, and although the information he was imparting had everything to do with one's personal survival, especially for a sister who could barely do the doggy paddle in the water, the rush that Tyrell had produced hijacked her focus nonetheless.

It was nearly impossible to be in the same room with the man without his charismatic way eclipsing everything else that was going on. He had *it*—Tyrell Ramsey had true star quality. Something she hadn't seen up close and personal, although she worked in an industry that produced *The It Factor*.

Repeatedly, Natasha tried to wrest her focus back to the safety lesson. But time and time again, Tyrell stole the show by asking a crazy question that made the crew chuckle, and even the other contestants grudgingly laugh. His self-deprecating manner drew them all in as he made jokes about being a kid from the 'hood who had never been on a boat, and truthfully, wasn't trying to be on one. She watched him confess to his disadvantage with humor, unashamed of who he was, and disarming everyone in the process.

When he stood up and repeated after the captain, "Okay, portside, star-something, helm, stern . . . Yo, man, if there's a fire or something, don't get technical—cool? Just tell a brother—*jump*, and I got you." The whole room laughed hard. And it was so utterly, absolutely sexy. . . . A man comfortable enough in his own skin not to care what people thought, confident enough to act a fool, but to also be shrewd enough to know that working the crowd in the dining room meant working a national audience. It was genius, subtle upstaging. He'd used the platform of his lack of knowledge and the other contestants' male ego against them. They sat quietly, looking intelligent and engrossed. Tyrell interacted, won over the crew, relaxed the entire group, and he'd have call-in support from viewers before the ship even pulled out of port.

Natasha shook her head. The man was on fire. The cameras were eating him up alive. When the female crew member put on an orange life vest, and upon the captain's instructions, showed everyone how to blow into the tube if it didn't inflate, and Tyrell closed his eyes, outstretched his hands and asked her to stop, the room erupted again.

"Ten weeks, sis. Don't go there," Tyrell comically pleaded toward the young woman who was now giggling so hard she couldn't blow up the vest. "I'm trying to at least make it to one round, girl. Fellas, tell her, we can't watch you do that." Tyrell pounded fists with several contestants at his table, who were doubled over laughing.

"Ms. Hicks," Captain Russell said, mirth disrupting the authority in his tone, "why not allow one of our other crew members to demonstrate that aspect of the life jacket."

Tyrell shut his eyes and covered them with his palm as the young woman handed the vest to a male crew member. Tyrell grimaced and then peeked through his fingers. "Oh, no, I *definitely* don't want to see that either, y'all. We get the picture."

Again, the room erupted into gales of laughter. Devon leaned in close to Natasha, still recovering as he tried to whisper.

"This guy is the show hook, you know that, right?"

Natasha simply nodded.

Her face hurt from laughing so much and she didn't really care that her mascara was beginning to smudge at the corners of her eyes. The tour had been a real trip. At every door entrance, Tyrell had something smart to say, drawing in the other contestants into his mischief one by one. At the shared contestant bathrooms, he held the doors open, shaking his head, talking trash about not having elbowroom to even handle his business. But when everyone's mind went south, Tyrell covered his heart with his hand, feigned innocence, and told them to get their minds out of the gutter, claiming he was talking about reading the newspaper on the john—that was all.

By the time the brief tour concluded, and the male contestants had been sequestered in their rooms so that the anonymous female contestants could board, Natasha had almost forgotten that she was indeed working. She had to get her head right, had to regain her professional distance and decorum, and mentally steel herself to deal with five new personalities.

Before she and Stephanie had had a chance to share a private high five on the successful taping of the male boarding segment, Devon was through their suite door.

"Don't you ever knock?" Stephanie asked him with a smile.

"Of course not, when I'm this overwhelmed," he said, swooning against the door as he shut it behind him. "We've got gold. Celluloid gold. Black gold, can't you feel it?"

Begrudgingly, Natasha nodded with a smile, not wanting to jinx the project. "We just got some pretty good stuff."

"Good stuff!" Devon shrieked. "Are you mad? Good does not even describe it," he said, waving his arms and imploring Stephanie to back him up. "Oh, tell her, Steph, just be honest. He'll decimate them. I'm seeing *People* magazine, after the show couple follow on shows, a new season!"

"Before you get all caught up," Natasha warned, "the ladies have to like him, keep him on the ship, and he can't mess up, or do anything that will—"

"'Tash," Stephanie said, her face serious, "he'll slay 'em."

For a moment they all fell silent.

"The underdog is gonna pull this out, you know it in your heart, 'Tash. This is cosmic justice," Devon said, rushing to Natasha and holding her by her upper arms. "Stephanie's psychic had a vision, right Steph?"

Devon was shaking her so hard and looking between her and Stephanie so frantically that Natasha burst out laughing.

"All right, all right, he has the it factor."

Devon dropped her arms and threw up his hands. "That, is all I wanted to hear." He fanned his face and took a deep, cleansing breath with his eyes closed. "Only once in a career, if you're lucky, do you run across one like this—a natural." He opened his eyes, put his hands on his hips and stared at them hard. "We have work to do, ladies. These females are duds, personality wise. Do you have the dinner cards?" he asked, his mood and voice instantly shifting to a drill sergeant's crisp, businesslike command.

"Right here," Stephanie said, swallowing a wide grin as she produced the ivory embossed invitations for Devon.

"Good," he snapped. "Now, let's see if we can get

these she devils to give us a half ounce of theater before we shove off."

He hated waiting and wondering and being locked in his room for an hour. What was worse was being trapped in a room with Mario Campanelli. His roommate seemed to know he'd been trumped, but it was obvious that Mario still wasn't exactly sure how. But the guy was clearly salty. As soon as they'd reentered the room, Mario's be-cool-for-the-cameras smile had faded and he'd donned a pair of headphones, laid down on the bed, and shut his eyes.

Cool, Tyrell thought. *No biggie.* He had headphones and a Walkman, too. In fact, the more he thought about it, he shoulda brought his boom box!

But he had more important things to worry about, and chilling out did seem like a good idea. As Tyrell reclined on the bed and shut his eyes, a hundred questions ran through his mind. Would Bernard remember the code if he got in over his head; one wink directly into the camera with a smile meant send in reinforcements? Would the wink hit the editing room floor, and his boy never see it? Would they send them somewhere so far and so exotic that it would be mad-crazy expensive and impossible to get a quick flight to it? And would Bernard be able to rally some of their artists to meet them in time? Would they be able to get through the security barriers? If they did, and he could arrange a special treat for the ladies, would that represent a breach that could get him put off the show?

Nagging doubts made it impossible to catnap, especially with the tense, bad vibes oozing off of Mario. What did they have planned tonight, anyway? Why did they have to wait to see the female contestants? What if this was one of those flip-the-script reality shows where every female on the boat was dog ugly, and only the guy who was really nice to them all would win? Tyrell opened his eyes and stared at the ceiling, wondering where the hidden cameras had been placed in their room.

So what if the sisters weren't fine. It wasn't about that, anyway. It was about treating them all the way every woman wanted to be treated—decently. That was the thing; he wasn't there to get hooked up with any sister. He was there to win the game by giving each woman the same time, attention, and courtesy so that none felt slighted.

As he allowed the thought to wash through him, calm befell him. Treat them all like the sisters he never had. Be friends. That was something women rarely got offered these days. They had heard the lines; he oughta know, having kicked enough lines in the past. If he kept it like that, sisterly affection at the forefront, treated them like family, then what could go wrong?

It was so simple a concept that Tyrell almost chuckled as he began dozing. He could remember the family reunions, the weddings, even funerals. If you were an available male, you danced with everybody, got drinks for everybody, helped the old ladies, teased your younger cousins and told them how pretty they were till they blushed. You pulled chairs for the matrons, offered your elbow up a church step for the elders, helped corral errant children, and tended barbeque grills. You pitched in and picked up the slack where missing husbands, AWOL lovers, and dead men walking left a void.

And as soon as the awareness gelled, he realized that the woman who'd conceived this show knew this secret, *had lived it.* In his very soul he knew you had to have experienced this to understand the complex simplicity of it. They were more alike than he'd cared to imagine. He could see her big, beautiful brown eyes get wide with fear that he was going to mess up her job, mess up her show plan, and now, with deeper understanding, he also remembered seeing the pain in her dark irises. It was all in her expressive face, an appeal for him not to blow it before he'd begun. She wanted him there, was trying to give him a chance to show them all how it was done 'round the way.

How could he have been so oblivious to the obvious? No ring on her finger, no tolerance for bull . . . if she'd been in his family, she would have been one of the women he'd tend to . . . she was a woman with a void.

Again, Tyrell opened his eyes, but this time sat up needing air. The room felt confining. He wanted to go to the top deck and let the wind hit his face. He wanted to feel the freedom of motion. One of the contestants, *who wasn't even a contestant,* was already under his skin and the ship hadn't even pulled up anchor.

Claustrophobia set in. He tried not to panic and took in slow sips of air. She was available, and smart, and funny, and sexy, and was from what he recognized in one word—home. She had made good in her profession, like he had. But had never lost her respect for the old traditions of southern hospitality, like him. She had skillfully hidden her message and methods in a game, like he had.

Maybe she did it because she, like so many of the women in his family, had lost hope? Or maybe she did it for the same reasons he was on the show? Like him, she needed just one more shot at the title before throwing in the towel . . . before resigning herself to working a regular job, behind the scenes for the rest of her life? Clearly, girlfriend was taking a career gamble, a big one, just like he was.

Tyrell stood and stretched, trying to seem casual when Mario glared at him for the disturbance, closed his eyes, and went back to ignoring him with his music. Tyrell walked over to his luggage to act like that had absorbed his attention. He couldn't concentrate on this new possibility. Now was not the time to allow anything to blow his head up with drama. He reminded himself that, although she might be what he'd been searching for and was right down the hall and around the corner, that corner was laden with hidden cameras. And, she'd get a bird's-eye view of who he was, what he was about, and how he dealt with women from a spectator's standpoint, judging, assessing.

He tried to banish the thoughts as he heard a slight rustle of paper slip beneath his door. No doubt about it, this ship was too small for him and Natasha Ward to be on together.

Chapter 7

"Meeeeow," Devon fussed, flopping on Natasha's bed. "Tell me, were we sniffing glue when we picked this bunch of—"

"Devon, please," Natasha begged. "What's done is done."

"I know, but after the men's tour, what the *hell* was *that*? It was totally flat, devoid of anything worthwhile, and just lackluster. No wonder they're still single!"

Both Stephanie and Natasha looked at each other, sharing a silent ouch.

"The dinner invitations have been delivered," Stephanie said crisply. "And, frankly, after that last comment, I need some space."

Appearing horrified, Devon stood quickly. "Oh, love, I was *not* talking about you or signifying about your status. Hell, I'm *very* colorful, and unfortunately, still single, too." He kissed her forehead and made her smile, even though she snatched away, determined to stay annoyed with him.

Natasha sat down heavily on the bed, truly knowing how long the ten weeks before them would be. "Devon is right. We'll have to fast forward through their boring ship introduction, and create some new twist to soak up some time."

"Like what?" Stephanie asked, leaning against the sparse wall space.

"We've given them the dinner invitations and seating arrangements where we do the whole roulette thing; each woman gets to share a dinner course with a two-man male table." Devon's eyes twinkled with renewed excitement. "We'll watch the guys duke it out for each gal's attention during five gourmet courses, the women in their finery, the men dressed to the nines, and everyone having now till the dinner to get to know each other . . . what more can we do?"

"Maybe we can stretch out that segment, if we get some interesting antics at each table?" Stephanie offered.

Natasha shook her head as she leaned back on the headboard and closed her eyes. "No, all you'll get is polite conversation. The dinner was just a little glitz and glamour filler until we get them down to the Bahamas, but I want this first show to pop with controversy. The women aren't giving us anything to work with."

"Nor are the guys, beyond that one catalyst we have," Stephanie said, her tone morose.

Natasha opened her eyes as Devon claimed the adjacent bed. "What's the funniest thing about cruising a club, Dev?"

He smiled and raked his fingers through his hair. "The opening line. Oh, and I have heard some beauts!"

"Have you told the guys they can go up on deck yet?" Natasha looked at Stephanie and grinned.

"Noooo . . . but why do I know you have something truly wicked running through your head?"

"Because I do, Steph." Natasha stood slowly and began pacing in the tight confines. "What if you give the guys express instructions that they can only wave, smile, wink, or whatever, but they are not to verbally interact with these women until they are formally introduced at dinner? They can look, leer, whatever, but they cannot talk to these sisters."

"Oh, that is insane," Stephanie said, covering her face with her hands.

"It's perfect," Devon exclaimed. "But don't tell the women what's up. Just tell them that they all have to stay together in a group until it's time to go down to change for dinner. Let them think whatever, and they'll believe that they have a group of too shy guys who won't break the ice to come over to their group, no matter what kind of come hither looks they issue. Now *that* will create some outrageous dialogue in their little huddle, I'm so sure, as they talk about these guys being losers, and I'm sure the guys will be dying as the women step up their seduction game, but they can't speak to them."

Stephanie clapped her hands, and then arched her fingers like claws. "Rrrrhhhh, hisssss," she said, laughing and imitating the sound of cats fighting. "I know what me and my girlfriends talk about when there's a club filled with cute guys who are too dorky or self-absorbed to walk over and buy a woman a drink! Oh!"

Devon clasped Natasha's face with both palms and gave her an air kiss. "Genius, darling, sheer genius. You are the master of mayhem, the mistress of the foul."

Natasha laughed, even though she wasn't sure

she liked the title that had been bestowed on her. A slight pang of guilt stabbed her in the side as her staff gabbed about the logistics and prepared to knock on each man's door with new instructions—cameramen in tow.

Tyrell listened intently as Devon breezed into his and Mario's room to release them from incarceration, but draped a new wrinkle in the game on them. He chuckled as Devon ranted on and on, and as each facet was revealed, it made him think of how Natasha Ward's mind worked. She was brilliant, and he could see it clear as day in his head . . . her and her girls, all fine, sitting in a club, sipping drinks, bashing the male species, waiting on somebody to have enough gonads to simply walk up to them—as a group—and be hospitable enough, like the old days, to buy all of the women seated a drink. It was strategically beautiful.

He calmly waited for Devon to leave, and watched Mario hustle out of the room behind the producer to make it to the deck before any of the others, obviously eager to see what the female lineup looked like. Instead, Tyrell hung back, found a pen and some paper, and wrote out five brief notes, and tucked them neatly into his pocket.

"They are sooo cute," Vera said. "I have seen a lot of executive types, given I'm in real estate and specialize in corporate relocations, and these guys are awesome." She wrinkled her tiny, button nose as she covered her mouth with her hand, giggling the whole time she spoke.

"Cute, girl—you betta stop playing. Their asses are fine!" Linda said, her head held high with sassy attitude, her intricate basket pattern of cornrows and chiseled, coffee-hued features making her look like a sun goddess as she placed one hand on her gym-toned hip. The statuesque beauty cut a knowing glance at the male group. "I have Wall Street brothers from the Big Apple come sit in my salon chairs, darlin', and I also know what a good suit looks like. But if they're too chickenshit to come over here, then, who knows, they might be on the DL?"

A series of high fives rippled around the five-woman team, along with whoops of laughter. Natasha glanced at her crew; the cameras were eating it up. Leave it to the New Yorker to serve it straight with no chaser. Excellent. Devon gave her a thumbs-up from across the deck, signaling that they'd found another live-wire in the bunch as Linda Jones strutted to a neutral position where the camera could get a full shot of her brick house figure in her white silk halter and hipster set. The navel ring was a killer, so were the woman's abs, and Natasha watched the men to see their reactions as they drank beers from their side of the deck, wondering what their conversation was about. But it concerned her that Tyrell had lagged behind.

"Well, maybe they're just intimidated and don't want to offend any of us by making an awkward approach," Michelle said, sighing and sipping her lemonade. "After all, this is stressful for them. They're the ones in jeopardy of being booted off the yacht, not us."

"Leave it to the Harvard psychologist to psychoanalyze these guys before they've even laid on her couch," Stephanie murmured in Natasha's ear.

Natasha swallowed a smile behind her bottled water as she took a sip of it. She had to admit thinking the same thing as the long-legged, trim Michelle tossed her D.C. perfect, auburn-highlighted tresses over her shoulder and adjusted the tasteful strap on her neat, white, cotton sundress.

"Well, I for one just wish they would stop being scared and come on over and say hello," Vera whined, pouting. "The way we were taught in the corporate real estate game was, you have to be aggressive and friendly if you want to meet people."

Natasha nodded and smiled and tried not to gag as she watched Vera Banks, realtor extraordinaire to hear her tell it, unnecessarily lean over the top deck rail, run her fingers through her short silky hair, and allow her too ample cleavage for her too petite frame to practically fall out of her fuchsia halter top just enough to catch the cameraman's lens. The only saving grace was that the New York salon owner, Linda Jones, had rolled her eyes at Vera's antics. Yeah, yeah, yeah, we've already done your bio, hon, Natasha thought, becoming surly. She couldn't help it. This woman was always selling, and always reminding them—on air—about her successful profession. The perky little cheerleader routine was wearing Natasha out as she chaperoned the all-female group.

"I'd love to hear their voices, though, nervous or not," Lillian, admitted after a while, glancing in the direction of the male huddle by the bar. "In telemarketing, you learn so much by the sound of a man's voice—but sometimes, the face doesn't match the voice."

"Word," Linda said, slapping five with Lillian, making the group laugh.

It was so strange, but Natasha could tell that Linda, with her crazy, outrageous self, and Lillian, who was dressed in conservative Docker shorts and a red tank top, were already bonding. Vera's squeaky voice had alienated the group, just as Michelle's air of intellectual superiority definitely had. And Kimberly Gibson from Houston was all steel magnolia.

The executive-wannabe-actress had shut out the group's conversation, simply smiling prettily as she took a pose in her lime green bikini top and Daisy Duke white short shorts, draping her to-die-for form against the rail in a way that would have rivaled a *Sports Illustrated* swimsuit issue. Natasha watched Kimberly work every gift she'd been blessed with, using everything from her Pocahontas length of sable hair to her caramel butter skin, and smoldering, Ethiopian eyes. Sister had it going on and knew it as her focus and gaze on the male group intensified without waver. She then leaned her chin up to the sun, the rays of it accenting the copper highlights in her flawless skin and bouncing off her long, brunette hair that blew in the breeze

"Oooooh, barracuda," Stephanie whispered as she passed Natasha again.

"Yup. Totally," Natasha murmured, and took another sip of water, her line of vision on the men's group and settling on Tyrell.

Okay, so he'd been wrong. Dead wrong. This was no script flip. The show had scoured the planet and found five of the finest sisters he'd seen amassed in one place at one time. He scanned the group of them, smiling at all equally and evenly, but his gaze settled on Natasha Ward.

To him, standing there in the sun, she looked like a wildflower amongst a bouquet of hothouse orchids. They were all powdered, hair spritzed for the cameras, the natural shine that came from just being out in the sun erased from audience view. He watched Natasha move quietly in the background. Occasionally he'd get a glimpse of her eyes. She was offering the professional mask. That much he could tell by the sad smolder that he saw within them. The contrast was stark, so different from the woman who had come alive with laughter when they'd all toured the ship earlier. But the fact that he'd been wrong about the potential five contestants had shaken his confidence a little. What if he'd been wrong about Natasha?

"Yeah, man, I hear you," Nelson Carter said. "The eye candy is off day heezy fo' sheezy, brother."

Rejoining the conversation, Tyrell chuckled and clinked his beer bottle against Nelson's, saluting the cool construction firm owner from Philly. Tyrell made his mind up right then and there—Nelson he could deal with, but he and the brother from D.C., who worked on Capitol Hill, Jason Fulbright, and the arrogant magazine publisher from New York, Anthony Adams, were not gonna get along, no more than he and Mario would.

Tyrell continued to study the group as the group continued to study the women, each man chiming in with his assessment, trying to guess professions, ages, and the kind of men each woman might go for. It was so ridiculous, but it bought him time. He felt like he was at a high school dance.

The engineer from Detroit, Floyd, and the blonde one from Colorado, Sam, were just too dry for him to engage in convo. Joe Scott, the auto dealer from St. Louis, was just too pimp style for him. Brother was playing the role so hard all laid-back and chill-factor till it didn't make sense. But, oddly, he could get some good jokes going with Mike Quazar, the Greek from Palo Alto—that was a funny dude. So was the wild Latino brother from L.A., Tony Rodriguez. Antonio was cool enough, like Quazar, to allow his name to be shortened to an around the way nickname. The big question was, however, when to make his move, and then, after he did, was he prepared for it to be on?

Antonio Rodriguez laughed and shook his head. "See that one on the rail in the green, how you gonna treat her like all the rest of them, man? Just look at her."

Tyrell felt his fingertips tingle as he touched the little notes in his pocket. "I'ma show you how to treat them all the same," he said, setting his beer down very carefully on the edge of the bar. "You do it like this."

He gave each woman an appreciative but respectful smile and walked up to Natasha Ward. "Ms. Ward, would I be violating protocol by offering to buy each of these ladies, you and Stephanie a drink?"

Natasha almost spit out her water, and she glanced at Stephanie for support. She was not supposed to be on camera, except as a background figure. Now Tyrell had cut a swath through the group and there were three huge lenses in her face.

Stephanie beamed. "We only told the men not to speak to the ladies until formally introduced at dinner, but there's nothing in the rules of this round that said he couldn't offer them a drink via third party."

Tyrell was immediately surrounded, and Natasha raised one eyebrow but her expression was pleasant. "Then, Ms. Ward, as the one who gave me my opportunity, I'd like to ask the bartender to fix you what you'd like, first."

She held up her bottle of water and her smile widened. "There's no money exchange on the ship for drinks. It's an open bar."

Tyrell rubbed his jaw and chuckled. "True, true, but is it about money or chivalry? I came to introduce myself to them, non-verbally."

"Touché, Mr. Ramsey," Stephanie said, delighted.

"You guys were told not to talk to us?" Linda asked.

Tyrell nodded his head yes and gave her a slight bow.

"Oh, my God!" Vera exclaimed. "No wonder!"

Tyrell took her hand and kissed the back of it like a gentleman, making her draw it back with a blushing giggle.

"That took a lot for you to come over here," Michelle said, her voice low and sensual.

Tyrell nodded and winked at her.

"Did you know you have the most awesome voice?" Lillian asked with a slight sigh.

Tyrell shrugged and looked at Natasha. "Please tell the lady I said thank you," he murmured, an octave lower than normal.

Natasha smiled. "Mr. Ramsey, this borders on fraud."

"But his voice is fabulous," Lillian argued, laughing. "Thanks for sharing it with us."

"And so wickedly creative," Kimberly said, moving away from the rail to enter the small ring of women that had formed around Tyrell.

He could feel the vibration shift as the other women backed up, seeming defeated, to let her near him. The only one who hadn't budged was the tall pretty sister with the cornrows. The way she'd cut her eyes at the one in the bikini top made him chuckle.

Again, he addressed Natasha. "Sometimes, when you want something bad enough, and it's that important to you, you have to be ready to take some risks."

He extracted the five identical notes from his pocket and placed them in the center of Natasha's smooth, delicate palm. He savored holding her hand, and truly enjoyed staring into her eyes. The irony of it was, each woman assumed that the unspoken message in his gaze was destined for her, with Natasha as the mere conduit. He just hoped that Natasha Ward could see beyond all that. "You read the notes and let me know if this is a violation—as I'm not trying to be put off the boat before dinner. But I would like all the lovely ladies on this boat to know my name, hopefully get to know who I am . . . and I don't want to waste time during dinner talking about me. I want to know about them and what they want out of life. Is that cool?"

"Brother, you ain't *neva* getting put off this boat, hear!" Linda exclaimed, slapping five with Lillian.

"Can we see what he wrote," Vera said, nudging her way to Natasha's side like an excited puppy.

"That was definitely smooth, Mr. Ramsey," Kimberly said in a sultry, seductive tone. "I won't forget your name."

Michelle looked down, seeming flustered. "We have to give the man points for chutzpah."

He almost blew it by saying "thank you, ladies," and the only saving grace was Natasha's big brown eyes. He stared into them and then glanced at Stephanie. "Thank you ladies for couriering my note and drink orders." With that he left the group, feeling the center of his back grow moist from perspiration. But triumph had a way of making a near miss worth it all.

"I don't believe it," Rodriguez shouted as Tyrell went to the all-male side of the deck. "Trumped!" He laughed and handed Tyrell a beer.

Nelson slapped him on the back. "See, where I'm from, we woulda kicked your natural behind, brother—but you did that mess so smooth and all pro, all we can do is laugh. Dayuum! And pulled the superfine one off the rail, too? When this is over, I want your number so we can run the clubs together in Hotlanta, boss."

"But you know it's on now—ain't no friends in this game," Rodriguez said, laughing but serious as he clinked Tyrell's bottle and the others offered him grudging congratulations for breaking the deadlock.

"Never was, *hombre*," Tyrell said in good humor, pounding Nelson's fist, and his gaze never leaving Natasha.

Chapter 8

"Wait till Nathan sees this footage," Devon said, fanning his face as he walked in a tight circle around the room. "He'll freak. Between Tyrell and Linda, that sassy salon owner, we have got us a show, people!"

"Can we get dressed, Devon?" Natasha fussed, trying to work around him and find her outfit. "We have a half hour to be at the captain's table and—"

"Oh, just get dressed, please. There's nothing you girls have that I haven't already seen or am interested in seeing. But this is just so exciting, I can't begin to—"

"Devon, out," Stephanie said, laughing and pushing him toward the door. "You also have to get yourself dressed. Now shoo."

"I love you, too," Devon said, tossing his head in mock indignation, then slipped out the door and slammed it.

"Dra-ma," Stephanie exclaimed with a sigh. "But he's right, it was fantastic. Your idea worked like a charm. I can't wait till we lay in the voiceover narration. Can't you hear it? There's Tyrell Ramsey, breaking away from the pack, and he's out, coming around the deck, making strides away from the group."

Both women laughed as Stephanie mimicked a racing announcer.

"That man is a trip," Natasha said, willing away the butterflies that were still fluttering in her stomach for no reason.

"Yeah. Too bad he's a show contestant, huh, lady?"

Natasha refused to look up as she dug around in her suitcase. "Be serious, Steph. Don't even go there, mentally or otherwise. That guy is a serious player. He probably shot himself in the foot with every woman on the boat." When Stephanie didn't respond, Natasha glanced up, then straightened and placed her hands on her hips. "Think about it. If he was able to do what he did, he's probably done it before, and is used to having a crowd of fine women around him begging for his attention. He is, after all, in the whole music and entertainment scene, undiscovered label or not. And once the ladies caucus about it and put two and two together, they'll be salty."

"They didn't look too salty to me," Stephanie said, her grin widening. "As a matter of fact, I'll bet you a five dollar chip at the casino that when we get the hidden camera tapes back from their rooms, we'll see that they've been discussing him and making comparisons to the others."

"But will it be positive?" Natasha argued, folding her arms over her chest.

"Five bucks and a drink say yes."

"You're on," Natasha replied with confidence, going back to her search.

"Tell me your stomach didn't flip-flop when he held your hand."

"No, it didn't," Natasha lied.

"I thought I'd pass out," Stephanie said, leaning against the door with a thud. "It was the way he looked at you . . . wow . . ."

"Oh, pullease, girl. Get dressed," Natasha said, yanking clothes from her suitcase. "I'm not talking about this any more."

Tyrell sat in the ballroom, just as the others did, quietly, waiting, expecting. This was the big round; the others had been practice. All of the guys had their line of vision trained on the door. There were so many different scents of cologne mixing in the air that it was giving him a headache. They'd drawn straws on the shower. By the time he'd gotten his, the water had run cold. It didn't matter, he was used to that at home. All it did was keen his senses and wake him up, make him sharper. It was every man for himself. Every guy in the room had pulled out a casual but fly suit. Every man had shaved. They all passed muster. Was this what women went through . . . putting their best foot forward only to be left sitting and waiting and wondering if she'd be picked? This sucked.

As he watched the ballroom doors open, he was on his feet. It was an instinctive response, nothing he had to think about. Then, from the corner of his eye he noticed Captain Russell in his nautical dinner whites, and his first mate, had also instantly stood. However, the thing that bemused him was the gathering of women at the door allowed their gazes to rove to the late-standing guys at the table.

It was in their eyes, and the way they tipped their chins up a little higher. Any man scrambling to his feet was late on the basics, and it was clear that a negative mental hatch mark had been placed beside them. You slow, you blow. Tyrell said a silent mental thank you for all the years his mother had pinched a frog into the tender underside of his arm for such boyhood offenses.

He kept his eyes straight ahead, military style, affixing a name to each woman as she was introduced by name, profession, and state. Indeed, it was like a beauty pageant; Miss D.C., Michelle Tyler—long, lean, leggy, almond toned, bourgeois and highly educated, tasteful in turquoise. Miss New York City, Linda Jones, tall, statuesque, coffee brown fine, doing black diva, deep plunge, makeup flawless, hair beat, all city, and built to stop traffic. Miss Chicago, Vera Banks, cute as a button, brandishing red against her dark almond skin, dangerously hugging her petite curvy frame in a no back number, stiletto heels making her best asset bounce as she sashayed to the captain's table. Lawd.

Miss Boston was no slouch, Lillian Reed had it going on . . . he hadn't noticed how much with her in Dockers and a tank top. But she wore peach righteous, her figure was well proportioned and she had a friendly, pretty smile. Although he had to give it to Miss Houston, when Stephanie, a producer, announced her . . . dayum . . . Kimberly Gibson had missed her calling. What was she doing working in anybody's office building? Sister could do runway in Paris, the way she slinked in with a midnight blue, beaded number on, nothing but s sheer drape of fabric, no back, no sides, and an endless slit to expose a flash of thigh with each step as she glided to the captain's table.

As the last woman sat, all the men sat. But his legs wouldn't obey him. He had his eyes trained on the one who was talking to the camera guys. He couldn't help staring at her as she bent her head to give them instructions, the delicate nape of her neck seeming so graceful from across the room. Her skin against the white . . . her mannerisms so efficient yet ladylike . . .

"Mr. Ramsey, is there a problem?" Devon asked, coming to the table.

"No problem," Tyrell said calmly. "I'm just waiting for the last beautiful woman to take her seat."

"Oh, and right you are," Devon said theatrically, placing his hand on Tyrell's shoulder. "A true gentleman to the end," he said loud enough to cause a stir. "Miss Ward, would you please come to the captain's table so this man can sit down and we can begin serving?"

She thought she'd die a thousand deaths. Again, cameras were on her and a scene had been created. The other male contestants were awkwardly scrambling to their feet. "Oh, gentlemen, it's all right. Camera two, cut this out, I'm not in this." Flustered, she hurried to the table and allowed a server to pull her chair out for her before sitting in it hard. She tried to force herself to laugh it off with a brittle comment. "Okay, there, are you satisfied?"

Tyrell nodded, smiled, and sat down. The rest of the men followed suit. Mario, his table partner and unfortunately his shadow for the evening, was grinding his teeth. From the corner of his eye he saw Nelson and Tony chuckle. Mike Quazar gave him a discreet thumbs-up. The other guys seemed dazed as his line of vision slid to the long head table populated by crew, show staff, and the female contestants.

Linda, from New York, gave him a nod of appreciation from the captain's table. Kimberly, the supermodel, issued him a sly wink. Vera and Lillian had bright, expectant smiles just like Stephanie, and Michelle, the psychologist, kept glimpsing him from a long, sideways glance. But Natasha Ward refused to glance in his direction.

The conversation at the table was putting knots in her stomach as the women whispered about the good-looking eligible bachelors in the room. Tyrell's antics had them all buzzing. She was losing the bet to Stephanie; the women thought he was awesome. Every time they mentioned his name and glanced at her, she twisted the napkin in her lap. Her nerves were fried; this man was outrageous. Natasha willed herself to breathe as Devon made the logistical announcements.

"The ladies will dine with the captain through the appetizers and drinks, then a server will come to the table and allow each lady to take a scroll from beneath a silver platter. Once the appetizers have been cleared away, each woman will then, and only then, unroll her parchment to see which table she's to visit first. Each time a course is cleared away, a server will present each woman with a new scroll, then it will be time to switch tables until each woman has visited all five tables. Think of it like a game of musical chairs over fine wine, and a wonderful gourmet meal."

Heads nodded as all show contestants kept their

gazes fixed upon Devon. The set up was mad-crazy, and Tyrell had to remember to breathe. Two guys at each of five tables, an open seat for a visiting lady—musical chairs style, while trying to eat, be suave, talk, get to know her and get her to know you, without looking like a jackass while subtlety competing to shut out the other male at the table. This wasn't musical chairs, it was freakin' Russian roulette. One false move and a brother could be done.

"Now, obviously," Devon said, his sly smile growing as he continued to explain the rules, "those two lucky men who have the pleasure of spending the entrée portion of this dinner with a given lady at their table, have more time to make a good impression with her. The shorter courses mean you have to talk faster, gentlemen, so that the ladies who grace your tables during the shorter courses can get to know you in a shorter amount of time. And we did this by design so that the women who've spent the entrée with the male teams will have a deeper perspective to bring to their final caucus tonight, which the others may not have— which also means theses ladies will have to lobby for guys using insights and cues their teammates don't possess."

Devon paused, allowing the concept to sink in, clearly enjoying the tension of the moment. Natasha could almost hear the theme music he'd use to score the footage for the segment. The soundtrack from *Jaws* came to her mind as she watched Devon circle the male tables in a slow figure eight.

"And," Devon said with a melodramatic sigh, "*that* will require the female contestants to trust *each other*, even though they, too, are in competition with each other to be picked as a final choice by one of you gentlemen—the guy left standing at the end. We foresee heavy negotiations that may keep the female team up half the night until one of you guys gets the axe. But we'll allow our female guests to at least have a chance to all sit together and to strategize at the head table before investigating you guys. Remember," Devon warned, "whether the time is short or long, each of these ladies has to walk away with a good impression of you, and each has to come to consensus about whether you stay or leave. Bon appétit!"

Each man put a napkin in his lap and watched the head table for any sign that could help him. Every one of them had a stricken expression on his face. Tyrell could feel the muscle in his jaw pulsing. When he was offered wine, he said yes, forcing the server to repeat the question, red or white. He glanced at the head table and then at Mario.

"Red," Mario said, appearing perturbed.

"What's the appetizer?" Tyrell asked.

The waiter smiled in a way that let Tyrell know that every person on the ship was part of the game. "A nice shrimp presentation served in a cilantro mango chutney."

Tyrell nodded. "Make it white, then."

She took a spectator's position, listening to the women's assessments, wondering which woman would be the chosen one at the end of the ordeal. She also watched which woman got her glass repeatedly refilled and who didn't. She watched who laughed too loud or too shrilly, and wondered if any of that mattered to the ten men scattered around the room. Stephanie shot her glances that let her know the camera was getting it all. But she was thankful for the captain's ebullient presence, and his first mate's as well.

It was as though somehow she had been unwittingly drawn into this very public nightmare, and now couldn't wake up from it without losing her job. So she refused comment, only laughed with the group, and repeatedly reminded the five contestants that no matter how any of the male contestants acted toward her, trying to win favors, perhaps because she was the producer, that she had no opinion.

The moment the words had leapt from Natasha's mouth, she wished she could have retracted them. Stephanie gave her a lethal glare—she'd possibly polluted the control group, when that hadn't been her aim.

"Now, Ms. Ward, you have to admit that your statement about Tyrell Ramsey's possible motives for standing up and offering you a gesture of respect, could be construed as a negative comment," Michelle said.

Mortified, Natasha tried to redress the slight and set the record straight with the psychologist. "No, no, no, no no. I am not in this debate at all. You ladies have to assess for yourselves why any of these contestants does whatever he does. If you like it, I love it."

"Chile, she may be right, though," Linda argued. "What if he was only doing all of that to get on her good side and to blow our minds?"

Natasha wanted to crawl under the table. The New Yorker would never turn the suspicion loose now.

"Frankly," Kimberly said, tossing her silken hair over her shoulder and looking at Tyrell from a sidelong glance, "I'm just glad you're not in the final lineup." The contestant with supermodel grace returned her gaze to Natasha and beamed. "The way he looked at you was electrifying."

Without warning, Stephanie let out a weak, strained chuckle, entering the fray to try to assist Natasha. "Or, ladies," she offered, leaning in and dropping her voice to a conspiratorial whisper, "what if he had to look at her like that up on the deck and now to channel all that heat to a noncompetitive source? Guys do that, you know . . . uh, transfer like that, when they can't feel safe letting it be known who they really want."

Natasha could only stare at Stephanie. That was such a crock that if these ladies bought it she'd spit out her sip of wine.

"That's true," Michelle said, nodding. "It was transference."

A coughing fit gripped Natasha as her sip of wine went down the wrong way. She noted that the captain and his crew had shied away from even venturing near the discussion.

"Like I said, I'm not in this." Natasha wheezed, gulping water as she brought the napkin to her lips. "He was only trying to get his little notes delivered to impress you ladies, which is what he should be doing as a contestant."

"Oh, and they were sooo cute," Lillian crooned. "They said, 'Hello, my name is Tyrell Ramsey. I can't talk to you right now—it's against the rules. But I would like to find out more about you at dinner. See you in the ballroom at seven. It's a pleasure to meet you.'"

"I think Michelle and Stephanie are right," Vera whispered loudly, hailing the waiter for her third glass of wine. "That one is a keeper, and everything he says to her or does in her direction is a safe way to send one of us a message without letting any of us know which one he really wants."

"Very, very sly . . . and very, very intelligent," Kimberly said, slowly sipping her wine. "I like it."

"I don't like no game-playing man," Linda said flatly. "For real." She rolled her eyes in Tyrell's direction, and then a half smile came out of hiding. "But his fine ass is so tricky that I'd keep him on for a couple of rounds just to see what he'd do next. He is interesting, Kim. I'll give you that."

"Ladies, there're ten of them and you haven't even been to the tables," Natasha said, still intermittently coughing. "Keep an open mind, and keep your wits about you. Find out as much as you can during dinner, because after that, you've gotta huddle and make a hard decision."

"Okay," Stephanie said, so brightly that her singsong voice rang out through the ballroom. "Time for us show staff to huddle, too. Madame senior producer, may I see you in the wings?"

Natasha stood calmly, reading the rigidity in Stephanie's back. A subordinate, who was also a good friend, was gonna try to read her while appetizers were being served?

"Steph," she said quickly, as soon as they were out of earshot and camera range, "don't get started."

"Don't get started?" Stephanie hissed through her teeth. "What are you trying to do, derail your career with a lawsuit?"

"A lawsuit?"

"Yeah, that bull caught on tape with you making

a disparaging comment about Tyrell Ramsey, when we're supposed to be silent, objective observers!"

"I didn't make a negative comment about him!" Natasha fussed, her voice low and warning as she whispered her complaint in self-defense.

"You practically said the man was trying to garner favors from the senior producer to get over! What was that, huh?"

Natasha slapped her forehead. "I know that's how it sounded, but that's not what I meant."

"Then don't say anything that could be misinterpreted to sound any way, no matter how he makes you feel. Got it?"

Natasha opened her mouth and closed it, too stunned for a moment to speak.

"Listen, 'Tash," Stephanie said, as she glanced around quickly and stepped closer. "You and I have known each other a long time. This guy was in your face from the auditions. He smiles nicely and whatnot for the others, but when he looks at you, it's like he stops breathing—okay. The girls are picking up vibes, and everybody can't be wrong. But he's so funny and such a cut up that he plays it off. Now you have to walk a very careful line here not to upset the apple cart. Later, you guys can hook up and—"

"What!" Natasha nearly bit her tongue as Stephanie covered her mouth quickly and pulled her deeper into the serving wings. She struggled to untangle herself from Stephanie's well-meaning but misplaced grip. "Have you lost your mind?" she whispered fast and hard through heaving breaths. "There's no way in the world I'd do something like that! Do you think I'm—"

"Blind? No!"

"I would never, ever in a million years—"

"Be human?" Stephanie folded her arms over her chest. "Why not?"

"You need to stop going to soothsayers and doing séances, or whatever you do. It's making you live in a fantasy world, and your brain is getting corroded by all that metaphysical, astrological connections junk you read."

"Are you finished?" Stephanie asked, the mirth returning to her twinkling eyes.

"Yes. And we should send out the servers with the dag-gone silver platters so at least it looks like we were back here working instead of arguing."

"Okay. You're the boss," Stephanie quipped, but hadn't moved.

"That's right. I'm the boss," Natasha said. "We may be friends, but there's a line while we're working."

"I know," Stephanie said. "But I saw what I saw, boss lady, and I know what I know . . . and I also am telling you that I have it on tape—the way you looked back at him for just a *little* too long—which will hit the electronic trash can before it goes to Nathan. So, yeah, we can be professional," Stephanie said, making quotes in the air with her fingers as she said the word professional, "but sometimes it's good to have a true blue friend in your corner behind the scenes."

"Yeah, it is," Natasha finally said, looking at the floor before closing her eyes. "I guess I've just been under a lot of strain and working so hard that I'm a little on edge."

"Yeah," Stephanie said, giving her a brief hug. "That's all it is."

As they dispatched the servers with the num-bered parchment beneath silver domes, she took slow breaths to try to bring her racing pulse back under control. As she watched Stephanie walk into the room and work it with Devon, allowing her some mental space to recover, she also silently thanked Steph for not mentioning her return glance again.

That was a *real* friend, someone who set you straight but didn't rub your nose in your own vulnerabilities. What was happening to her? Getting all gaga over a show contestant—especially one who was a bonafide player? Natasha covered her face with her hands for a moment and breathed into her palms. For this round, she'd stay in the back, watch the monitors, and pull herself together.

Mario had been predictable. The guy was blowing it, big time. Tyrell was thoroughly disgusted by the time the lobster bisque came. He'd suffered through the second appetizer of miniature conch fritters with papaya marmalade, listening to this guy go nonstop about all he'd done by age thirty. Vera, who was a motor mouth in her own right, never stood a chance. The best Tyrell knew he could do was to interject with a question about her real estate knowledge and tie that to whatever bull Mario was spouting regarding Chicago. So he found himself asking about relative real estate values between the club districts in Chi-town versus other cities—a question designed for Vera, but that Mario would wind up hogging and answering.

Then there was the mixed green salad with a creamy goat cheese that they called by a name he couldn't pronounce. Two serving changes and his cellmate still didn't get it. Both a psychologist and a telemarketer had been to the table, two women who threw probing question after probing question, designed to go deeper beneath the surface, and Mario kept on with his agenda. The only thing that surprised Tyrell was that one of those ladies hadn't slapped that fool by now.

As soon as a lady approached the table, Mario almost knocked over his wine trying to beat him in standing first. Then, before the poor woman could draw a breath, Mario had her by the hand, and was running his mouth a mile a minute about all of his possessions and clubs in Chicago, never letting the sister get a word in edgewise. And each time it was so ridiculously bad that he had to literally make the time-out sign with his hands, apologize to the woman visiting their team, and put Mario in check.

Tyrell glanced around the tables, again sweeping the ballroom for any sign of Natasha. Yeah, he knew she had things to do and behind the scenes stuff to handle, but the room seemed so much bigger and emptier without her giving him a fishy look for pressing his luck too far. He already missed her arched eyebrow, the scowl that contained a droll smile. He liked the way she sucked her teeth and said, "Oh, brother, pullease." It was so familiar, and her laughter was like music. That was genuine. Now here he was stuck at a table with a true jerk that in all likelihood, he was gonna soon come to blows with. Tyrell stood and looked Linda in the eyes as she came to their table. The entrée was definitely going to be a trip.

"Hi. I'm Mario Campanelli," Tyrell's roommate said, "let me get your seat for you."

"Save it," Linda said with a wave of her hand, getting into her own chair without Mario's assistance.

"I already know I'm not your type. Kimberly has already blown your mind, and you're dying for her visit to your table for dessert. It's all over your face. So, let's just have the lobster stuffed with crabmeat, chitchat, and if you can keep your focus at this table as to not embarrass me, I'd appreciate it."

Both Mario and Tyrell sat down slowly.

"Have you ever been to Chicago?" Mario said, as soon as he'd recovered. "There're some really hot clubs there and I own a good deal of them."

Tyrell just looked at his partner in sheer disbelief.

"I'm from New York, and have been to hot clubs. Thanks just the same," Linda said, her attitude sharp as a razor. "But since we're talking business, if you ever get to New York, look me up. I have a chain of salons that could get you hooked up right."

"That was cold, girl," Tyrell said. It was reflex. What else could he say? He was tired, all of this was stressful, and Mario had behaved like a smacked ass.

Mario gave him a look that was unreadable. It was between relief for having someone at the table that had his back, and anger because Tyrell was in a position to do so. Tyrell braced himself, waiting for Linda's tongue lashing, but instead, she laughed. She covered her mouth and simply laughed. She peered at Tyrell and then glanced at Mario and laughed harder.

"Okay. I'm blunt," Linda said. "I tell it like I see it, but that was out of order. Mario was only trying to get his rap on before Tyrell blew him out, and I shouldn't have jumped on you, dude. My bad."

"It's cool," Mario said, focusing on his plate.

"Aw, c'mon roomie," Tyrell said. "You know

Linda was just . . . I don't know. Just keeping it real." He glanced at Linda for support, but she only shrugged.

"Look, you know Linda is from where they don't play and sister is handling some thangs, with salons strung across the city. So, you have to step to her with respect as a serious businesswoman. She doesn't want anybody in her face talking yang about what they got, what they can do. You needed to ask the sister what was on her mind, where she's taking her salon business, and then you wouldn't have gotten put on blast. It doesn't necessarily mean she doesn't like you . . . but that you have been checked, so cut the crap." He looked at Linda and then opened his arms wide in Mario's direction. "Am I wrong?"

"Screw you, Ramsey!" Mario shouted.

The room went still; the cameras went into overdrive.

"Yo, man, not with a lady at the—"

"Shut up, Tyrell. If the lady can dish it out then she ain't no—"

"Oh, so now because I put you on blast, I'm not a lady?" Linda looked at Tyrell.

"She said it, I didn't," Mario muttered, taking a liberal sip of his wine and then stabbing a hunk of lobster with his fork.

"I do not believe he even said something like that." Linda's gaze narrowed. "You are too rude."

"Don't go there, man . . ." Tyrell warned. "Do not make me get up over here."

"What? You threatening me!"

"No. But I am telling you that if you continue to offend this lady by saying she isn't a lady, just 'cause she checked your punk ass, then me and you can step outside."

Mario was on his feet in an instant, as was Tyrell. But Tyrell went to Linda's chair as her attention ricocheted between both men. He pulled out her seat and thrust his elbow in her direction.

"Listen, baby, I'm going to escort you back to the head table before this drunk fool does something stupid, like splash your pretty dress with his wine. Then, I'ma wax his ass regular."

"Upstairs! Me and you, Ramsey," Mario shouted, walking away from the table.

Tyrell felt Linda's hold on his arm tighten. "Don't do it. He's not worth your getting kicked off the show behind no mess. He was drunk by the time I sat down."

The tables cleared as Mario stormed upstairs and the contestants gathered. Cameras were on the periphery, security watching and readied. Ship crew were standing, also waiting, for anyone to make too emotional a move.

"Did you see that?" Vera said. "He said one of us wasn't a lady?"

"Seems like Mr. Campanelli just self-selected out of round one," Devon said coolly, his gaze going toward the ship's security team, and then over to the captain, who nodded.

"That's ball game," Stephanie said. "Where's 'Tash? We have to get a final on this."

"Damn, man. What'd you say to set him off like that?" Jason asked, his tone defensive.

"*He* didn't say *anything* that wasn't the truth," Linda argued. "*I* said something that jerk didn't like. That's what kicked this whole thing off. And he got all salty with me, but Tyrell wasn't having it and he set him straight at the table. Then, he got all pissy and wanted to fight."

"Hey, well, if he offended the lady and the brother stepped to him," Nelson said with a shrug, "I don't see what the issue is."

"That's what I'm saying," Rodriguez chimed in.

"I ain't in it," the auto dealer said, walking away. "You all got this nonsense."

"What is *wrong* with all of this," the engineer from Colorado began, but then a female voice cut him off.

"Tyrell was actually going to fight for—"

"The whole fighting thing is unwarranted," Anthony Adams said, straightening the front of his suit. "Totally unnecessary and street thug–like. I thought everyone here was beyond all of that."

"I'm not talking to you, Adams," Linda said, flipping him the bird as she sent her line of vision toward the female contestant he'd interrupted. "Michelle, the man was gonna protect my honor and stood up when that drunk bastard offended me. Period. And y'all need to dig it."

"Wow . . ." Kimberly said, as she looked Tyrell up and down. "Been a while since any of us has seen a guy go there over a verbal infraction. And I was supposed to have your table for dessert. Guess I missed out."

Tyrell's head hurt. This thing was not supposed to go down like this. He was sure half the female team thought he and Mario were both drunk, but he hadn't consumed seven or eight glasses of wine like Campanelli had. The only one who could vouch for him as an eyewitness would be Linda, and Vera and Lillian and Michelle had seen him wrest the conversation away from Campanelli so they could talk. But, at the same time, this kind of Jerry Springer mess had a way of going through selective memory filters. It was possible that the other women might say he had been messing with Campanelli all night, therefore, he'd strategically egged Mario on and had made him lose it. But that's not how it was. When he said what he'd said, it was from a very true place in his heart. He was trying to school the guy on how to treat a sister like Linda, while giving Linda her props, so that everything could remain peaceful for at least one more round. Now his momma was going to have to read about him fighting on cable TV?

The worst part of it all was finally looking up and seeing the expression on Natasha Ward's face.

Chapter 9

It was all she could do not to scream as she stood at the opening to the ballroom watching a travesty occur. She'd seen the slow storm building at Tyrell's table. Video monitors didn't miss a thing during dinner. Sure, she could see Tyrell baiting the man, trying to detonate his suave, but she'd never expected Campanelli to blow, no more than she'd expected his outright disrespect of Linda—no matter how caustic the sister had been.

Steadying herself, Natasha strode across the room with authority. "Okay, people. This behavior is problematic." She watched everyone become silent and still. That's right, dammit. This was *her* show!

"Ladies, we caucus in here." Natasha motioned for a cameraman to follow the small group of women to the head table. "Devon and Steph, you take a couple of bouncers outside on the top deck. I want footage of Tyrell's side, Mario's side, and a take from the rest of the male contestants. Tell Captain Russell that when he drops anchor in the Bahamas tonight, one of these gentlemen will be escorted from the ship." Natasha was talking with her hands as she walked and the group of very nervous female contestants followed. "This was unnecessary!"

As the group of women settled themselves at the long table draped with white linen, Natasha could only shake her head. A yacht, full silver service, linens, and folks were still acting crazy. In her mind it was as though everyone had reverted back to being a kid. "Bring me a video monitor please," she said on a weary sigh to a technician. "We're going to first roll tape and then dissect what went down."

"I can tell you *what* went down," Linda said. There was slight attitude in her voice, but not as much as usual.

"All right," Natasha said, as the technician set up a nearby monitor for them to view, and handed her the remote control. "Before we view tape, maybe you're right. Let's get your version of what happened."

Cameras angled toward Linda, and then panned the rest of the group as she spoke, trying to capture facial expressions, tone, any nuance that could be spliced and edited for more controversy.

"It's really simple," Linda said, sounding exhausted. "Mario and Tyrell are two aggressive competitors. First, Tyrell had beat him out by ordering the right kind of wine, had been on his feet first when all the ladies came in the room. Basically had chumped him at every move."

"That's right," Vera said, butting in with her perky perspective, clearly unable to sit still. "You could see the way he looked at Ty when he made that first bold move up on the deck and came over to our group."

"Very true," Michelle said quietly, but the fact that the psychologist was so moved to speak before she'd been called on made everyone at the table crane their necks to hear her take on it. "At the table, even though I was only there for a shorter course, Mario was arrogant and very offensive. . . . I believe in some circles it's called 'tacky rich,'" she said, making quotes in the air with her fingers upon saying the phrase. "He wouldn't let me get a word in edgewise, asked me nothing about myself, and boasted nonstop—which is a sure sign of narcissistic insecurity. But then Ty interrupted him and said, 'Please, man, let the lady speak. Give her a chance to process what you've told her.'" Michelle covered her heart with her hand. "He stood up for me and was trying to allow me to *process* the information—do you understand?"

"Oh, my God, yes," Vera said quickly. "He stood up for me, too. When that jerk just went right past what I'd told him about what I wanted to do one day in real estate, Ty said, 'Yo, man, so what you've got all these clubs, the lady is talking about building a real estate empire with all sorts of properties—not just clubs.' And then Mario said, 'Yeah, well, it takes significant capital to make that happen.' Okay, I know it was a dig toward Tyrell, but Mario was so interested in fighting with him that he never realized, or seemed to care, just how much he'd offended me."

"I know how they feel," Lillian added in. "I know I'm not the prettiest one in this group, and I know I'm not as educated as some, but Ty was so nice—just made me laugh—whereas Mario was cordial, but you could tell he was glad I hadn't gotten put at their table for the longer entrée." She glanced around the group. "Do you know what I mean, like, you can't exactly explain it, but you can tell when a guy is tolerating you and is looking at another table."

"Girl, dealt with that all my life," Linda said, putting an arm over Lillian's shoulder. "Now you and me probably won't get picked by whatever one of those fools is left standing, but I don't ever want to hear you saying all that negative stuff about yourself."

Two big tears welled up and rolled down Linda's nose as she hung her head and the other women gathered around her—everyone except Kimberly, who had been unusually quiet.

"I told myself that I was not going to cry on television," Linda said in a quaky voice through a forced laugh as she dabbed her tears. "I was so surprised when I made it, and then when I saw you all, I was like, what *am* I doing here?"

"We all felt the same way," Michelle confessed. "I looked at you all and thought, I'll never stand a chance. This is worse than the clubs."

"You, girl?" Linda scoffed. "If I had what you had I would floss it so hard you'd have to arrest me."

Everyone laughed as Michelle battled tears and tried to laugh.

"That's why when Mario kept looking at Kimberly while I was sitting there with him and Ty, I just lost it. I admit it. The claws came out, I hated being dissed right to my face, and I didn't want to be made to look stupid on national TV. So, it was me or him." Linda drew a shaky breath. "That shit hurts when it's done to you, and I didn't like it." She swallowed hard and then laughed through a sniff. "Good thing we have a psychologist in the house. Damn, this was some therapy."

Again, the group laughed a cleansing, relief filled round of chuckles. Hugs got passed, and in that moment, Natasha knew why she'd created the show as she watched the group bond through the first crisis. Just like she'd always claimed had been done to her and her girls, she'd judged these women, had grouped them by stereotypes, but when you peeled back all the layers, they were just vulnerable human beings.

But she had noticed two very key issues in the exchange; Kimberly never said a word and all the women had nicknamed Tyrell, Ty. In one afternoon, brotherman had gone from Tyrell Ramsey to Ty? Wow . . .

"Kimberly, this has to be voted on by consensus, and you've been awfully quiet," Natasha said, bringing the group's focus around to her.

Kimberly released a long, bored sigh as she raked her perfect French manicure through her silky hair and leaned back. Natasha noted that, even when being a pure bitch, she was still gorgeous and the camera loved her.

"Well, I for one thought the whole escapade was juvenile on everyone's part."

"What?" Linda was on her feet with two other women holding her back.

"This is why I didn't say anything, so I have no comment."

"Hold it, hold it, Linda, please sit down," Natasha said firmly. "No, you have the right to speak, Kimberly. In fact, you have to weigh in some so we can determine what to do."

Kimberly dramatically held up her hand. "I do not want to be put at risk for being ostracized from the group, just because I have an unpopular perspective. I'll pass."

"No, Kimberly," Michelle said, playing peace-maker. "We want to hear how everyone saw this."

Linda sucked her teeth, Lillian folded her arms over her chest, and Vera pouted. Kimberly gave them her back as she turned to face Michelle, Natasha, and the camera at just the right angle.

"Well, first of all," Kimberly mewed, "if Mario was watching other tables, that's not his fault—that's the fault of the contestant who obviously couldn't hold his attention."

Natasha held up her hand as the women behind her erupted with a series of sounds of discontent.

"And if Linda would have kept her cool and not said nasty things to him, because she was jealous, then the whole thing wouldn't have escalated between them. That's number one," Kimberly said, ticking off the charges on her long, manicured talon. "Then, if Tyrell Ramsey wasn't such a . . . I don't know . . . roughneck, then even if Mario did say something a little out of line—albeit it said because he was provoked, then he wouldn't have outright threatened the man. That was so wrong and so street, and frankly, I'm just not used to dealing with men who aren't polished. As a personal preference, I like them sophisticated."

Even if Natasha were an NFL linebacker, there was no way to hold back the verbal assault that ensued. It was pure chaos as the sides polarized, Michelle standing in the middle trying to hold back the impossible. The cameras were running tape so hard and fast the shoulder-mounted Betas were smoking. Every profanity registered in Natasha's mind as a bleep. They were going to have to give her boss smelling salts, not from anger but because this was the stuff he loved. But it shamed her no end. Her mother had been right. This was unseemly, as the woman had called it, and yet, it was her job to dredge through the most outrageous, painful, ugly portions of these interactions and serve them to the public raw—right after dinner, at eight.

"Yeah, you like 'em polished, like that publisher from New York!" Lillian shouted. "He's arrogant and nasty and thinks he's all that, too. Just a more chocolate version of Mario!"

"Why you hating so hard on Ty, just because he doesn't do like the other men and give you more than your fair share of attention? Is that it?" Vera hollered, jumping up and down so she could be seen above the other towering beauties.

"Anthony Adams and Mario Campanelli are *worlds* apart," Kimberly shrieked in fury. "If you had any class, you'd know!" Veins were standing in her once graceful neck that now bobbed as she spat every word, her finger in Lillian's face as she delivered her litany. "Anthony is fourth generation money out of New York. Campanelli can only trace his folks back to Sicily, need I say more—that idiot didn't even know which wine went with fish—and, and, despite whatever was going on, Tony would have simply gotten an attorney to settle a serious dispute, and wouldn't be in a ballroom about to turn over tables behind something as trite as a verbal slight. If either one of them had more verbal dexterity, they could have sliced each other with a verbal redress—but no! They couldn't do it because of their limited vocabulary! Throw them both off the yacht and stop wasting our time."

They watched Kimberly storm out of the ballroom. Her outburst, and the venom contained within it, had taken them all aback. Plus, Kimberly had lost her head and alluded to a serious personal preference for one of the male contestants—in front of the entire female group that despised her. Natasha just hoped that the poor brother would be judged on his own merits, and not fall victim to the backlash from something he wasn't even involved in. But even she knew better than that. Anthony Adams was toast, especially if the other women felt like he'd been picked to be sweet on. It was a no-win situation for any of them, and Natasha shook her head as she suddenly realized that she'd concocted this fiasco as entertainment. What sickened her more was the fact that, the more drama erupted, the ratings would soar . . . to her thinking, she'd helped reinstate the old Roman coliseum blood sports. Only this was watching emotions and people's personal dignity get ripped to shreds.

"Okay," Natasha finally said, attempting to insert some decorum, "everybody's emotions are running hot right now. Let Kimberly go off and cool down. We should all get ourselves together and be calm. We have a decision to make."

Natasha handed Linda the remote control for the monitor. Everyone knew Linda had risen to the fore as the group's leader; there was no need to clarify that. "Do you all need to watch any footage?"

"No," Linda said, setting the remote control unit down hard. "I'll cast my vote. I was there and saw it up close and personal. Keep Ty, give Mario the axe."

"Done," Lillian agreed.

"I'm with them," Vera said, nodding.

Michelle let out a weary sigh. "I have to vote with the group. He self-selected out."

"All right. Then we all go up and inform the

male team." Natasha set her shoulders square, glanced around the group, and began walking. Instead of going up to the top deck, she felt like she was walking the plank, and yet, wasn't exactly sure why. But she did know that this was the part she disliked the most about the rules of her ill-contrived game show. No matter how crazy a person acted, she still didn't like hurting people's feelings, creating an inside group and an outside group, an *in* crowd and *wannabes*. She'd lived that reality all her life as an outsider, and now she was the architect of a nasty human dynamic.

Every step she took gave her pause. There was a time when she thought that it would be wonderful to be able to ostracize the cheerleaders, the pretty girls, the stuck up girls with pedigree, and to make them have to answer to her. As soon as the memory entered her, she thought of Camille . . . one of her best friends, who was so much like a combination of Kimberly and Michelle that it wasn't even funny. And then there was her other homegirl, Jorgette, who reminded her of both Linda and Lillian, with a little Vera to add spice. It had also been a mad-scientist dream to be able to make a successful, arrogant, polygamist male who thought he was all that, experience the insecurities and pain of being slighted, having to compete, and ultimately be passed over.

Yet, as the group of women assembled on the top deck, and she stared at the frightened sets of male eyes, saw pure and honest requests for compassion etched within each handsome expression, suddenly it all became such a hollow quest. There was no joy whatsoever in any of this. Serving comeuppance raw, slicing the in crowd's emotions into human sushi, offered nothing redeeming. Rather than making her own pain and loneliness lessen, seeing theirs and having a hand in creating it, only made her feel more isolated.

If the cameras hadn't been rolling, she would have simply walked away.

Tyrell looked up at the female group. He, nor any of the men on their team, bothered to stand. It was a messed up situation. Chances were great he was off the boat—which suited him just fine. Through all the arguments, back and forth verbal self-defense he'd lobbied with the male team, along with all the after-the-fact who shot John, the one point remained, the money wasn't worth all this.

True, he'd entered this whole escapade for one reason—to get paid. He wasn't there to make friends, get caught up with any woman, or get involved in these anonymous people's lives. But it was strange how in one day, just how much and how little you got to know about people under deep immersion conditions. If circumstances had been different, had their lives intersected a different way, a few of the guys he'd met were cool people, people he'd like to hang out with, maybe do business with.

Just thinking about that made him realize how empty his life had been and how much he missed his brothers, before things fell apart. As he sat waiting for the inevitable verdict, it reminded him of sitting with his family in courtrooms as his brothers, one by one, were locked away for offenses created both by them and their environment. If he thought about it hard, Bernard was the only real friend he had . . . the only brother left standing. The big fam-

ily meals were no more, his mother didn't participate with the extended family out of shame and
grief for what had gone wrong with her boys, and
she only held one up as her icon, him, and now
he'd shamed her on national television.

The thing that kept nagging at him during the interminable wait for his sentence was that he became aware of how empty being the one held up as
the victor truly was. All he did was work. Where was
the joy, the laughter, the friendships, the barbeques, the gatherings, the cookouts, the kids . . . the
person whom one built a future with?

Tyrell's gaze swept the boat. He'd been chasing
the almighty dollar and had wanted fifteen minutes
of fame. But it wasn't what it had been cracked up
to be. He allowed his line of vision to settle on
Natasha Ward. If he'd only met that sister under
different circumstances. . . . Now she probably
thought he was a total fool.

"After much debate and discussion, the female
team has come to a consensus," Natasha said, her
voice firm but compassionate. "Ladies?"

She looked at Linda, who oddly looked away. The
other women sent their gazes to the deck floor.
Michelle stepped forward, which made the men
pass nervous glances between each other. Again,
another dynamic was unfolding. Linda was the in-
formal group leader, but Michelle had just been
dubbed the group's spokesperson.

"We've all weighed in," Michelle said in a soft
voice. "The fight was ugly, and on day one, never
should have happened."

Mario looked away, tears of humiliation and rage

glittering in his eyes. Tyrell just nodded and stood to go get his gear.

"My apologies," Tyrell said, his voice quiet and resigned. Defeat claimed him as he lifted his chin and straightened his spine. "You're right. I was wrong. And I'm sorry that I offended you ladies by telling dude that we could settle it outside."

"Oh, man," Rodriguez muttered. "That's a good brother."

Several of the other male contestants simply shook their heads. Nelson came over to Tyrell and offered him a handshake. Anthony Adams hung back, along with Jason Fulbright, and Joseph Scott. But Mike Quazar was on his feet and had begun pacing.

"It wasn't all his fault," Mike said, talking with his hands.

"Oh, so now it's back to that shit," Mario said, standing and raking his fingers through his hair. "He provoked me!"

"Hold it," Natasha said, watching the group begin to unravel again as her gaze darted to Devon and Stephanie. "Let the ladies deliver their decision, and then we'll go from there. The rules are clear—once the female team has reached a consensus, then the decision is final."

Only the breeze could be heard as everyone became still. All eyes were on Michelle.

"We have decided that Tyrell Ramsey, although he did help provoke the incident, did so because one of our team members had been offended. Therefore, Mario Campanelli will be asked to leave the ship."

"What!" Mario yelled. "I do not believe this bull! You picked *him* over *me*?" He walked in a hot circle, tears streaming down his face. "Screw all of you, then!"

The teams parted as Mario stormed past them and went belowdecks to collect his gear. Intermittently the sound of a wall being punched echoed behind him. No one moved, as though too fatigued to do anything but stand still while they absorbed what had just happened. Then, one by one, smiles slowly dawned on several of the male team members' faces. Tyrell was rushed by hugs, slaps on his back, high fives and fist pounds.

"I have a question, though," Anthony Adams said, his voice controlled yet issued with enough force to cut through the din. "If this was done by consensus, where's Kimberly?"

Again, the group stopped. Nervous glances passed between all contestants. Natasha could see mental gears engaging as people began to process the question and the intensity of it. Oh, boy, it was true. There was already a couple forming on the ship.

"She self-selected out tonight," Natasha said coolly.

"Self-selected out," Anthony said, stepping closer to Natasha. "What does that mean? Is she off the boat?"

"No," Linda said in a lethal tone, her narrowed gaze raking him. "It means girlfriend threw herself into such a tizzy that the thing she voted for wasn't allowable, so her vote didn't count—that's A, and B, she stomped her spoiled, yellow behind out of the meeting when we weren't having it, so she self-selected out. Period."

Anthony folded his arms over his chest and looked away, but the relief in his expression about the fact that Kimberly was still on the boat, wasn't lost on a soul.

"I'd be interested to know what she voted for that was so untenable that her vote would be disqualified?" Jason Fulbright asked, his glare toward Linda almost withering.

"Leave it to the engineer to get all technical," Vera scoffed.

"What goes down in our meetings, stays in our meetings," Lillian shot back.

Stephanie and Devon shook their heads discreetly. Natasha sighed.

"No, tell him," Linda fussed. "I don't care. They need to know how girlfriend operates."

"I don't think that would add value to an already tense situation," Michelle hedged. "Let's just drop it. Okay?"

"No, it's not okay, *Michelle*," Linda challenged. "Girlfriend was trying to throw both Tyrell *and* Campanelli off the boat, when the rules clearly state that only one guy gets the axe per test. And she thought that if she flounced her behind up in our faces with a tantrum that we'd go for it—when you and I and all the rest of the women know that she only did that to improve the chances of *her man* getting picked as the last guy standing!"

"Who's her man?" Rodriguez murmured to Tyrell, who simply shrugged.

Confusion ricocheted around the top deck as the cameras worked overtime to capture the new tantalizing bit of dirt that had just been yanked from beneath the rug. Pure excitement glittered in Devon's eyes as he tilted his head and issued a silent question to Natasha and Stephanie with one glance.

"Okay, okay," Michelle said, again trying to restore the peace. "We don't know that, it's sheer speculation on our part. All we do know is that she proposed something improbable that could set a bad precedence." She looked at the male team. "In all fairness, if we cut two members or more per challenge, then there's no safety factor . . . we couldn't allow her to do that."

"Yeah, but I bet if Anthony Adams was involved in the argument, she wouldn't have gone there," Vera spat, hands on hips.

"You got dat right," Linda said, still puffing with anger.

"Y'all better watch your backs, because girlfriend already has her pick," Lillian said.

"Whew . . ." Mike Quazar said, shaking his head. "Well, fellas, forewarned is forearmed, if that's the case."

"Hold it, people!" Devon finally exclaimed, clearly unable to contain himself. "Every one of you has your favorites from the first impression. But it's waaaay too early in the show challenges to begin freezing people out and making assumptions." He placed his hands on his hips and cocked his head to the side and studied Anthony Adams. "All right, so he made a good first impression with one of the female contestants." Devon's gaze shot to Tyrell. "And, Tyrell has his fan club, too. But the key is going to be, will these first two front runners be able to stay in the lead?" Devon smiled and gave the group a jaunty pose. "Maybe, maybe not. Ten weeks is a long time to keep your footing at the top of the proverbial mountain. My suggestion is that you all get a good night's rest and be fresh in the morning. The first show will be edited tonight and will air tomorrow night. You'll only have a couple of days to regroup before the next challenge."

Chapter 10

"Would you look at this stuff we've got!" Devon said, buzzing from monitor to monitor as the technicians loaded the videotape for edit. "Stop right there . . . oh, 'Tash, Steph, this is golden!"

At two o'clock in the morning, she didn't care if the footage would win an Emmy. Natasha stretched and sighed. Yeah, it was great emotion, poignant, and drama-filled, but she hated it all. "Nathan will love it," she said flatly.

"He'll cream his jeans," Stephanie said, slurping her fifth mug of coffee. "The show is gonna open with a bang. The voting lines for most favorite, least favorite, and the whole Internet connection to the show are going to pop!"

"You've had too much coffee, kiddo. We're competing with some really big shows, and if we do half of what we promised in the boardroom, maybe we'll get to keep our jobs." Natasha stood. She needed air. More than anything she needed to stop looking at fear and pain and people bickering. At this point, she really didn't care how they finished editing the tapes for satellite feeds. The core was laid, now there were little nuances and touch ups that would be added at the station all morning to get this madness in the can and ready to roll by an insane deadline. One human being had been crushed and put off the boat. Another had had his fate hanging in the balance. And one had been exposed for being sweet on one of the contestants. The rest of the guys had been demoralized by knowing that they had an uphill battle before them if they wanted to make it to the finish line. All in a day's work. She hated her job.

"I'm out," Natasha murmured. "I need a cup of coffee and some sea air to clear my head. I'll be back down to finish up in fifteen or twenty."

"Cool," Devon said, engrossed in a section of tape.

"We got this," Stephanie said, not looking at Natasha as she left. "We know exactly what you want, boss lady."

Natasha poured herself a mug of coffee without responding and slipped out of the suite that had been temporarily converted to a video edit chop shop. It felt so eerie to pass silent rooms, nothing moving except the gentle sway of the moored yacht. Loneliness and yet a sense of peace collided as she mounted the stairs and climbed up to the first deck.

Alone with the wind on her face, she studied the stars. They were so crystal clear within a dark blue velvet horizon that their beauty almost made her weep. She wanted to reach out and pluck one down, just to wish upon a twinkling jewel from heaven. "God forgive me," she murmured. "It wasn't supposed to turn out like this."

In the distance, she could see Paradise Island,

knowing that as soon as dawn rose, the ship would come alive, as would the small Bahamian towns. She envisioned the small pink houses, and impressive government buildings that had withstood the test of time, hailing from old colonial days. The conflict of beauty created by sadness struck her as she began walking to alight another bank of stairs to the top deck, just needing to elevate herself and go higher above the madding crowd.

She stopped abruptly as she saw a lone male figure. He was leaning over the rail, studying the water. While she had sought solitude, strangely she was glad that Tyrell Ramsey had been the one to disturb her peace. A slow smile crossed her face as she neared him.

"Don't jump," she said in a soft tone. "I know this is horrible, but don't do it."

He chuckled and kept looking down at the water. "I've never experienced anything like this in my life."

"If it makes you feel any better, me neither."

He nodded and let out a long, tired exhale. "Are the cameras rolling up here?"

She shook her head no. "Only in the bedrooms, the hallways, and the common eating areas. The camera guys have turned in for the night. They aren't secretly roving the decks looking for the forlorn—that's why I came up here to get away."

Tyrell pushed away from the rail and looked at her. "Good. Your secret is safe with me." He rubbed his jaw and glanced up at the stars. "I thought I could handle this. Guess I learned something about myself today. I don't think I have what it takes to be a bug under a microscope."

"Well, take heart. You're not alone. I don't think

anybody can deal with that, really. I didn't know how crazy it could get, even though I orchestrated all of this."

He stared at her for a moment. "Can what we discuss be off the record, 'Tash? I mean, if you can't, then cool. I know you have to remain impersonal, and this is your job, and all . . . but I just need to talk to somebody who's not in this whole game."

She stared at him for a moment, truly knowing how he felt. "Yeah. Off the record. On both sides, deal?"

"Deal," Tyrell said quickly, his smile competing with the stars.

Looking at him was disorienting. She wasn't sure if it was his relaxed countenance, or the honesty within his handsome face. He'd changed and had on a green, collared T-shirt and a pair of raggedy, comfortable gray sweatpants . . . just as she imagined he might wear around the house. His smile was so genuine and his manner so easy that it was as though she'd known him all her life.

Yet she cautioned herself that it also might have something to do with watching him defend someone he didn't even know over and over again as she'd edited his video segments. The repetition had burned the sound of his voice into her mind . . . his laughter, the way he teased good-naturedly, and made improvisational jokes. She loved his conversation, which was open and upbeat, and even when he got angry, there was still a quiet dignity about the way he did things. Rare. Still, nothing beat his handsome smile and easy manner, or the charismatic way he endeared almost everyone to him.

The way he was staring at her made her look away. It was both electrifying and terrifying as she waited for him to begin. Stephanie had been so right, but the timing was so wrong. All she could think to do was defuse the tension with light banter.

"Well, if you're not jumping tonight, and we have a pact to talk . . ." She cocked one eyebrow up and looked at him over her coffee as she sipped it slowly. "You keep standing here not talking and I might have to call a cameraman on my two-way to get rare footage of a quiet Tyrell Ramsey."

He chuckled and leaned against the rail, but he never stopped looking at her. "I just don't know where to begin," he said, telling her the truth. "There's so much going through my mind at the same time that it's all jumbled up." He paused, hoping she could relate. "You ever feel like that?"

"Are you kidding," she said, blowing out a long breath and leaning against the rail beside him. "All the time." She glanced at him, the gentle, balmy breeze feeling so good against her back. "I keep waiting for them to peg me as a fraud at the job and yank my position. So many things run through my head all day every day that most of the time I can't begin to sort it all out. Welcome to being young, black, and corporate."

He nodded and ran his palm over his hair. He knew exactly what she was talking about, but had never articulated it that way. Standing next to her, keeping an appropriate professional distance was also running through his head, but he dared not begin to unravel that train of thought. Yet, the breeze wafted her creamy vanilla scent his way, and she'd put on a pretty, powder blue tank top with her jeans . . . and it left her smooth, glistening shoulders exposed to be kissed by moonlight and starlight. Right now he wished he were a star.

"You know, 'Tash, the only reason I did this was to save my struggling label. The only reason I was trying to do that was, I wanted to work in an environment where I didn't have to hide who I was, follow somebody else's rules, and be somebody who I'm not. Plus, I wanted to give some brothers and sisters who had music and creativity in their spirits a chance to do their thing, the way they wanted to do it, without getting that crushed out of them by a dead end day job." He chuckled sadly and closed his eyes. "Then I find myself on the auction block, my pride, my whole life, under a microscope all because I didn't want to wait for it, wanted to break out now rather than wait." He opened his eyes and stared at her, searching her face for understanding. "I realized when I went back to the room that I had pimped myself."

Natasha lowered her coffee mug slowly, one hand covering her mouth.

"Think about it, 'Tash. I went out on the street, like a hoe, to earn money, doing stuff that would shame my mother. I'm supposed to woo five women at once on national TV, get them all hot and bothered so they'll pick me and I get the money. If that ain't a hoe, what is it?"

"Oh . . . my . . . God."

"Right, sis. That's why I'm having trouble sleeping at night. Because if I had told my sister or some girlfriend or some female I knew to do this to bring the money home, I'd be called a pimp, right? Like our boy from St. Louis, who owns the auto dealership . . . before I get bounced off this boat, I'ma ask Joe Scott how he fell into his business start up money, because boyfriend looks like Snoop, to me."

They both laughed, but they both also knew it wasn't funny.

"Until you said that . . ." Natasha closed her eyes . . . "I never thought about the implications, I was just—"

"Sis, I ain't judging you. You were trying to follow the trend, do your job, come up with some new TV show to compete with what's already out there. But it's like what I always tell my artists, just because that's what's already out there and people are getting paid from it, still doesn't mean you need to go hard core. Be creative." He touched her cheek with his knuckles as her expression became pained, but drew away the caress that they both knew was too familiar.

"Naw, don't be hard on yourself. I'm the biggest hypocrite around. I tell my artists not to go down that path, then as soon as I need money, I'm out hoeing," he said with a sad chuckle and shoved his hands in his pockets. "Now I've gotta sleep in the bed I've made."

Her face burned where his fingers had gently stroked it, and it sent a slow smolder through her. "We all have to sleep in the bed we've made, I suppose," she said quietly, trying to fathom how, amid this madness, she'd discovered a man with a conscience. "My mother is horrified by this show, and so am I, now that I really see what things like this do to people." She sighed and held his gaze. "I just asked God to forgive me for playing with people's lives and hopes and dreams for profit. I never meant to hurt anyone . . . in fact, when I went into this business, I never thought I'd be doing shows like this. But somewhere along the way, in that quest to be successful . . ."

"You lost your way," he said, finishing her sentence. "We all do."

His tone was so mellow and was so nonjudgmental that, were it not for circumstances she would have stepped in closer and hugged him. But propriety held her back.

"I hope you make it to the end, Tyrell Ramsey," she admitted. "I can't or wouldn't influence that, but you're a real decent guy. I like the way you treat people." That was as much as she dared to explore, and needed to get the conversation back to something safe, like the show—anything but deep philosophies about life.

"That means a lot coming from you, 'Tash. For real."

His gaze was so intense that she had to look away from him. Again she could feel her body temperature rising and responding to his voice and what he'd said, despite the gentle sea breeze.

"I'm serious," he said.

She didn't know what to say. He'd spoken so softly that she could barely hear him.

"I come off as an opportunist, I know that," he murmured. "And, truthfully, I am one. I used to believe in walking through the door of opportunity, by any means necessary. But along the way, I've been finding that even I have my limits."

He waited for her to look up at him and he offered her a sad smile.

"Like, when I saw my brothers go down the wrong road—and you know my history from your investigation when I applied for this show . . . I knew that was a road I wasn't going to travel. I had my limits." He let out another hard breath and turned to rest his elbows on the rail while studying the horizon. "I thought that I could come on a show, talk some smack to five women, and be out. But, today, I found my limit."

"You're not thinking about quitting the game, are you?" She was mortified, and not sure why. But she was quite sure she didn't want him to jump ship.

"No, not all the way. I'm torn," he said, his expression pained and earnest. "See, here's the dilemma. I like people. I don't like playing them off one another." He turned and looked at her to be sure what he said sank in. "Vera reminds me of a perky little sister. Annoying, got too much energy, but nice. She's ambitious and has a good heart and doesn't deserve to be messed over. Linda is *cool* people, yo. Just got it going on, and folks can't see beyond her hard edge. But you can tell that sister had to scrape for everything she's worked hard to have, as well as every shred of respect she's gotten— which is why Campanelli pissed me off so bad and I had to step to him."

Natasha kept her gaze steady on the man beside her, even though his words were buckling her knees. The depth she'd only imagined he had was being slowly revealed, and it was like watching him disrobe, one article of clothing at a time as he spoke. She held onto the rail for support as his brow furrowed in deep contemplation and he spoke from his heart.

"Then there's Michelle . . . she's as crazy as she can be, shy, nervous, but you know that somewhere, somebody hurt that girl bad. I can't explain it but, with all her education and good looks, it's as though she's fragile. Does that make sense?"

Natasha only nodded and took a sip of her cool coffee.

"And, Lillian . . . man . . . she wants the basics. That sister just wants to get married, move to the suburbs, and be a soccer mom and get out of the rat race. I can dig it. My best friend, Bernard, is the same way. Good people, just wants to be about family and no drama, doesn't want to get burned. Knows she ain't the sexiest woman alive, but would be a great wife and mother, and would be the family rock. Now tell me a woman like that deserves to be kicked to the curb, all because she isn't eye candy like a Kimberly? That ain't right."

"No, it's not," Natasha whispered.

"And, Kimberly . . . Lawd, have mercy. She's in the worst shape of them all, emotionally speaking."

That was the last thing she expected Tyrell Ramsey to say and the question flew out of her mouth before she could censure it. "How so?"

Tyrell shook his head. "Women like Kimberly wind up having nervous breakdowns. She's beautiful and knows it, therefore feels entitled. But she also feels gypped by life, so now girlfriend is on a mission to snag what she thinks she should have—namely, a high-powered brother, who can set her up in her profession as a model. That's a high maintenance challenge to take on, because it ain't about working with him to build. She wants everything hand delivered on a silver platter. When it comes time for kids, she'll freak, because kids are not convenient, prepackaged, predictable, and they require that you step into the background so they can get what they need." He rubbed his jaw and let out his breath and then looked at her. "Think about all your momma probably sacrificed so you could be where you are today. Do you think a sister like Kimberly has that level of unconditional love and willingness to sacrifice in her?"

"No," Natasha said, her voice distant as her thoughts traveled with it. "I hadn't considered all of that."

"You're not alone. I didn't think about any of that, either. No more than I thought about what I'd do if I ran into some really cool brothers whom I'd have to try to beat out." Tyrell pushed away from the rail. "I like Nelson and Tony and Quazar. They are funny guys, just trying to make it like I am. Sam Hartman is deep—quiet, but that white boy from Colorado got something going on in his head to even deal with this whole thing. Floyd, the other engineer, seems like a momma's boy who was raised in the church, scared of everything, and the fact that he's on this show is making me wonder. All I can figure is that he was so ready to settle down, and so hated the unpredictability of the dating life, that he'd subject himself to this travesty to help him sort it all out—so I don't wanna burn him, but the way the show is set up, I have to." Suddenly Tyrell laughed. "But Anthony Adams, and that arrogant brother, Jason Fulbright from D.C., them I'll do in a heartbeat, just like Campanelli was expendable."

Natasha was glad he laughed. It relieved so much tension that she found herself wiping her eyes. But the sound of his warm voice washed through her hard. It made her remember just how long it had been since any man had truly made her think and laugh and be so comfortable in her own skin.

"You know," she said, recovering slowly, "you should have been on the show design committee as one of the producers, brother. You would have been the voice of reason and maybe derailed this very bad idea."

He was laughing, but her comment stole some of his mirth. "But then I wouldn't have met you."

She just looked at him. His smile widened.

"Don't you know by now that you're the complete package?"

"What?" she whispered, glancing around the deck nervously. "You need to stop playing. Just because we're cool doesn't mean—"

"Aw, girl, relax," he said, putting one foot up one the rail and chuckling. "I'm an opportunist, but I'm not working you for favors. I know that what goes down on this top deck stays here—but the opportunist in me would jump overboard if I didn't take this rare chance to get this off my chest."

"It's late and I'm going down to finish—"

"Okay, run away if you want to, but you'll miss an opportunity to hear some male science."

Natasha laughed and folded her arms over her chest, gripping her mug while trying not to slosh cold coffee on her top. "Male science?"

"Yeah. You're the complete package. You constructed all the phases of dating into one mad-crazy ship adventure, with all the fragments of the complete package on it like a giant jigsaw puzzle."

"I did?" Natasha laughed hard. "Oh, Tyrell Ramsey, when it comes to talking trash, you, my brother, are good!"

"No, for real, hear me out, then decide. Cool?"

"All right. Shoot."

"This is how I see it," he said, pushing off the rail and walking around her. "You have everything any man would want bundled in separate packages."

"Huh?" She followed him in a circle as he walked around her till she was dizzy.

"Kimberly is for the libido. Those driven blindly by that, will go for her—ignoring the other finer elements."

Natasha stopped turning with him as the information took root. "Whoa . . ."

"Yup. And Michelle is the sensitive one, the nurturer to listen to all your darkest secrets—that's why she's the psychologist. The quiet guys on the team are blown away by her."

"Oh, now that is deep. Stop walking and talk to me," she demanded with a smile.

"See, I told you I know people," he said triumphantly, and stopped before her. "Linda represents the strength element, that sister who you know will be the rock if you go to jail, get shot, your business fails, you get sick, she is *there* for the long haul and that's worth more than money."

Incredulous, Natasha opened her mouth and then closed it.

"I already told you, Lillian is about kids and family, hearth and home, mom extraordinaire type. You're ready to have the big cookouts and barbeques, Lillian will make you go to her like a moth to a flame . . . that's why if my boy Bernard were around, brother would be booted off the show for proposing."

"And Vera?" That was all Natasha could say.

"Oh, she's your fun and party and run the streets woman. That's the one who likes to hang out, will even go camping and do extreme sports with you—might try bungee jumping and all that."

They both laughed hard.

"So, you see, 'Tash, what you did was bring all the

various elements of what any man could possibly desire under one roof. Then you put him through accelerated paces." Tyrell used his palms to paint an invisible picture against the horizon. "We have to pass the bar test—literally walk up to them in a group and risk getting flat blasted. Did it. Then we had to go to a highfalutin dinner and know how to behave—aw'ight, so I messed up—but with cause."

Again they both laughed hard, and she was holding onto the rail. "Okay, what else did I do, since you're reading me so hard?"

"See, that's just the thing. I don't know what else you have planned, but if each challenge is going like I think it is, it's going to be designed to show how we respond under each one of the major dating hurdles." He smiled wide as she covered her mouth. "Bull's-eye. Lemme see," he said, his tone teasing and triumphant. "Somewhere down the path, it'll be about money. That always comes up. Then there must be something to show how brothers deal under stress . . . I don't know, but I do know that you've also added the celibacy clause, so that these women get to make choices without the one crutch we often lean on to sway the balance in the equation."

"Oh, stop!" She was laughing so hard her mug went over the rail and hit the water with a splash. "Oh, no!"

"See, you're throwing dishes because you know I'm right, girl. If a brother can put his thing down hard enough, sometimes if he doesn't pass the other tests, well . . . all is forgiven, temporarily, at least. But your rules done messed that all up."

"You are terrible, Tyrell, seriously!" Natasha

peered over the edge of the ship, lamenting about the lost cup. "This don't make no sense."

"But it was brilliant," he said, his tone growing more subdued as he watched her laugh and shake her head. "It made me see some things that I hadn't seen before . . . I was blindly just going through the paces until you set up this mad-crazy dynamic."

When she glanced up at him, she was surprised to see that his expression had grown serious. Instinct told her it was time to go back downstairs and finish the edit; she'd been alone with a show contestant longer than was advisable. She knew that her time spent with him could be misconstrued as preferential treatment, and she didn't need another layer of complicity to be added to the already volatile situation. But try as she might, her legs would not obey her. The things that he was sharing, and the temporary joy that he brought to her spirit, made her want to break the rules and soak in their private moment.

"I said I was an opportunist, girl . . . so I had to take this opportunity to tell you that, from what I've seen, you are that foundation type sister who will weather storms. You've built your career, and I know that was no easy feat, but you don't wear it like an S on your chest, even though you're brilliant at what you do. Your kindness with people tells me you have a sensitive ear . . . tonight, you listened to me and proved me right. I've seen you run around this ship and attend to so many details that you could double as the Energizer Bunny; Vera ain't got nothing on you as far as spunk. And, 'Tash, you laugh . . . deep and warm . . . real. I don't know if you're into family and kids, but I have my strong suspicions." He let out a long breath through his nose and his smile mellowed as his voice dipped. "And, sister, I'm not being fresh when I tell you, *you are fine* . . . messed me up in the auditions and I ain't been right since."

He allowed his gaze to burn her before he put more distance between them. "It's easy to deal with passing on the buffet when it doesn't have anything you really want on there. If you're real hungry, you might sample a little of this, a little of that, but you still have to keep going back to the long lines . . . sometimes what's on the sternos is hot, sometimes the stuff has been messed over. Ain't the same as having everything you ever hungered for served up hot, on one plate, in the right environment. Hence my dilemma. Everything I want, is right there—but bad environment." He glanced at her and gave her a wink. "That's why I moved over here. I ain't trying to mess up your job, 'Tash."

She didn't know what to say. "I'd better be going back downstairs. Bad environment."

He smiled. "Yup. Real bad."

She nodded.

"Maybe when the environment isn't so bad, with hidden cameras everywhere, you'll tell me, off the record, if you've seen anything on this buffet you like?"

She chuckled. "I haven't been to a buffet in years."

What she said stole the air from his lungs. "Neither have I."

"Yeah, right," she scoffed, her smile now shy.

"I've been working very hard *for years* . . . no trips to the buffet, because I was tired."

She just stared at him. "For real?"

He nodded his head. "Believe what you want, but that's the truth."

"Me, neither," she finally said, unable to stop looking at him framed by the midnight Caribbean sky and stars.

"Then, you might wanna go on downstairs like you're supposed to . . . before I mess up your job."

She nodded, but was slow to begin walking away from him. "The problem is, everything I've had a hanker for is all on one plate . . . but the environment is very, *very* bad."

Chapter 11

When Natasha entered the editing suite, Stephanie and Devon were still hunched over the monitors fine-tuning the raw footage. She needed a cool shower in the worst way, but dared not leave her colleagues for any longer than she already had.

"How was the break? Get your head clear?" Devon asked brightly without glancing up.

"Yeah," Natasha said slowly, moving toward the coffee service to get a new cup. Get her head clear? Was Devon kidding? It was more like getting her mind blown.

"Sometimes all you need is a short change in routine to get a fresh perspective," Stephanie said on a yawn as she stretched. "Without it, this is murder."

"Yeah, it's definitely murder," Natasha murmured, slurping her coffee to drown her thoughts.

"All right, Steph," Devon said, working the kinks out of his neck. "Run the tape from the top. I think with one more pass it'll be ready to transmit to Nathan. If he doesn't like it, screw him. I'm beat."

* * *

She felt like a zombie, but made her body move when the alarm clock sounded. They'd shut down the monitors and had crawled into bed at three A.M., but after her talk with Tyrell, and watching him over and over again on the screens, sleep was the last thing she could do.

It was as though the man had sent electric current through her. Parts of her body and spirit were coming alive that had lain dormant for years. And they weren't just waking up, they where rousing and shouting and demanding attention. This was so bad, so terribly awkward. How had she allowed herself to get in *this* kind of position?

There was no private space, no place to sit quietly and figure this all out. The boat was loaded with people and cameras and drama. She had a roommate, for chrissakes, who talked nonstop and who was already getting *vibes*. To make it even more complicated, now she had it bad for a man who was clearly off-limits. There were legal and career implications, and all she could do was sit on the sidelines, act like there was no chemistry . . . in exotic, sensual, wondrous locations. She'd have to listen to his warm rich laughter, yet couldn't participate in his humorous banter, or get into his deeply philosophical conversations. . . . Then she had to spend nights revisiting all of his images and content over and over again to edit him to perfection. Worse yet, she knew he'd be feeling it too . . . if he'd been honest when they'd talked. The way he acted at breakfast would tell her that much.

The only saving grace was that his roommate had been put off the ship, otherwise he might have embarrassed himself in his sleep. But sleep, what was that? Natasha Ward had him tossing and turning all night.

It had been a long time since a woman had messed him up that badly, if ever. The alarm clock was stabbing him in his brain. But he didn't want to get up, wanted to savor the last remnants of the dream a little longer. Then his eyes opened instantly. Cameras were everywhere, including in his room.

Tyrell sat up slowly, making sure he was covered. The last thing he needed broadcasted was a morning erection; the only thing he could hope was that he hadn't been talking in his sleep. But that settled it. No more interactions with Natasha Ward like he'd had last night. He had to put some distance between them, if he was ever going to survive ten long weeks wondering, hoping, and jonesing for her like he was. Last night was too intimate and too close a call. He'd done something that no brother should ever do on the first real conversation, just flat-out told the woman she had his nose wide open!

He rubbed the sleep from his eyes and turned off the alarm. Group breakfast, then the day's itinerary would unfold—whatever that would be. What had he gotten himself into!

Natasha held the phone away from her ear and then put Nathan Greenberg on speakerphone so that Devon and Stephanie could hear. Their boss was shouting and having a mental meltdown, but with no sleep and everything on her mind, she couldn't take the decibel level impact directly against her eardrum.

"This is pure art!" Nathan yelled. "Fabulous, fabulous, oh, this is going to be *big*!"

"Glad you like it, Nathan," Natasha said without emotion.

"Like it? Are you nuts? I love it!"

Devon gave Natasha a high five and Stephanie gave her two thumbs up.

"Devon and Stephanie really worked the edit," Natasha said. "The camera guys outdid themselves, and I think we've got ourselves a solid first show."

"The network is going to go insane. We need to add more trunk lines on the 1-800 voting line, and more intern staff to cover the E-mail responses. Carry on, people—and bring me more of the same for the second episode."

The threesome stared at each other as the call disconnected.

"Well, you heard the boss," Natasha said, forcing herself to smile. "We've done good, Nathan is happy, now all we have to do is be sure that we send him more of the same."

"Yes!" Devon yelled, doing a little jig and sweeping Stephanie up to dance around the suite with him. She giggled and hugged him and then took Natasha's hand.

"Didn't I tell you this was cosmically correct?" Stephanie said, laughing.

"Yeah," Natasha muttered, laughing despite her exhaustion and worry. "The universe definitely has a perverse sense of humor."

By the time they joined the breakfast, all the contestants were milling about, gabbing excitedly, and had formed small clusters of affinity. Natasha watched the groupings as the cameramen got cameos and worked the room, and she simply stared at the buffet table that had been set, trying to keep her gaze from going to Tyrell.

He nodded and raised a glass of freshly squeezed orange juice in her direction, shot a knowing glance over to the buffet table, and then chuckled as his gaze slid away from her so that he could smoothly resume his conversation. The private joke between them about the buffet was not lost on her, she was just glad that he was discreet enough to leave it at a subtle glance.

But all that did was add more tension to her already wire-taut nervous system. He remembered. He'd picked up on the silent reference. There was a private bond that neither of them could explore. The forbidden knowledge was titillating. It wasn't even ten o'clock in the morning and the man had already turned her on.

"So," Devon said brightly, moving with Natasha and Stephanie to the buffet, "we let the kids play, go shopping, explore the beaches, we get some sexy wet bikini shots of the girls and guys, and we splice that down as the Bahamas intro. I see horse-drawn carriage tours, treks through the scenic old mansions, piña coladas, sunbathing, and we allow them to organically pair off in huddles to see who gets along and who doesn't, where bonds are forming or fracturing before we drop tonight's challenge on them."

"Yeah," Stephanie agreed, placing a bagel on her plate. "Look at Miss Kimberly," she added with a discreet nod. "The ladies have frozen her out, but she's graced Anthony Adams's table and is holding court with his crew—that guy Fulbright, the one from Colorado, and our auto dealer from St. Louis, Joe Scott."

Natasha just nodded as she put a small scoop of scrambled eggs on her plate, noting that Tyrell had the other men and all the women around his table, everyone laughing and talking animatedly. Somehow, nothing on the buffet appealed to her. But when she glanced up, to her horror, Tyrell had stood and was on his way toward the buffet. She said a silent prayer in her mind: *Lord, do not let this man start.*

"Good morning," Tyrell said, his smile bright and his tone upbeat. "I keep coming back up here, but nothing on this buffet seems to fill me up. God, I woke up with an appetite this morning."

Natasha swallowed a smile. *You need to stop,* she mentally warned.

Stephanie laughed. "Tyrell, where do you put it all? Remember, the camera adds twenty-five pounds."

"Aw, don't worry," he said, chuckling, and glancing at Natasha. "I've got a wooden leg."

Natasha almost dropped her plate but coolly recovered to select a blueberry muffin without comment.

Devon laughed and slapped Tyrell on the shoulder. "Honey, don't you ever . . . and washboard abs to go with it. But if you keep chowing down like this, after ten weeks, we'll only be able to do head shots."

Tyrell issued them a wink, and strode away. "See y'all later. Gotta make the best of what I have on my plate."

Stephanie sighed and moved closer to Natasha.

"God, that man has charisma. Every time he says something, I feel faint."

Natasha just smiled. "Yeah, girl, I know what you mean."

"I think we should send a montage of beach shots to Nathan so he'll have promo trailer for the upcoming episode that he can bumper in at the end of the day one episode before it airs this evening. I know it's a drill, sort of a real push, but after seeing what we got this morning and early afternoon, I believe it's a must-do."

Natasha nodded as she peered into the monitors under the beach cabana. "Yeah, you're right. This is great stuff. We've got to transmit ASAP so he can scrub this raw footage and give the audience a twenty to thirty second taste of what they'll see next week."

"Then, we should give them their challenge right here on the beach. Give them tonight to have the bonfire cookout, then do the casino challenge tomorrow. Whatduya think?" Stephanie asked, joining the huddle in front of the playback monitor.

"I vote yes," Devon said quickly. "Just look at all those buff, bronzed bodies . . . wow. Let's rein them all in, serve the challenge now, get the reactions, and during the evening bonfire, we'll really see alliances form as they digest what's about to happen."

"All right," Natasha said. "Let's do it."

Her production team shared a round of high fives like they were going into a championship sporting match. She was simply glad that she had something to do to keep moving. All morning and part of the afternoon had been harder than she'd imagined, as she watched the groups from her spectator's position. Secretly she'd yearned to be that woman sitting next to Tyrell in the horse-drawn tour . . . or the one on the beach playing volleyball with him. As she'd watched him strip off his shorts to uncover his bright turquoise swim trunks, she'd had to look away; it was pure torture.

Intermittently, he'd slid her glimpses to let her know he was feeling it, too, which had made the secrecy of it all the more daunting. And everything was unfolding, as Stephanie would say, organically, spontaneously, naturally in such an unnatural set of circumstances. Her libido was on fire. There was no denying it as she and her crew left the cabana to address the contestants, just as there was no denying how alive she felt. As much as she dreaded every potential encounter with Tyrell, she also yearned for it. The conflict going on within her was thoroughly exhilarating, while the warm breezes, beautiful locations, sumptuous meals, and close proximity to what she couldn't have was driving her insane. Watching him smooth on sunscreen had indeed been murder, as his dark brown skin glistened from perspiration and protective oils. But when he'd come out of the water, drenched, rivulets of the blue Caribbean surf just coursing down his body, she thought she'd need an ambulance.

"Okay, people, listen up," Devon yelled, gathering the contestants around him. "Have a seat."

Again, the cameras took position as the beautifully tanned bodies sank to pure white sand, creating a mosaic of gorgeous human hues against nature's backdrop.

"Tonight we have free time at the beach bonfire cookout. But we want to give you twenty-four hours to mentally prepare your strategy for the first really big challenge."

All eyes were upon Devon as he spoke. Natasha couldn't help allowing her peripheral vision to soak in Tyrell's marble cut ebony form.

"Each team has seen how individuals in this contest play a little bit today during downtime. But when tomorrow comes, we'll hit the casino," Stephanie said with a wise smile. "They say you can tell a lot about a man by watching how he interacts socially and how he plays. But you can see so much more when you understand how he handles his money." She paused for dramatic effect, as the cameras panned each facial expression. Heads nodded amongst the female group; the men sat transfixed, hanging on Stephanie's every word.

"Therefore, each male contestant will be given two thousand dollars to spend at the casino. Let's see how well these gentlemen do at the tables. Gamble well, take risks, or not, the choice is yours."

Devon motioned for the cameras and went up to each contestant, asking him how he felt. He smiled as Jason Fulbright explained how gambling was scientific, and a matter of statistical odds. Anthony Adams pontificated about being a risk taker, having to do so as a publisher, while camera two zoomed in on Kimberly's beaming reaction to his statement.

Tony Rodriguez swaggered about, knowing how to play a hot hand, and Nelson Carter told the camera that he could play a little somethin' somethin' and wasn't worried about it. The two engineers, Floyd Jackson and Samuel Hartman, said that they agreed, gambling was a matter of statistics, both droning on and on that a man had to know when to hold 'em and when to fold 'em. For them, it was about discipline and not getting swept up in the excitement. The women were listening intently, giggling every now and then, but studying the male group as though they were about to take a final college exam.

Joseph Scott and Mike Quazar went with the luck angle, stating that it would either be their night, or not. According to them, it was the luck of the draw. But when it was Tyrell's turn to speak, he simply looked directly into the camera, issued a million dollar wink, and said, "Me, see, I'ma put it all on red and let the chips fall where they may."

"We gotta watch the first show, baby," Bernard said, slowly extracting himself from Camille's lush, naked body as he reached for the remote control. "I told my boy I would tape every episode. C'mon, girl, stop . . . for just a minute."

Camille sighed and rolled over, happy and temporarily sated. "I guess I should be interested, given that I wouldn't be here if it weren't for Natasha's VIP pass to see the ship debark."

Bernard kissed the bridge of Camille's nose. "Remind me to lay palms at your girl's feet. I owe my boy, Tyrell, too. If he hadn't insisted that I see him off, I would have never met you."

Camille snuggled against Bernard's damp chest as they clicked on the television. "Man . . . I wish we could go down there and hang out with them, don't you?"

Bernard chuckled as he stroked her hair and focused on the show. "Yeah, baby, I do . . . but I've been in Miami for days, hiding out from the job. A brother does have to go to work sometime, you know? I've never done anything like this in my life—just up and called out sick and scammed so hard."

"If it becomes a problem," Camille said through a giggle, "you've got an attorney. We'll make it an EEOC issue and back 'em up."

He kissed the top of her head and sighed. "Damn, I'm a lucky man."

"Yeah, you are," she murmured, stroking his chest.

As the show unfolded, they laughed and screamed, and pointed at the set, commenting about whom they liked, disliked, and taking odds on who they thought would make it to the end.

"I don't like any of the women on the show, truth be told," Camille said with a wave of her hand. "My girl, Natasha, should have been a contestant—she's the best of the lot, all things considered, and Jorgette could have definitely been in the mix."

"There he is," Bernard said, whooping with excitement. "My boy is handlin' thangs, ain't he?"

Camille just laughed harder as Tyrell went into his antics, and she sat mouth agape as he approached Natasha on screen. "Oh, my God!" she screamed. "Natasha has to be dying a thousand deaths! She's so private—and I know for a fact that she hates to be on camera. This is wild! But girlfriend looks *good* on there!"

The couple sat spellbound, watching every nuance until the final credits rolled, and had almost missed the promo for the next show as they fell into each other's arms talking a mile a minute between kisses.

"No, wait," Camille said, trying to get Bernard's

attention to return to the TV. "Let's see what's going on next week. This is like a soap opera!"

"Next week is a long time away, baby," he murmured, nipping her earlobe. "I'm much restored after the hour break. I'll catch the rest on reruns."

"No, seriously," she said, giggling as she slipped from his hold. "They're going to the casino. Check it out." Camille pulled the sheet up to cover her bare breasts, and Bernard begrudgingly rolled over to watch the promo for the upcoming show with her.

"Now, in the casino, I could do some damage." Bernard listened intently as each male contestant's five-second cameo was flashed across the television set. But he stood up as Tyrell's segment came on, and Tyrell looked directly into the camera, winked, and then his image was gone.

"Code blue!" Bernard shouted, walking in a circle trying to find his boxer shorts. "My boy's going under. I've gotta make some calls, rally the troops, we're going in and—"

"What?" Camille shot up from the side of the bed and wrapped the sheet around her. "What are you talking about, code blue, you're going in?"

"You saw him wink, right? That's *our code.*"

Camille stared at Bernard. "You guys have a code? For what?"

Bernard sighed. "I swore I wouldn't tell another living soul, but, girl, you're not just any ole body."

She smiled and loosened her grip on the sheet. "I'm not?"

"Naw, baby . . . you're special, don't you know that by now?"

She came in closer and yielded to his embrace. "Tell me. What have you guys cooked up?"

"See, the rest of those brothers have serious resources, and my boy doesn't . . . so, we were, uh, just figuring out angles to level the playing field a little."

"Y'all are cheating and you know he could be disqualified if there's any impropriety discovered. I have to warn you that I cannot go along with any show sabotage, or—"

"No, no, no," Bernard said, sighing loudly. "It's not like I'd slip him money, or anything like that. But, we wanted to use all nonfinancial resources at our disposal to give him the cutting edge, you know? And since the Bahamas is only a hop, skip, and a jump away—as well as a cheap flight from Miami . . ."

Camille giggled. "Can I go?"

"Down to the islands with me to help out my boy?" Bernard smiled.

She leaned up and kissed his cheek. "You'll need a lawyer on your hip to be sure you stay within the show's rules and regulations. Plus, I have to be sure that what you do won't mess up my best girlfriend's job."

"See, I don't want to get you involved in this, if it goes down funky."

Camille allowed the sheet to drop to the floor as she briefly swept Bernard's mouth with a kiss. "I'm already involved, and I owe Tyrell and my best friend. If it can make Natasha's show better, and give Tyrell a chance against the heavyweight competition . . ."

"I appreciate your trusting me, Camille," Bernard said softly, tracing her face with one finger. "Dang, girl, how did this get so thick between us so fast?"

Camille shrugged and ran her hand down his

chest. "Guess we were both looking for the same thing at the same time."

"But I can't have your professional name tarnished if a scandal breaks out. You're a lawyer, and I'm just a—"

"A fantastic marketing executive with a vested interest in a hot, new label. Besides, two heads working as a team are better than one. That chick, Kimberly, is already in cahoots with that publishing jerk, I can tell."

"Yeah, I know, and they already tried to get my boy, Ty, kicked off the boat day one."

"Mmmm-hmm," Camille said, her voice filled with singsong mischief. "But Jorgette could pose as just an island sister in the casino to get a note slipped to brotherman, if necessary."

"See, this is getting complicated now," Bernard said, beginning to pull away from her. "We were just going to have a couple of the guys in one of the bands show up, offer to entertain—"

"I have Natasha's cell phone number and can get the scoop so you can better position your troops."

Bernard stared at Camille for a moment before a slow smile dawned on his face. "You, sister, are scary-brilliant."

Chapter 12

He'd ignored Natasha as much as was humanly possible all day, just joining in the frenetic activity of touring, enjoying the surf and sun, and keeping everyone laughing. But each time he glimpsed her, a current of desire ran through him. Now, with the sun going down and washing the brilliant blue sky rose orange, a beer at his side, a warm fire before him, listening to the waves, and watching her smooth body move beneath a hot pink sundress, he was burning up.

Every color she wore just made him need to reach out and stroke her butter-satin brown skin. Her laughter and the sound of her voice just ran all through him. He watched ripe island mango dribble down her chin, and studied her hands as she cracked crab shells and sipped a beer, her smile infectious, destroying him as she relaxed at the edge of the group.

When she sprawled out on a blanket, full, sated, peaceful, it took everything within him not to go over to her and just trail his fingers up and down her long lithe spine. He could imagine the feel of his palm tracing down it to the sway in her back, up and over her firm behind and back again. Tyrell closed his eyes briefly, trying to shake the sensation she'd produced.

From his peripheral vision he could see her tiny, pixie face held between her hands, as she lay on her belly, resting on her elbows, knees bent, legs crossed at the ankles, watching them all with a smile. Her petite breasts were partially exposed as the sundress took a serious dip at the cleavage, letting him know what he'd already realized, they were ripe and unfettered by a bra.

If he could only share her blanket . . . just sit beside her and talk to her some more. If he could find a private space to connect with her like they had the night prior. One kiss, that's all he wanted right now, just a sample of her lush mouth and smooth tongue to tangle with his to the reggae beat. The pulse of the music had the same rhythm as lovemaking. The islands were designed by the Creator for that, he was so sure. Paradise, no lie, this was it . . . a place to be fruitful and multiply with Marley crooning to lovers. A full disk of blue-white moon as a spotlight, white sand to cushion the impact of each thrust, and the steady beat of waves to keep time . . . This was not a place to be celibate and surrounded by people playing a game.

Tyrell shifted and poked at the fire with a stick. He had to remember to breathe when Natasha rolled over on her back and closed her eyes. Her expression was so serene, her gentle inhales and exhales creating a steady rise and fall of her breasts; he was losing his mind. It had been *years* . . . and it all hit him at once. *Years.* He needed to get with this sister. Years. She was the finest thing on the planet. Years. He hadn't found anyone else like her *in years* of searching. Years, since he'd been held. Years. Natasha Ward was off-limits, but damn . . . Years were making him dare to be stupid. He had to keep talking, keep joking around, before he just stood up and went over there and blew it.

She had to roll over on her back and close her eyes. There was no way she could continue to watch him and the group. The brush of the blanket against her breasts and belly felt like a hot caress, and she only prayed that the soft breeze coming off the ocean would cool her down. Her panties were wet and he'd given her gooseflesh with just a mere glance. In profile, the fire had bounced off his skin until he looked like an African king. If this were any other place, any other location, she would have just said yes. Take it. Damn, that man was messing her up.

Natasha looked up at the stars, Tyrell's booming laughter seizing his stomach muscles like it controlled the surf. Reggae was lovemaking music, and Bob Marley was telling it so real . . . oh, Lord, she had nine more weeks to go, if she made it through this one without incident.

She quietly fussed at God, explaining that there oughta be a law. Maybe the best thing would be for him to be booted off the show, just so they could end the torture and get together? She shut her eyes tightly and tried to breathe in slowly through her nose, knowing that wouldn't be right, either. But she already knew, ten weeks would feel like ten years, and it had been years since anyone had held her, had made all of her awaken like this. He'd made her come out of her self-imposed coma one layer at a time. . . . First, he'd made her laugh, then, he'd worked on her compassion, had instilled a level of trust that she'd yet to be able to explain. And the things she imagined he could do to her body made her almost shudder.

It was insane, but she'd been watching, waiting, mentally strategizing to find a way to slip off with him privately again, just to get another dose of conversation—since that's all they could do, and even that would be a risky venture. But as she lay there, the breeze kissing her hardened nipples, the sand beneath the blanket at her back, all she could envision was what his weight covering her might feel like.

Natasha sat up quickly to jettison the sensation. She was at work, had to be clear about the boundaries, and couldn't even allow fantasy to take root within her. However, as she rejoined the group with seemingly carefree conversation, the embers within her belly caught fire and began a slow descent past her navel, making her swell between her thighs until she had to crush the sensation between them.

"I don't care what they say, or how much hard work this had all been," Devon said, raising his beer to Natasha and Stephanie, "there are worse jobs in the world."

"Hear, hear," Stephanie said, flopping on the blanket as the camera crew circled the contestants.

Natasha nodded toward the photographers. "Those guys will need a vacation after this. They are working harder than any of us." She stood, needing to move, and headed for a cooler.

"Yeah," Devon said, standing and stretching. "How about if we give them a brewski?"

"I'm with you," Stephanie said, pushing up from the blanket slowly. "They can't miss any of this footage, but they've got to be exhausted."

When Natasha got to the cooler filled with ice and drinks, she rooted around in it for the selection she knew her guys drank. The icy water felt wonderful on her hands, and the difference in temperature made her realize just how flushed and warm her face had become. It was reflex to dribble a little of the cold water down her cleavage, and she patted her throat and neck with a damp, cold hand. Much improved, she straightened herself and walked to the cameramen, and extended beers to them.

"Oh, thanks, 'Tash," one photog said. "You must have been reading our minds."

"Right on time," another one said, and she leaned over and handed out another brew.

"I got your back, guys," she said, laughing, enjoying the way the sand pushed through her bare toes. "It's been a looong day."

You ain't said a mumblin' word, Tyrell thought as Natasha gabbed with the camera crew just out of reach. When she'd bent over the cooler, his stomach had clenched. When she's reached into it, and dripped cold water down the front of her dress, his heart went into mild arhythmia. When she'd patted her throat with a wet hand, sliding it slowly down to her collarbone, and then dabbed her cheeks, all he could think of was her naked, on the beach, a piece of ice in his mouth, making her arch and moan as he let it melt in a slow trail to where he knew she was burning up.

"You're awfully quiet all of a sudden," Vera said, nudging Tyrell.

"I'm just tired, girl," he said, forcing a chuckle. "After that volleyball game, and hanging out with y'all all day, a brother is beat—*plus* I just ate." He flopped back on the sand and shut his eyes. Vera just didn't know. He was worn out. He could hear her laughing, and felt a presence on either side.

"You don't look like you're all that tired," Vera murmured in his ear.

"Not at all," Lillian said with a giggle. "But your secret is safe with me."

Tyrell sat up fast, and started laughing with the two ladies beside him. He knew the cameras were on them, and humiliation made his face burn.

"What did you guys say to him?" Michelle asked, chuckling and leaning forward.

"Not a thing," Vera said. "Don't ask, don't tell."

"Oh, so it's like that," Linda said, downing her beer with a wink. "Bet I can guess."

"Don't," Lillian shrieked, covering her face as she giggled hard. "Mind your beeswax."

"No private jokes," Quazar said, his tone teasing and good-natured, as the other guys offered shrugs of confusion.

"They just wanna know why a brother is beat," Tyrell said, trying to deflect more inquiry, "and are on my case because I was trying to slide in a cat-nap."

"Good save," Vera whispered. "But, later, if you really want to play with kitty . . ."

Tyrell took a deep swig of his beer and tried not to choke on it.

Lillian's gaze swept his body. "I won't tell," she murmured when no one was watching. "I woke up feeling the same way this morning, and the islands are so romantic."

Tyrell only smiled and continued to sip his beer, joining in the conversation with Lillian, but not without giving both Vera and Lillian a nod. It was an *I heard you gesture* that was left wide open at the end as to not offend, but wasn't a commitment. This was a helluva position for a brother to be in. Two beauties, one on either side, making grand offers that could get them all put off the show. The woman who had actually caused his body to salute her was across the beach, with a blazing bonfire between them. Nine jealous male contenders just waiting for him to mess up. But one of them, he noted, looked like he might not make it through the night.

Tyrell allowed his gaze to casually scan over to where Kimberly was sitting just a little too close to Anthony. The brother's eyes were nearly half-mast as she giggled and cooed and passed little private glances his way. Oh, yeah, Adams was done. The island night was killing him, especially after watching Kimberly squeal and splash half naked in the water all day. But he almost spit out his beer as he noticed Michelle lean back on her elbows next to Jason Fulbright. If he wasn't mistaken, he saw the muscles in the brother's biceps twitch, as though it had taken his all not to roll over on top the girl.

Sure, everybody was talking and laughing, but the chemistry was thick. The wildest thing was watching Nelson ease up beside Linda and just flatout start rapping. Now *that* he had not expected, no more than he'd expected to *ever* hear Linda giggle and glance away, seeming bashful. Linda?

It was more than his nerves could bear, and

Tyrell got up and headed for a cooler. "Anybody want a beer? Name your poison," he called over his shoulder. He glanced around as the men each lifted a beer and showed him their labels, then nodded to the female beside them. "Well, dang, y'all, why don't I just bring the whole cooler over, huh?"

Everybody laughed and slapped five. From the corner of his eye he saw Tony Rodriquez immediately claim his space next to Vera, and then moments later, Sam Hartman sidled up to Lillian and plopped down. Go Colorado. Dang, even the white boy was feeling it. "I knew he was deep," Tyrell said, talking to himself and chuckling as he bent to gather an armload of drinks.

"Who's deep?"

Tyrell started at the sound of Devon's voice, but relaxed as he hoisted up his beers.

"Colorado. Don't count him out. Dude took my seat and busted a very smooth move," Tyrell said with a wink.

"We almost missed that!" Devon said through his teeth. "Excellent!" Then he was gone.

Part of him felt bad for sicking the cameras on Sam Hartman, but Tyrell rationalized that he probably saved the man from being booted off the show tonight. Tyrell chuckled to himself as he struggled to hold all the cold beers in his arms. The fact was, if Hartman was feeling half of what he was, add that to Lillian's state, the scenario would be volatile. Rodriquez was probably history, as hot as Vera was at the moment. The only brothers who seemed to have their heads on right were, ironically, the guy from St. Louis, Joe, the engineer from Detroit, Floyd, and the Greek, Mike Quazar.

"You seem awfully amused," a soft female voice

said, making Tyrell turn quickly and almost drop a sliding beer.

The cold against his stomach was helping, but not much, as he righted himself to peer into Natasha's warm expression.

"All of this is crazy," he said, pulling up his T-shirt to carry the beers in it like an apron. "Real crazy."

It was reflex. As he'd lifted his shirt to expose his damp abs, her gaze went right to it before she could stop herself. If he'd just kept joking around, she could have recovered with something witty about hogging all the beers. But he'd watched her face, his eyes sliding to where hers had, and his expression had become stone serious as he swallowed hard. That had been her undoing.

"I have to get these beers back to the group before somebody says something to me . . . and before I lose my mind around you. Cool?"

Cool? Anything but, she thought. *Oh, why did he have to acknowledge it?* A hand on her shoulder made her jump and turn around fast.

"You okay?" Stephanie asked. "Have another beer. Your nerves are bad."

"I've already had over my quota," Natasha said, reaching for a Snapple iced tea, and wanting to splash her face with cold water. "Those Red Stripe beers sneak up on you."

"As do many things," Stephanie said with a sigh.

Natasha's body froze as she peered up at Stephanie. *Please, God, no, don't let her colleague have seen anything untoward.*

Stephanie gave a discreet nod toward the fire and then grabbed Natasha by the elbow. "I need to talk to you ASAP," she said in a harsh whisper, giggling the whole time.

Natasha stood fast and hurried behind her crew mate. "Girl, what's up?" she said, almost out of breath as they went to the monitors to try to pretend they were talking show business.

"Oh, my God, that guy Mike Quazar . . . after the show, 'Tash, I'm . . . I cannot explain . . ."

Natasha laughed but shook Stephanie hard. "No, no, no, no no! Girl, you cannot mess with a contestant, you know that," she said between her teeth, looking around five ways as she kept her voice barely audible.

Stephanie covered her heart with her hand and then reached into her pocket and produced a note. "I know. Not now, but for once in my life I want to be Cinderella." Hot tears rose in Stephanie's eyes and glittered as she weaved.

Natasha snatched the note from Stephanie and blocked her view to the bonfire with her back. "Steph, you've been drinking, the environment, and—"

"Read the note," Stephanie urged, her gaze darting around in all directions to be sure the coast was clear.

Slowly, Natasha opened it. The writing was bold and plain. "I've seen the others, but I want you. Period." She folded up the note quickly and shoved it back into Stephanie's pocket.

"Look at him, 'Tash," Stephanie said, practically swooning. "Six feet six, black curly hair, gray eyes, and a wonderful sense of humor . . . he looks like a Greek god, I tell you! And he wants me?" Stephanie allowed her gaze to wander toward the group and then she swept her hand down her front. "I have a mess of bleached blonde hair on my head, three silver earrings in one ear, I'm short, my figure is okay—but not supermodel like those ladies, and, he wants me? I've never in all my life ever pulled the linebacker, or the prom king, or the guy with a great career. I've *never* been *picked*, 'Tash—ever. Do you know what that's like? Even if it doesn't last, one day when I'm an old lady I can look back and say, down in the Caribbean, a Greek god picked *me.*"

Hot tears streamed down Stephanie's cheeks as Natasha pulled her into an embrace and patted her hair. Oh, Lordy, what was happening? Her crew was now bugging, the emotions were running hot, people were losing their grip, and a potential lawsuit was everywhere.

"I know, I know," Natasha whispered, trying to get Stephanie to calm down. But her tipsy colleague began to quietly sob, then the sobs became a hiccup-crying jag; Natasha rubbed her back as she dragged her into a cabana. As Devon peered into the tent with two cameramen in tow, Natasha put up her hand and blocked the entrance.

"Tell them that we had a crew meltdown. Kill the cameras. The stress of doing the show under heavy deadlines without sleep just got to one of our own. That's the only aspect of this you can broadcast, or I'll kick yours and Nathan's butts myself!"

Yanking the blue and white tarp shut, Natasha drew Stephanie into another embrace, rubbing her back and talking to her like one would address a frightened child. "It's going to be all right, sweetie. Now, we'll wash your face, get you some coffee and a good night's rest. Tomorrow, we'll think about this, but you will not leave my side—understood? No going off even to the Coke machine in the hotel. You're not stable."

Stephanie laughed and sniffed and wiped her face as she nodded and clung to Natasha. "I've lost my mind, 'Tash. This is the gig of a lifetime, and I freaked on national television. What is wrong with me?"

"You're human and exhausted and have been sleep deprived like a POW. Anything is liable to happen under these circumstances."

Stephanie looked at Natasha, searching her face with a furtive gaze. "Do you think that's the only reason he picked me, because he's sleep deprived and exhausted, and . . ."

"No," Natasha said firmly. "Whatever he saw as he watched you work is why he picked you. But neither one of us can fall off the wagon right now."

For a moment, neither woman spoke. Natasha started wiping Stephanie's tears and then turned away, too embarrassed for words. She'd only meant to support her coworker, not confess. But everything was too close to the surface and spinning out of control.

"*Neither* of us?" Stephanie murmured. "Talk to me, 'Tash."

"I can't go into it, but—"

"I wasn't wrong about Tyrell, was I?"

"There's some chemistry," Natasha admitted, downplaying the potential, "but that cannot happen right now."

Stephanie nodded and blew out a long sigh. "It has to be the beers and this freakin' Caribbean music," she said, chuckling and wiping her face. She raked her unruly pixie haircut and closed her eyes as she shook her arms to release the tension. "You've always had more discipline than me, 'Tash. I always get myself into trouble with my crazy adventures." She opened her eyes and looked at Natasha squarely. "I'm so horny right now I could scream."

Again, both women stared at each other and then burst out laughing.

"It's de islands, mon," Natasha said through a belly laugh, wanting to just go ahead and admit the same to Stephanie, but she just couldn't bring herself to say it.

"Stay with me, and don't let me make a fool of myself. Promise," Stephanie wailed, still giggling.

"Go over to a cooler, splash your face and get something with caffeine in it to sober you up."

"Yeah, I need to dunk my head in the ice." Stephanie sighed. "What was I thinking?"

"He's very cute," Natasha admitted, "and so are you . . . just be cool and do it after the show."

"Think he'll wait for me?"

Natasha's hands went to her hips. "He'd better. If not, then he wasn't worth it anyway, right?"

Stephanie gave her a halfhearted shrug. "I guess not."

"I know it's been a long time, but—"

"*Years,*" Stephanie said, her gaze intense. "Years, 'Tash . . . with all the women getting diseases, getting beat up, killed, abducted, left in Dumpsters, identities stolen, credit cards jacked. I've been a walking nutcase, afraid to go home with anyone I didn't know. And how do you get to know someone, working all the time, and everyone lying to each other with no frame of reference, family history, or neighborhood histories to fall back on? It's terrible out there, scary. Insane," she wailed, grabbing her hair in her fists. "The dating process is all screwed up—black, white, old or young, widowed, divorced, single, men are gay, crazy . . . oh, my God—axe murderers, serial killers . . . I haven't slept with a man in years. I'm going through batteries at the drugstore like I own stock in coppertops!"

Natasha was laughing but it wasn't funny. Tears had risen to her eyes, although she played them off like they'd come from their crazy banter. She, too, wanted to run shrieking into the night from it all. That had been the genesis of the whole show!

Before she could stop her, Stephanie had grabbed her by the shoulders. "'Tash, he's eligible, *not gay,* not married, been investigated, AIDS tested negative, credit checked, and we have his whole Greek family on tape—and *they're normal* . . . and he wants to be with me? I haven't been laid in so long that I might have a heart attack when he takes off his clothes—did you see his body today? And he's a nice guy . . . great conversationalist, is stretched out by the fire with a hard on, for me!" Stephanie dropped her hold on Natasha and laughed till she began crying again. "Do not ask me to be rational, 'Tash. In fact, if every woman on this show gets hooked up, *c'est la vie!* The cosmos dictated change. What can I say?"

Stephanie stood before her, breathing hard, her face flushed, her nose red, her expression pained. What was there to say, truly? She intimately understood exactly where Stephanie was at, but as the show's senior producer, she couldn't have it blow up like that. But as a woman, she wanted to rush over to Stephanie and tell her, *go for it, gurl.* Just take the plunge, consequences be damned—if he's the one, then grab the brass ring. Watching Stephanie was like looking into a crazy, Alice in Wonderland mirror. How could she begrudge any

female on the show for coming away with a very
rare find? Yet it hurt her soul to know that she'd
constructed a no-win scenario if they did

"Then, don't be rational," Natasha said slowly
and carefully. "Just try to be patient and very, very
discreet. Can you try to do that?"

Stephanie relaxed, sniffed hard, and smiled.
"Yeah. I just need some air and a good night's
sleep."

"Okay," Natasha said, her voice faltering. "We
both do. So, we'll go out there after you fix your
face and stay on the periphery as much as possible.
We'll edit tomorrow and get our heads together."

"Thanks, 'Tash," Stephanie said, her shoulders
dropping two inches with relief. "I know some of
what I shared could be considered too much information, huh?"

Both women laughed.

"I didn't need to know about the coppertops, but
your secret is safe with me."

Intermittently, Tyrell kept glancing at the cabana
off in the distance. He knew he'd said too much,
but never imagined that it would totally freak
Natasha out. A mild buzz had gone through the
group when the two show producers suddenly exited the scene, and he also noticed that Mike
Quazar had gone ashen. What was that about?

The only thing that made him feel a little better
was that Devon had come over and made a comment about producers being human, too, telling
them all about how hard the show staff had been
driving themselves toward perfection. He could
definitely understand it, and knew Natasha had a

lot on her plate. The woman seemed to drive herself nonstop to be the best, but could he blame her? It worried him no end that perhaps his inability to keep her blocked from his mind may have made him push the edge of the envelope of decorum just a little too far, and she'd wigged. That, he was not trying to do.

This time, when he stood to go get a beer, Mike Quazar offered to help him. He could tell the guy wanted to talk, but hadn't realized that they'd bonded like that. The only saving grace was that the cameras were still over by the others, who were engaged in a lively debate about the merits of playing truth or dare.

"Uh, Ramsey, can I ask you something?"

Tyrell looked at Mike Quazar as he bent to search for a selection of beers. "Yeah, man, what's on your mind?"

Quazar nodded toward the cabana. "I may have messed up real bad, and even though we're competitors, I just wanted to say that, sometimes there's something worth more than money."

Tyrell stood slowly with only one beer in his hand and offered it to Quazar, who accepted it, twisted off the cap, and guzzled it.

"Okay, I hear you," Tyrell said carefully.

"I'm already rich," Quazar said. "My software company survived the dot-com fallout, I've done all the islands, did the whole travel thing. I came on this show because I was looking for a wife. I didn't feel like sifting through the morass out there, I wanted one already investigated, certified, and if we clicked, I was gonna do it—black, white, green, or purple. As long as she was a good person . . . am I making sense?"

"I know that's your eighth beer, and the islands are talking to everybody, so maybe you oughta go for a ginger ale before you shoot yourself in the foot. I like you, man. If you get put off the boat, let it be because I beat you fair and square."

They both laughed as Tyrell found a beer, twisted off the cap, and saluted Quazar with a clink.

"That's why I'm telling you. I'm getting off the boat before the casino gig. I've found her, that's all I came for, and I'm out."

Tyrell held his beer midair and gaped at the man. "You serious?"

Again, Quazar motioned toward the cabana. "The blonde. She's funny, and nice, and sexy, and my mother met her when she visited the family to take the bio shots—looks like my dad's side, could be a cousin. My people liked her; the old ladies said they had a good feeling about her and not to blow it. I'm going for it."

For the first time in his life, Tyrell was speechless.

Mike Quazar pulled him into a bear hug and released him. "You're good people, we should stay in touch. You remind me of my family—the laughs and the way you treat the ladies. If you're ever on the West Coast, look me up . . . and I'll root for you on the call-ins. I have a lot of friends on the Internet; we'll be sure to vote for you, man. But I've gotta go so I can . . . ten weeks is a long time, that's all I'll say."

Tyrell just stood there as he watched the large Greek stride away, raking his hair, guzzling a beer, but seeming as though the weight of the world had just been lifted from his huge shoulders. There were no words as he saw Quazar plop down by the fire and meld with the group again, his disposition

vastly improved. The entire brief but very profound
incident gave him pause. Mike Quazar was indeed
a free man . . . free enough to not have to worry
about scrambling for a dollar, trying to build a business; he already had that under lock.

A deep level of respect for the man who would
throw a chance away for something more important held Tyrell where he stood as he sipped his
brew quietly, just thinking. What must that feel like,
to be in that position? Courage was relative. It required coming from a platform of strength. Conversely, his platform was shaky. If he gave up now,
he'd be another unemployed black man. If he quit
on his own before the ten weeks were up, he
wouldn't even have the twenty-five thousand—a
caveat in the show's compensation structure. He
wouldn't have the bills covered, and that would get
old with a sister he was trying to woo. His struggling
company would fall apart, and Natasha Ward would
probably be done with him for bailing out and po-
tentially compromising her job. He, unlike Quazar,
had shackles on his feet.

The only thing that made him feel halfway okay
with what he'd just heard was that Mike had trusted
and respected him enough to pull him to the side.

Chapter 13

This could *not* be happening! Her best producer/editor had gone AWOL, Devon had taken to his bed from the news that Mike Quazar had quit the show, citing a family emergency, and Nathan was on the horn wanting footage of the scandal that was erupting, not realizing that it was coming from inside the crew.

Natasha sat on the side of her bed in the semi-abandoned ship suite, holding her head. What was going on in the world? They hadn't even made it to the real first challenge, and the dynamics that were unfolding were so bizarre even she couldn't have architected the drama, had she been so inclined. Now her cell phone was blowing up?

She groaned as she crossed the room and retrieved it from the dresser. "Oh, hey, Camille," she said, trying to sound upbeat, but needing in the worst way to cry. "You good, lady?"

She listened to Camille go on about the first episode, her mind a million miles away. "Yeah," Natasha said, trying to seem cheerful, "the first one was a doozy, but we're planning on taking the teams to the Atlantis Hotel and Casino tomorrow night to see what the guys can do with some gambling money. As crazy as things have been unfolding, who knows what will happen?"

Camille's voice seemed to be getting farther and farther away as she found a chair to flop in, pure exhaustion making her bones feel liked they'd become wet sand on the beach. "Yeah, girl," Natasha said by rote. "I'll call as soon as I can, and give Jorgette my love, too." She closed her eyes and leaned her head against the wall. "I love you, too. Bye."

When a light tap at the door sounded, she didn't even move. She just blindly placed her cell phone on the coffee table and quietly told Devon, "Come in." What was the point of locking the door? Devon was always buzzing in and out like a bumblebee.

"Hey," a male voice said, much deeper than Devon's ever was.

Natasha opened her eyes and just stared up.

"Listen, I just wanted to tell you I was sorry that Quazar quit, and I know this thing with him and Stephanie has to be bugging you out—but I'm not saying anything to the group about it. Whatever his story was that he told us after the beach bash, is what it is. And, I know I made some moves that made you nervous . . . but, especially now, I know you can't act on them. I guess I just came to say I was sorry for anything I could have done to make your job harder."

"He told you?" Natasha stood slowly and kept her voice at a near whisper. "Does anybody else know?" Panic ripped through her. Stephanie could not be put on the firing line like that.

Tyrell held up his hands and leaned against the door. "Yeah, he told me, but nobody else knows. He doesn't want her business out, or her hurt, any more than you do, and he trusted me with the info."

Natasha immediately relaxed. Somehow, just knowing that in such short order, Tyrell had inspired trust from what should have been a competitive adversary, made her both curious and comforted at the same time. "But when could you guys have even discussed it?"

"When you two went into the cabana, he joined me at a cooler and we shared a beer. He let me know some things, and I could understand where he was coming from."

Natasha came in close, to keep their conversation as private as possible, motioning to him with one finger over her lips that he should be sure his voice stayed low. "Like what?" she finally murmured.

Tyrell sighed. "Dude was right, 'Tash. He said he was already wealthy, had only come on the show to find a wife, and screw scrambling for money and fame. Your colleague blew his mind and he was out. It made me think about a lot of things . . . I have to hand it to him, it was a bold, outrageous move that you have to respect."

Natasha's eyes widened. "You're not thinking of bailing, too, are you?"

Tyrell shifted nervously and pushed away from the door. "I wish I could," he said, "but I'm not in his position."

She watched his gaze drift toward the porthole and go somewhere far and private beyond it.

"I'm happy for Steph, if that's what the man said," Natasha admitted. "She's a sweetheart."

Tyrell nodded and turned to leave. "Yeah, and he's a real prince, not a pretender. So, it's all good."

She wasn't sure why, but her palm found his

shoulder. Maybe it was the defeated look in his eyes
that made her want him to linger and talk. But the
sad register in his voice had drawn her touch up
and out of her slowly. She felt his back straighten
beneath her touch as though she'd burned him,
and a hundred connected muscles beneath his taut
skin locked.

"I wish I could have been in a position to do what
he did—basically." Tyrell turned and held her
hand, staring at the floor instead of into her intense
eyes. "He said he was rich already, had made an assessment, and was going for it. Me, if I quit, not
only would I have messed up your gig, since being
with you would be the only reason I would bail on
the show, I'd be an unemployed, ragged record-
label-owning, broke-ass black man . . . and that
would not go over well with an ambitious sister
who's got it all going on. So, I'm stuck. I have to
play out this hand and hopefully hit jackpot, while
I watch the one I really want from a spectator's position."

She squeezed his hand for support, knowing exactly what it was like to not be in the right position,
not to have the options that others had, and always
having to do things the hard way just to be considered equal.

"I want you to play your best hand, then," she said
gently, knowing the professional line between them
had been crossed a long time ago. "Not because I
care about this job, per se, and not because I care
whether you have a bankroll or not, but more so
you can have your record label fly and so your
dreams can soar." She sucked in a deep breath, and
dropped his hand, simply because she had to stop
touching him.

"Tyrell, you deserve a chance, and if this insane show I've concocted offers you that, then grab the opportunity with my blessings, brother. You've got a very good shot at winning this thing. . . . I'm not saying that because I'm partial, I'm saying that based on the reaction everyone has toward you."

He looked up at her and studied her face for what seemed like a long time. Never in his life had he had a woman tell him that it didn't matter if he had money, didn't matter if he won or lost, but what was important was that he tried. And the fact that she was standing there, giving him a pep talk while her show was falling apart, made him want her all the more. Rather than simply give in to the impulse to kiss her, his fingers found the soft side of her cheek. He could feel them tremble as he glided them across the satiny surface, the smooth texture of it exquisite . . . just like he'd imagined. But the softness of her skin couldn't compare to the softness of her heart. He could see that in her searching gaze, the way her caring came through within her big, brown eyes.

"You deserve to be swept away by a prince," he said, his voice becoming gravelly. "But my carriage is a mirage, and everything I have is a shell game that transforms after midnight. I've been given a ticket to the ball under a lot of grace . . . and right now—"

She pressed her fingers to his lips, discarding the final barrier of propriety. "You already swept me away on the beach with one glance. Every time you stole a look all day, I thought I'd . . ."

"Yeah, I know," he murmured, kissing the center of her palm and covering it against his chest. "All day, every new thing we saw, I wished it was just me and you there . . . no cameras, *no teams,* no groups . . . just us. Does that make sense?"

She only nodded because standing so close to him, she could barely breathe.

"I'm not trying to play you for any show favors, or anything. I just hope you believe that at this point."

"I know," she whispered, "but you do have to leave."

He nodded, but didn't move. "You've gotta keep your job and rep intact."

She nodded, but didn't move. "I just want you to know that I feel it, too . . . but I have a job to do, and I have to stay impartial."

He nodded and stepped closer. "I know, and I'll try not to look at you when we're in the group . . . I'm sorry about doing that too much on the beach."

"Me, too," she whispered. "I was as much out of line as you were."

"I couldn't help it," he said low in his throat. "The colors you wear are so pretty on your skin." He touched her arms and ran his hands down them slowly. "It's so even, and beautiful, and brown . . . like dark, perfect, chocolate . . . I . . ."

"And you should see it get all ashy when I get out of the water," she said, forcing a chuckle to try to break the tension between them.

"If somebody told you your skin wasn't pretty, they were crazy . . . and I'd love to put oil on every inch of you one night . . . so let it get ashy, and then come knock on my door so I can fix that problem."

She could only stare at him as he took in a shallow breath, the edges of his nostrils flaring ever so slightly as he breathed. She watched him tilt his head, his eyes absorbing every inch of her as though he were memorizing a pattern.

"Damn, girl, you're fine . . . eyes, and your mouth . . ." He touched her collarbone with the pad of his thumb and let it linger at her shoulder before gingerly trailing it down the inside of her arm till she shivered. "Then you dripped water, here," he said, drawing a line between her breasts a millimeter over her skin without touching it, stopping where the edge of her dress created a border. "It messed me up. I knew I needed to stop watching you, but couldn't help it," he admitted quietly. He neared her hairline and breathed in. "You smell so good, too." His hands found her hips and caressed them for a moment, running the outside length of her thighs before he pulled them away. "I have to go, because my imagination was working overtime when I saw you sprawl on that blanket under the moon. When you turned over on your back and closed your eyes . . . Every time I see you walk, and your body moving underneath the sheer fabrics you wear . . ."

Her skin was on fire. The places he touched and didn't touch had become a diffused ache on her entire surface. His near touch between her breasts had made her quietly begin sipping air through her mouth. The touch of his thumb at her collarbone, and then down her arm had made her nipples sting so badly with need that she'd almost gasped. Now the heat from his body was so close and intense she thought her dress would catch fire.

"I can't watch you, either," she said, her voice hoarse. "But I have to, every day, over and over again on video after I already have . . . all night," she whispered, "in the editing bays. Tyrell . . . listen, this is an intense situation and—"

"I haven't been with anybody in years, and never anyone like you." He stared at her, unable to move.

"Years?" Her voice was a harsh whisper.

He shook his head.

"Me, neither."

"For real? Years?"

She closed her eyes and took in a slow sip of air. "For real . . . that's why you have to leave before I lose my job."

Finally she gathered her resolve and looked at him to convey her seriousness. Her hand found the center of his chest to back him up. It was meant as a placement to communicate not to move in closer, but the effect of touching him there made his eyes slide shut upon a shaky inhale. The expression on his face, his ragged breaths, and the rock solid formation of warm sinew beneath her palm made her want to trace the entire structure of it, despite the dangers. It was impossible not to as he stood there, trembling, not moving in toward her, backed up against the door, waiting for her to make the first advance. Something fragile within her psyche snapped as her other palm found his chest, both hands fanning out slowly to brush over the surface of it lightly until they scored his nipples.

She watched him swallow a moan and open his eyes, his palms again finding her arms, the edges of his thumbs moving over her breasts till her head dropped back. The pull against him was instant. The palm at the small of her back was a heated, flat grip that soon covered her backside while his mouth found hers. The kiss produced delirium, a level of insanity that she hadn't expected or experienced. The soft wetness of his mouth made her pelvis fuse to his. The hardness against her belly nearly made her cry out, but his deepening kiss smothered it. She broke away from his mouth needing air, only to find her breath halted by the long, wet, burning kisses he landed upon the swell of her breasts. The sensation he created made her turn into the attention, lift herself, panting, edging her breasts up to the low cut top of her dress . . . if he would just take the sting away with his lips . . .

She covered her mouth with her palm when he read her mind and obliged. The walls were too thin to be carrying on, but Jesus. His strong grip at her back, her pebble-hard nipples peeking over the edge of her dress, his kisses and tongue flicking away all rational argument, a pulsating suckle bringing tears to her eyes, him moving against her like the Caribbean surf . . . hard, long, and slow, the sound of his deep moan a thunderous wave through her womb—what job? The one she was destined to lose tonight? The one she hated anyway, when this man felt so good? But a push against the door made them both go still.

"Love, do you have anything stronger than Tylenol for this monster headache?"

"No, Devon, and I'm not dressed!"

"Oh, pooh . . . just open the door and stop being silly. I'm worried sick about Steph. It's not like her to—"

"I can't, and you cannot come in."

"Would you stop it and open this door now. I'm just not in the frame of mind."

Tyrell had closed his eyes and was leaning against the door like a SWAT was on the other side. She watched him quietly breathe through his mouth, at times halting his breath to sync up with hers. Frantic, her eyes scanned the room for options. High theater was the only way.

"I've got cramps. Please. In the midst of all of this, I'm about to have a nervous breakdown, so is Steph . . . and . . . and I'm changing. You do *not* want to see that."

They could hear Devon sigh loudly. "No, I *really* don't. God . . . But we have to find her."

"She needed space and decided to sleep at the hotel tonight. She's fine and she called me, okay. Give her room. Both of us could not be in here under these conditions, so she left. We'll catch up with her in the morning, 'kay?"

"Oh, all right," Devon finally said, sounding dejected. "And neither of you girls has anything stronger to kill the pain—"

"Midol," Natasha said fast, "and you don't want that."

"I'm going to bed," Devon replied with curt attitude. "I cannot take another thing tonight."

Natasha and Tyrell stood very, very still as they listened to Devon's footfalls fade. She stepped back from him and straightened her dress. He tucked in his T-shirt, glanced down at his pants for a moment, and then sent his line of vision out of the porthole window.

"I guess I should—"

"Yeah, you have to."

"I got kinda—"

"Crazy. Tomorrow—"

"We'll act like nothing happened," he said slowly. "I'll try to keep my professional distance."

He nodded. "I'll try to keep my focus."

"Yeah, we both have to do that." She nodded.

"You should wait till the coast is semi-clear. Not much we can do about the cameras, but I'm not trying to look at anyone in the face."

He nodded. "I know, but I have to get out of here."

"Give it a second to be sure Devon is gone."

He rubbed his palms over his face. "I have to go now to walk this off, 'Tash."

She quickly glanced down his body and then toward the floor. "Oh, yeah . . . I understand."

"No, you don't. When I go back to my room, I have to pass cameras, might bump into drunk fellow contestants, maybe some of the female contestants, and in my room, there're cameras."

Natasha covered her mouth and stifled a squeal.

"I know. Too embarrassing. You can play it off, but I can't. My issue is highly visible at the moment."

"I'm so sorry," she said, laughing quietly to keep from crying.

Tyrell leaned against the door, turned the doorknob, and chuckled. "I don't think he's coming back tonight, though."

She walked away from Tyrell, shaking her head and waving her arms. "It was a sign," Natasha whispered through the giggles. "This was out of order, and it was a sign to stop or get busted."

He sighed and turned the lock, peeping down the hall through a sliver he made when he silently pulled the door open a crack. "Coast is semi-clear, at least of people, cameras notwithstanding," he whispered sadly. "Guess that'll have to last for ten weeks."

She became thoroughly morose as she watched Tyrell slip through the door and silently click it shut behind him. By rote, she went to the door and turned the latch, needing space from any intrusion. As she walked back to the bed, she wrapped her arms about her waist to help stave off the tremors he'd created within her. The interruption was like a dash of cold water, but she could feel the slow burn beginning to smolder again, coming back with a vengeance. She sat down slowly, breathing slowly, carefully, assessing the damage to her credibility and reputation. But staying focused on that was near impossible just now.

His hands had covered her like warm velvet. She closed her eyes at the memory. His body was made out of granite, but moved with such fluid grace that he had to be a child of the sea. Where did this man come from, really? His resume said Atlanta, but Atlantis was more likely. A Pisces, a water sign, made sense, if she asked Steph . . . but his mouth, and his hands . . . the way they could elicit a gasp without actually touching her, rising tides within her that had flooded her valley, still wet and throbbing, wanting to wring Devon's neck. Years. Long, dry, desolate years of barren terrain, and then came this flood . . . bringing emotion, and washing jewels ashore at her feet, till her body bubbled and foamed with anticipation.

Never had she felt like this . . . a voice creating internal thunder, shockwaves and riptides of want washing through her system. Her mind taking whirlpool spins out of control, eddies dipping into broad brush fantasies about doing him on the beach au natural . . . She had to stop thinking about it, had to make her hands stop trembling, let her body cool off, will her tide to recede. All she had to do was take a shower, and stop squeezing her thighs together to the rhythm he'd created. But he'd said she was beautiful, and in the depths of his eyes she could tell he'd meant it.

No one had really ever seen her as pretty before, least of all herself. He'd also seen her many deep layers in such a short time, had said she contained all facets of what made a woman beautiful. This man had made her move to the ocean with all her clothes on, reggae inspired cosmos, and she wasn't supposed to go there with him. She breathed in deeply, still able to smell his beach-salty, masculine scent mixed with fading Cool Water. Another shiver ran through her; she glanced at her arms. Gooseflesh from memory, Lawd. Ten weeks of look but don't touch would be just long enough for a sister to lose her mind.

It was the most difficult walk he'd had to make in a very long time. She'd been right there, in his arms, ready, willing, feeling it with the same intensity that he had . . . and he had to walk away. Damn! This was crazy, made no sense. But he would do it all again if another chance to touch her presented itself. *Please opportunity knock, and knock hard.*

But it was also about more than touching her, getting with her, having sex. The whole package intrigued him—he wanted the full platter she offered, not just buffet samples. She'd believed in him, vouched for him, encouraged him to compete—not for her, but for himself. It was such a slow burning implosion that she was now fused to his psyche. No woman had ever taken him there, and he would have never believed one could so fast. But Natasha Ward had drilled right through all the armor he had and simply melted his ass down like quicksilver.

Unfortunately, Mike Quazar had trumped him, added a ridiculous variable. Her colleague had interjected possible scandal, one that Natasha had to stay far away from. One contestant had quit the show; another had been booted off before they'd anticipated. His best friend might not have gotten his code blue message. The walk to his empty room was very long, for real.

He was too weary to think about any of it. His body ached too badly; 'Tash felt better than he'd dreamed. He was still getting phantom sensations of her firm, round behind clenching and releasing, her tight thighs rubbing against his. She felt like satin, tasted like island spices and fruit . . . smelled so good she'd made his eyes cross when he'd kissed her mango-butter smooth skin. And her reaction to being touched, just so . . . just there, at the border of her dress, hard coffee beans pouting and waiting for his mouth; just remembering was making him breathe hard again. All of it was giving him a headache.

He just prayed that he didn't dream too hard about her . . . at least not with the cameras rolling.

Chapter 14

She awoke with a start to being violently shaken. Groggy and annoyed, it was all Natasha could do not to sit up and slap Stephanie. Five o'clock in the morning? Had Stephanie lost her mind?

But as she peered at Stephanie's beaming face, Natasha simply opted to wipe the sleep from her eyes.

"We're getting married, 'Tash," Stephanie whispered hard and climbed into bed with Natasha.

"You just met the man," Natasha said, stunned. She looked at Stephanie's neck. "You have a hickey the size of a fifty-cent piece on you, girl! How are you gonna play that off with the cameras rolling, the casino . . . ? Oh, *Lord have mercy.*"

Stephanie giggled and covered her neck with a gentle cup of her palm. "He's *wonderful*, 'Tash. I know it's fast, but I don't care. Be happy for me. We're gonna have us a big, fat Greek wedding, and you have to be in it."

Natasha smiled as she stared at her crazy friend and colleague. "You're really serious, aren't you?" A warm sense of joy filtered through her, stemming the panic as Stephanie nodded and sighed. "I am truly happy for you, then," Natasha said, meaning it. Then she burst out laughing and covered her face. "Devon is going to have a coronary, and Nathan . . . oh, no!"

"Yeah," Stephanie said, hugging Natasha quickly before she popped off the bed. "I need about four layers of pancake makeup and a very long, creative story."

Natasha threw her legs over the side of the bed. "Now how did I get involved in concocting your story?" She playfully sucked her teeth and stood as Stephanie made little mewing sounds of contrition. Natasha scratched her head, fussing as Stephanie began to laugh. "Chile, it's too danged early in the morning for all of this, and I bet you didn't get an ounce of shut-eye, did you?"

Stephanie shook her head, closed her eyes, and smiled. "Not a wink . . . *God* . . ."

They both laughed as Natasha held up her hands. "TMI. That's all I need to know." She let out her breath hard. "Okay . . . uh, we can say that, after he had a panic attack, because things were going on in his business and family that made the stress of being sequestered on this show too emotionally challenging . . . uh, lemme see . . . he, uh, went to the hotel to make his arrangements to leave." She began walking in a circle as she rubbed the nape of her neck. "Then, what happened was, on Nathan's orders to get the scoop about what was really going on, I dispatched you to go talk to the guy to see if you could dissuade him from making the decision to bail."

"Yeah," Stephanie said, her eyes alight with excitement. "Then, once there, and hearing his long story and talking until the wee hours, a bit of chemistry happened . . . you know, that we're-in-the-same-foxhole thing that happens to people who are sharing the same stress type of thing."

"Right," Natasha said, her confidence waning. "And you learned about his life, by sharing yours, found all these things in common, the fire was lit, and then, kaboom. It wasn't supposed to happen, but he was already off the show, so what can Nathan say?"

"Think he'll buy it?" Stephanie waited, her gaze furtive.

"No," Natasha said, laughing, "but at five A.M., it's the best I can do."

Stephanie hugged her so hard and fast that Natasha nearly lost her balance.

"Mike's and my biggest problem is going to be staying away from each other for the duration of the show."

Natasha could relate, boy could she ever, but she tried to keep the rational side of her brain functioning. "Listen to me, Steph. That man has *got* to get on a plane, go home, and y'all talk on the phone, whatever, but you *do not* want this to go on tape." She looked at Stephanie hard when her friend closed her eyes. "I'm serious. There are paparazzi *everywhere*, even if our crew turns a blind eye. Not to mention, what if one of the other contestants sees you, huh? Then, what? Or, worse, what if one of the disqualified contestants says there was insider stuff going on and wants an investigation into the integrity of the game show? If you guys keep sneaking and creeping, sooner or later, you'll get busted—and that will get splashed across every gossip rag in the nation."

When Stephanie's eyes widened, Natasha nodded.

Finally, it was sinking in. Yet she wasn't sure if her litany was more for Stephanie or herself. She, too, had to keep all the dangers in front of her, had to remember what was at stake—because if she didn't, she'd be in Tyrell's arms in a heartbeat. Last night was too close a call, and her body still ached from the near miss.

"Can't you just see it?" Natasha said, with a dramatic wave of her arm. She mimicked reading a tabloid. "Nation's number one dating show producers caught on tape, keeping it real."

Stephanie's rosy complexion went ashen, but then a slow smile crept across her face. "You said, 'produc*ers*,' as in plural."

"I did not," Natasha fussed. "I said producer."

"Did not." Stephanie argued, chuckling. "I may be many things, but I'm not deaf. How Freudian, Ms. Ward."

"I did not, and you're reading way too much into anything I may say at five o'clock in the morning. Pullease."

"Okay . . . if you say so," Stephanie teased.

"Yes, I say so," Natasha replied, growing indignant. "There is *nothing* going on."

"I didn't say there was," Stephanie said with a wide grin as she adjusted one of her many earrings. "My, aren't we touchy."

"I'm not touchy, just sleep deprived. I'm also having a mild nervous breakdown—why? Because my best producer/editor has lost her mind, fallen in love during a ten-week shoot, and has come back to our room with a monster hickey on her neck, and we have nine more weeks to finish this show! Nine weeks, Steph!" Natasha said louder than intended. "Do you know how long nine weeks is?" She wasn't sure why she was breathing hard when she'd finished her statement, or why her blood pressure was making her ears ring.

"It's a very, very long time," Stephanie said with a quiet smile.

"It's an eternity," Natasha said, raking her fingers through her twists. "I don't know if I can take it. My nerves are shot." She went to the mirror. "Look at this, I'm starting to break out from this mess." She released a long sigh. "Nine weeks . . . I don't know if I'll make it."

Stephanie came to her and laid her head on Natasha's shoulder. "I know, lady. Whatever happens, I'll support you and will be there."

Although they both knew they were talking about the speculative, unspoken topic, they also both knew it was way too volatile to name. Natasha silently thanked Stephanie simply by turning around to give her a hug.

"Let's get some makeup on that huge strawberry on your neck," Natasha said as she pulled away from Stephanie. "Devon will keel over and will worry you nonstop till you tell him who."

They both put their hands on their hips and laughed, speaking in unison. "And *that* cannot happen!"

It felt like the longest day of his life. He tried to keep up the façade of being crazy Tyrell, but nothing that was going on held his interest. The group scene made him feel claustrophobic. The beach was a place to sleep. Taking a short cruise over to Bimini and flying back on a puddle jumper with everyone talking and laughing and drinking just wore him out.

Looking down at the awesome blue water only made him want to drown within her. Parasailing with the wind lifting him to aqua sky freedom made him want to cut the line to the speedboat and keep going to land safely, privately, somewhere away from the cameras . . . with her. And every time he glimpsed her long, brown, sunscreen-slicked legs in her swimsuit or shorts, or got a glance of her high behind working beneath the wet fabric, a shiver claimed him even though it was ninety degrees in the shade. Watching her eat with the show staff from afar was pure torture. He could remember every nuance of her mouth, the way it felt, her lips . . . the way she smelled. Seeing her dip and sway and hustle about her daily activities, orchestrating the teams, dispensing orders, moving, moving like pure poetry in motion; heaven help him, he'd never make it for nine weeks.

By the time they'd been told to dress for the casino, he was sullen and quiet and evil as all get out. When people gently inquired about his strange mood, it took his all not to just holler and tell them to get out of his face. But opting for an acceptable defense, he simply lied and told them it had to do with his casino strategy, his mental process of getting ready to hit the tables hard. To his relief, Devon accepted that response, as did the camera crew and the others. However, he almost lost his cool when Natasha issued him a long, knowing glance, then turned away. It didn't help in the least that she was obviously feeling it, too.

* * *

Four, white stretch limousines pulled up to the dock, creating a media frenzy. Tyrell stood amongst the male contestants, each man donning his best casually elegant gear; collarless silk shirts in every hue imaginable beneath lightweight linen suits that ranged from khaki to black, seemed to be the order of the evening. Every man was freshly shaven and barbered to perfection, waiting to descend the ship's ramp, and make their way past flashbulbs and glaring video lights.

Oddly, although he appreciated the spectacles of beauty as the female contestants passed by, each wearing a filmy, spaghetti-strapped number, every color for the choosing, spike heels to show off their lovely legs, Tyrell could only offer a mild nod of appreciation. Where was Natasha?

Thoroughly disinterested, he waited for each woman to pass, as he and the other men began the slow descent down the ramp to the limousines. He pasted on his best corporate smile and waved at the cameras, not caring one whit about all the frenetic activity around him. Then he saw her.

She'd come up on deck with Stephanie at her flank, Devon before her. She was wearing a simple raw silk, strapless mini the color of burnt gold. A sheer, oblong scarf was draped about her back and rested within the bend of her elbows. The setting made the dress's fire-gold tones glisten against her skin. He stopped and held onto a limo door, offering to allow another contestant to enter the vehicle before him. He needed a moment, just a little while, to stare. Natasha looked like dark, sweet, Hershey's chocolate that had been poured into a golden mold. At her ears were small teardrops of amber. Her throat was naked. A sheer hint of bronze covered her mouth, her cheeks, and seemed to make her dark, sexy eyes smolder. Her twists were threaded up to a high crown atop her stately head, held only by two long tortoise shell sticks.

His gaze raked her without censure. There was no way to make his line of vision cooperate or yield. In her hands she clutched a tiny beaded purse encrusted by miniature cowry shells. His gaze slid down her body; she was Egypt, a goddess. The breeze blew her scarf as her proud carriage descended the ramp, one long, shapely leg gracefully maneuvering her short walk. Her delicate ankle was highlighted by a thin chain, and he indulged his vision to witness how each toe on her pretty feet was polished bronze, held captive in an open, thin strapped sandal, one row of beads, nothing else but her naked, oiled skin. He had to get into the limousine before he lost his mind.

To distract himself, Tyrell joined in the banter. They were pouring champagne, laughing, and pressing their noses to the glass, gawking. He repeated the mantra to himself, not to turn around. He would not look at the limo behind theirs. He would focus on the game, not her.

Relief swept through him as the vehicle finally came to a stop. Even he had to gawk when the driver opened the door, a hundred camera flashbulbs went off, and they stood before the massive glass mirrored doors of the Atlantis. True, they'd been experiencing VIP treatment all week, but the game had just kicked up a notch. This wasn't private beaches, bungalows, or sand. This was the red carpet treatment: crowds held behind velvet ropes, *Access Hollywood*, *Extra*, and a full complement of media were there, along with the ever-present crews that lived with them.

Questions from reporters pummeled the group. Tyrell watched Natasha's staff accept and decline interviews as her crew ushered them into the lobby. The hotel management had come down to greet them, effusively thanking the *Keepin' It Real* producers for selecting their establishment as a venue.

The whole thing was like an out of body experience for Tyrell. He suddenly realized what a taste of fame felt like, and he wasn't sure it sat well with him. This was what his artists craved, what he'd been trying to create for them all. But the question was, was it worth it? The money, he knew, was great—but he also realized that it came with a severe price. No privacy. Every aspect of one's life under a microscope. People feeling that they had a right to watch every detail of your joy, and pain, and mistakes, triumphs, and failures. No wonder the stars lost it, he thought. No wonder they did drugs, numbed the pain, has nervous breakdowns, or went off the deep end . . . what human being could take this constant scrutiny?

As he watched the whole process from a very distant place in his mind, he also watched Natasha handle the pressure. What if they were rich and famous? What if they were trying to have a secret, private moment? What if they were having an intimate conversation, or if their emotions spontaneously erupted on the beach? What if it just happened to be one of those bad days when all couples fight and get on each other's nerves . . . or if they were going through a bad family time? What then?

Would incessant cameras be in their faces, stealing their private love to splash across a page or screen for a dollar? Would their private failures be the subject of interviews, speculation, talk shows, and jokes on late night television for sick entertainment? A sense of indignation spiked within him. It wasn't right. He understood why stars went to jail for slugging an intrusive journalist. It was a human reaction to being pushed too close to the edge—and what gave them the right, anyway? Because you'd entertained people, had done your job and were paid well for using your God-given talent, you became public property? Bull. He'd never allow that to happen.

Tyrell's thoughts went to Mike Quazar as he pushed to the front of the contestant huddle. The man had done the right thing by opting out. Quazar was already rich; fame was simply a nasty by-product. Anonymity was a gift and something to be cherished . . . just like Natasha Ward was.

He wasn't exactly sure what he was going to say, but he was out. Elbowing to the front, Tyrell took a deep breath and headed straight for the group of producers standing within the glare of the lights. As he was about to open his mouth, from the corner of his eye he saw Bernard and froze.

His best friend was waving frantically. He had a very fine sister on his arm. Bernard? Here? With a woman like that?

Immediately, Tyrell felt someone tugging on the back of his suit jacket. He looked over his shoulder just in time to see a short, pretty woman with braids slip a note into his pocket before security moved her back. Now he had groupies? Insane!

Again, he glanced at his friend across the throng, and there was something in Bernard's expression that told him to read the note. As Tyrell extracted the slip of paper, a reporter was instantly in his face.

"So, Tyrell," the reporter said, "how's it feel to have all this attention? We see that you fellas have admirers on and off the yacht."

Tyrell forced a million-dollar smile as he unfolded the paper. "Yeah, guess so. Go figure. But I've just been invited to a hotel suite party"

"Ooohhh . . ." the reporter said, making other journalists leave their posts to gather around Tyrell. "A new twist has unfolded right here, and you've seen it first on our network, folks."

Tyrell's gaze carefully scanned the group and then went to the production team as all eyes focused upon him. "I can spend my money in this hotel any way I want, right?"

Natasha, Devon, and Stephanie came forward with caution.

"I suppose so, Tyrell," Devon said, his expression curious and confused.

"The challenge is to see how each man will handle his money," Stephanie said, her gaze darting between Natasha and Devon.

"I don't think there's anything in the rules that stated otherwise," Natasha said carefully as the other contestants came closer.

"Then, since I've been invited to a party, I'd like to share that with the group before gambling—that cool?"

"Aw, man, that's da bomb!" Rodriguez said. "What kind of party, man?"

Tyrell shrugged and glanced at the woman who'd given him the note. "You'll have to ask that sister over there."

Immediately the female contestants bristled as

Jorgette edged Camille forward and the cameras focused upon her. She produced a stack of postcard-size invitations from her purse and smiled.

Natasha almost fainted. What were Jorgette and Camille doing at the hotel! Oh, my God . . . please, girl, don't!

Laughing, Jorgette extended the invitations to Tyrell. "We met these brothers from N-Progress band, and they are doing a VIP gig up in the penthouse. You and all the show contestants and crew are my guests. We love the show, my girlfriend and I, and we know that only one of you guys are going to make it to the end—and, hey, we're single, too." She smiled at the female show contestants. "Y'all have nothing to worry about. Just like half the women in America, we'll be happy to take whomever you ladies kick off the yacht. Y'all keep the ones you want, and a couple of sisters maybe have a chance. What do ya say?"

The female contestants laughed and slapped high fives. Natasha held onto Stephanie and Devon's arms to keep from falling.

"There's a live, hot, band . . . champagne flowing, food, open bar, no cameras—except the ones from the show, and last I looked," Jorgette said, laughing, "the gaming tables ain't going nowhere, but this band is on tour and out in the morning."

"I'm down!" Linda exclaimed, giving Jorgette an high five.

"Me, too." Lillian giggled. "No cameras—oh, yes, count me in."

"It sounds like fun," Michelle said quickly, glancing at Vera who was nodding adamantly.

"A live band in a penthouse, *here*, girl? I'm in!" Vera said, twirling around and doing a little dance.

"Fellas?" Tyrell asked, looking at the men, but noting that Kimberly hadn't spoken.

"You ain't gotta tell me twice," Joe said, slapping five with Floyd. "Then, I'ma show you how St. Louis does gambling. I'ma hurt your feelings, boy."

Tyrell just laughed. "Okay, we'll see, brother." He looked at Sam, Nelson, and Jason, receiving fist pounds and slaps on his back as a response.

"All right," Anthony Adams finally said. "I'll go with the group for an hour, then I will show you skill at the tables." He glanced at Kimberly, who smiled and perked up.

Kimberly nodded. "It was an unexpected diversion, but I'm always up for an adventure."

"Good," Tyrell said, ignoring Natasha's stricken expression, as he smiled brightly at Jorgette. "Then let's doooo this thang!"

Chapter 15

"We couldn't have made this happen, if we'd storyboarded it," Devon whispered through his teeth, clutching Natasha and Stephanie's hands so tightly that their limbs were losing circulation. "It's like that Tyrell Ramsey is a good luck magnet," he said, swooning as they bustled through the penthouse suite door and the cameras went into overdrive.

Yeah, it was impressive, but it was also a set up, if ever she saw one. Natasha's gaze swept the sumptuous environment of white-on-white furniture, Oriental rugs covering glass-like hardwood, flowers everywhere. Her line of vision went to the expansive open terrace as the contestants ooohed and ah-hhed. The members of the band nodded with knowing smiles, their equipment all placed just so, wires strategically taped to the floor, bar loaded with seafood and hors d'oeuvres, champagne in silver stands strategically near love seats, sofas, and overstuffed chairs, while a very smug Tyrell Ramsey stood in the background with a sly smile.

She couldn't even look at her girlfriends. Good thing Stephanie was cool and Devon had never met them. Every now and again Stephanie gave Natasha's hand a little pat of support. The cameramen were going nuts as each contestant ate, laughed, relaxed, and vibed, slowly finding seats. She now remembered from the bio tapes that the guy going to the front of the room and dimming lights was Tyrell's good friend. A sickening feeling tensed in her gut as her girlfriends began lighting candles.

"This, ladies and gentlemen, is for you. A lovers' private party, courtesy of my band, N-Progress. So I want all the ladies to sit up front, and we're gonna sing these songs for you."

A series of giggles rippled through the group as the ladies made their way to the most prominent seating.

"Now, you all sit back and relax. Don't worry, brothers, we're not stealing your thunder. We're going to sing the things you can't say to each of these lovely ladies, without getting booted off the show."

She knew this had to be Tyrell's handiwork. It had his signature all over it. Natasha glanced at him, and he wouldn't even look at her. That confirmed her hunch. This was just like day one when he'd circumvented the system with little notes and a third-party exchange. Now it was third-party music. The combination of being both annoyed and flattered made her head spin.

The bandleader winked at Jorgette and the contestants clapped and raised champagne flutes to him. Natasha watched the lanky, chocolate-hued bandleader throw his shoulder-length locks back and pick up a microphone, sure that her girl-friend's knees had buckled. It had to be something in the air. Camille was hugged up to Tyrell's friend—*when* did *that* happen? Jorgette was obviously hooked up with an artist from *his* band—how? When! Her producer, Stephanie, had landed a fine Greek, gotten laid, and was engaged—overnight?

"Hold up," the bandleader said, looking toward the back of the room. "Now didn't I say *all* ladies to the front?"

Stephanie smiled and waved him off. "We're not a part of the show, we're just staff."

The bandleader's voice dropped to a sexy octave. "But, baby, you all women, too, right? You all betta act like you know and c'mon up here."

Linda and Lillian had stood and walked toward the show staff amid whoops of laughter and encouragement.

"You heard the man," Linda said, dragging Natasha by the hand.

"Come on up front with us. You're holding up the show," Lillian teased as she pulled Stephanie forward.

Natasha gave in. What else was there to do? Refusing was creating an even bigger spectacle than just obliging. She'd read Tyrell Ramsey later, in private. But for now she had to simply settle herself quickly with a soft groan. It was happening again. The spotlight. Her camera crew had taped her reaction just like she was also a contestant. It was insane.

When the band struck up a classic Barry White ballad, she almost covered her eyes with her hands. She watched helplessly as the women in the group settled back in their seats and became liquefied. This was not fair.

She put up her best defense, an emotional steel

wall to keep herself professional, detached, determined to stay piqued and aloof. But as the sexy crooner went down on one knee before Linda and made Linda nearly slide out of her seat, Natasha couldn't help but smile. Then, in a wicked turn of events, the vocalist served them Sade—sung with the lyrics reversed for a female crowd. Natasha watched him work Michelle into a puddle . . . yes, brother, it was a crime. Natasha shook her head. Without a break in focus, he began singing Norman Connor's blow-your-mind song of all ages, "Starship," to both Lillian and Vera. Natasha was sure the two female contestants would vaporize from the heat as he touched their cheeks, ran his hand down their backs as he passed them, and then returned to the small band area at the front of the room.

Her gaze casually went to the male contestants. She was sure they had stopped breathing, two songs back. Their faces were stone serious, muscles pulsing in their jaws. It was so outrageous that she could have jumped up from her seat and screamed—and the cameras loved it all.

Her girlfriends were so mellow that the very conservative Camille had given up all pretenses. She was leaned up against Tyrell's friend with her eyes closed. This was bad. If it had seduced Camille— Camille . . . the rest of the people in the room were goners. She refused to glance over to Tyrell, at least that's what she kept telling herself the whole time her eyes slid toward him and drank him in.

Nope. She was not going to fall under the spell of champagne, sensual sounds, and low lights. No indeedy. She was not going to get caught up in the drama. Not her. Stephanie was practically breathing through her mouth when the bandleader came over to her and began singing *One in a Million*, by Larry Graham. She could see tears glittering in Stephanie's eyes, and had to concede that she'd just lost her producer on tape.

When the musicians wrapped up the old wedding hit from yesteryear, Natasha had to quietly admit that she was relieved. Professional distance was hard to come by at the moment, and she needed air. But as the strands of the next classic began to filter into the room, and all the women swooned upon loud verbal appreciation for where the band was going next, Natasha could feel her steel barrier begin to come off its hinges. "Reasons," by Earth, Wind, and Fire? They *had* to be kidding. It just wasn't right.

No more than it was right that the bandleader was heading her way, was now holding her hand, and singing the song slow, and sexy, octaves lower than it was originally designed. Why did the brother have to go down on one knee, putting enough gospel elements into it to make a woman wanna jump up and shout hallelujah? No, that just wasn't right. And it didn't make sense when he pulled a cold, dripping bottle of champagne from an ice bucket, wiped his face with the wet exterior, and overpoured Natasha's flute till the foam ran down the sides of her glass.

Linda literally screamed. Michelle just covered her face and moaned into her hands. Lillian was shaking her head so hard and waving a hand, the chile seemed like she needed smelling salts. Vera had slid out of her leather chair and was now sitting on the floor, while Stephanie was laughing quietly and fanning her face.

Natasha took a quick sip of champagne, swallowed it with difficulty, and sat mesmerized, looking into the bandleader's eyes, his voice and the words of the song making her insides vibrate. When he was finished, he sauntered up to the front of the room and glanced at his band members.

"That, ladies, is what I believe these gentlemen would tell you, if they could. Right, fellas?" he said, grabbing a champagne flute from a stool and raising it toward the fellas.

Every man in the room shouted his assent. Guys were shaking their heads, dabbing their brows, laughing, punching each other's arms in secret but readable codes.

"Now that we've gone down memory lane, let's update this gig a little and paaaartay!" the bandleader shouted, cueing his band for a fast number. "Y'all ready for the casino?"

A resounding "Yeah!" echoed back to him.

"Then let's kick this off with a little Nellie, folks, 'cause I don't know about you, but it's getting *hot* in here!"

With that, everyone was on his or her feet, the band was rocking, and people danced whether they had a partner or not. Even the camera crew was jamming, Beta cameras bouncing as they got angles and went in low to capture booty shaking, sexy snippets, suggestive movements, but couldn't seem to help bopping to the music themselves.

She had to hand it to Tyrell. Scam or not, it was definitely a party. It was all the way live, and she instinctively knew her boss would love every moment of the footage. Devon swung her around, disco style, and hugged her before they broke and began free styling.

"This is two segments, 'Tash. You know that, right?" Devon said, laughing and dancing hard. "We have enough, just right here, to whet the audience's appetite, and do the conclusion of the casino challenge in episode four."

"I have to admit, this was a stroke of luck. Yeah, episode four," Natasha said, feeling light and free as she laughed and jammed to the music. "I haven't done this in years."

Devon smiled brightly. "Me, neither, love. Oh, honey, me, neither!"

Reluctantly, the show contingent said their good-byes as an exhausted band wrapped up. No one really seemed interested in going down to the gaming tables, and individuals had discreetly paired off, the effects of the champagne beginning to tell on them as they slowly filtered toward the original objective—gambling.

Natasha watched Jorgette slide against the band-leader near the slot machines. Camille was draped against Bernard over by the bar, not even pretending that they were going to play any games of chance. Each woman in the competition had a gentlemen by her side, some even had two men, openly competing for her attention, and each lady unabashedly loved every moment of it.

Linda was bookended by both Nelson and Joe Scott. Philly and St. Louis almost seemed like they'd come to blows to get next to girlfriend, so she'd attend them both during their game of choice, poker. Kimberly was body blocked by Anthony Adams, who made it openly clear that he was on her, because he'd dropped all façade and had put his arm around her waist, shutting out any other contender as he led her toward the blackjack area. Jason Fulbright from D.C. was going head-to-head with the engineer from Detroit, Floyd Jackson, keeping a very flattered Michelle between them, blushing, and each requesting that she blow on their dice at the craps table. When Tony Rodriguez walked toward Vera and Lillian, Sam Hartman blocked his shot, grabbed Lillian's hand, and took her toward the roulette tables. Appearing all right with the outcome, Tony smiled and gave Vera his arm, which she accepted with a wobbly giggle to follow him to the big wheel. Then she noticed the oddest thing. Tyrell was alone.

"Now, I would *not* have expected *that* in a million years," Devon said, nodding in Tyrell's direction, as the lone contestant buzzed around the groupings, laughing, making jokes, and buying drinks.

"Well just bowl me over with a feather," Stephanie said, her brow wrinkling. "He, of all people, I would have thought, could've snagged one of the girls—especially after that fabulous party he accidentally hosted." She shook her head. "I don't understand it. Go figure. None of us would have been invited if the cute chick with the braids hadn't gotten interested in him. Whassup?"

"The bandleader, obviously, beat him out for the attention," Natasha said, sipping a ginger ale. "It's hard to compete with a vocalist."

Devon nodded. "But it's strategically brilliant," he said, watching Tyrell like a hawk as the cameras followed him. "He's playing this game to the bone. Look at him. He's unattached, has made no affiliations, and is treating each woman with the same amount of attention, without threatening the male contestants' position. Those guys are messing up,

big time. In the morning, each lady will have a
vested interest in her specific pick—and won't be
able to come to consensus about who to kick off the
yacht. The only one who they'll be able to agree
upon who showed them each an equally good time,
is . . ."

"Tyrell," Stephanie and Natasha said in unison.

Natasha chuckled. "Freakin' brilliant."

"Damn," Stephanie said, her voice awed. "And
he's not gambling, which means in the morning,
he'll still have money in his pocket."

"Yep," Natasha murmured, her gaze raking
Tyrell. She watched him near the bar, discreetly
sidle up to Bernard and Camille, and give them
seemingly newfound friend handshakes. "Boy . . .
he's good," she whispered. "A media pro."

He tried to keep it casual as he leaned in and
collected a round of drinks. True, the floor cock-
tail waitresses kept anyone at the gaming tables
juiced, but it was about providing an extra layer
of service—besides, he needed to get a word to
Bernard.

"Yo, man, can't thank you enough for inviting us
to the private party," he said to Bernard in code, in
case cameras were in microphone range.

"Hey, we wanted in on the show . . . I had a hot
new band, this show is off da hook, and so it was a
win/win situation."

Tyrell chuckled. "Can I buy you and your lady a
drink?"

Bernard introduced Camille with a wide smile.
His eyes communicated to Tyrell that even though

she was trophy material, she was more than a trophy. Tyrell took note.

"Camille Johnson, Tyrell Ramsey."

"Pleased to meet you," Tyrell said, taking her hand and kissing the back of it. He smiled at her and then gave his friend an even wider smile of appreciation. "What you guys did for us tonight was awesome. Can't tell you how much stress being on this show is, and the break did everybody's head good."

Camille swallowed a smile, and discreetly motioned toward Natasha with her chin. The gesture was so slight and indecipherable that, Tyrell almost missed it. "We were happy to do it," Camille murmured. "We could tell that everyone on the show needed a break . . . some have been working *for years*, without respite." She sipped her drink, her hazel eyes blazing a silent message as she peered over the top of her glass to allow the seemingly benign comment to sink in.

Stunned silent, Tyrell slowly accepted his drinks with a nod. Years. This was obviously a connection to Natasha at an intimate enough level to have said something like that.

"Well, I've gotta go get these drinks over to the teams," Tyrell said. He had to get away from the bar before he seemed too familiar with Bernard and Camille.

But Camille's statement created a slow burn in his groin. *Years*, had been the operative word, and she seemed to know that. It was the sly way she'd said it, coated with innuendo and a breathy release of the word.

Years was a catalyst; the fire was simply dormant. The music had added kindling, as did the champagne. And seeing Natasha's quiet reaction to the songs had made it flare up, blaze, and nearly smoke out of control in the penthouse. How in the world was he going to get close to her tonight just to drop that bit of reality in her ear?

As he made the rounds delivering drinks and commenting on the games, he watched Natasha steadily from the corner of his eye. Her expression was mellow, but unreadable. He could tell she'd erected her steel wall again. The fact that she had, inspired hope. The only way he could process her reaction was to pray that she'd been so touched by the performance that putting up a barrier was the only way she could survive the evening. Moving, laughing, joking, staying neutral was the only way he could cope, that was for sure.

The songs had messed all of them up. He wasn't immune. The music had filtered inside him and lit a fuse. Finally unable to take it much longer, he approached the show staff, appearing casual, offering a bright smile.

"Everybody over here all right?" Tyrell asked. "You guys need a drink?"

"I sure could," Stephanie said. "You buy, I'll fly."

"A Manhattan, right?" Tyrell said, laughing. "And a blue martini for you, right, Dev?"

"This man was a bartender in his other life," Devon said, sighing. "Yes, absolutely—tell them with Stoli."

"You got it. And brews for the camera crew, no doubt. They're working." Tyrell looked at Natasha for her approval.

She smiled. "We're still working, too. But I know the guys would appreciate a beer."

Tyrell could feel the smile on his face fade. He couldn't help it. Staring at her and hearing the soft timbre of her voice had run all through him. It broke down his game for a second. He wanted her so badly that he couldn't even fake it. "And what do you want, then?" he asked, his voice going deeper than he'd wanted in front of her crew.

"A ginger ale would be nice," she said after a moment, her gaze sliding from his to a nearby table.

"You sure that's all you want . . . because you know if you want something stronger, I can make that happen."

She couldn't even look at him. His voice and his words had paralyzed her.

She shook her head, and willed her voice not to squeak when she answered him. "For now, that's fine."

When he walked away, she let out her breath in slow increments.

"Houston, we've got a problem," Devon whispered. "Oh, shit!"

"Don't say it, Devon," Natasha warned, gripping her glass. "No more drama on the set."

"Did you see the way he looked at you, girlfriend? I might have an alternative lifestyle, but some things are readable whatever your persuasion."

"Let it rest, Devon," Stephanie said with a cheerful rebuff. "You heard the boss. No internal drama on the set."

"Your secret is safe with me," Devon whispered, coming in closer. "I wouldn't *dare* put that on tape or tell Nathan, you know me better than that!" Appearing thoroughly indignant and flustered, Devon straightened the collar of his designer suit as he stared behind Tyrell. "But, that is *all* man, honey. No wonder he can keep his distance from the others. I must be losing my skills of observation. Oh, my, God . . . when did *that* happen?"

"Nothing happened," Natasha said, panicking. "Listen, it's very simple. Tyrell is the odd man out. Everyone is feeling the effects from close quarters and the environment, plus the serenade. He's at loose ends, and—"

"Me thinks the lady doth protest too much. But who am I?" Devon said with a sly wink. "Okay, so nothing has officially happened . . . yet. But, be honest, if we weren't doing this show and you met him . . . ?"

"I might be blown away," Natasha said, laughing despite her alarm. She had to give Devon some validation, or he'd worry the issue like a dog worries a bone. "There. Satisfied?"

"Thank you for seeing my point," Devon said, winking at her. "So, love, what are you going to do?"

Stephanie's eyes searched Natasha's as Devon hung on her every facial expression.

"We're working," Natasha said in a weary tone. "Yes, there's a chemical reaction—a mild one—but I'm not about to embroil this show in scandal and controversy. You oughta know *me* better than that."

Devon sighed and Stephanie relaxed. "Okay, Miss Professional," he said, sounding dejected. "You're right. But all work and no play makes Jane a very dull girl."

"It keeps Jane working and not getting fired, too," Natasha said, as she watched Tyrell head toward them. "Now, let it drop. There are plenty of other women on this boat for him to get next to. What you just saw was only a result of good music, good food, and perhaps a little too much champagne."

"If you say so," Devon replied, sounding unconvinced. "But, if it heats up, we'll strip it in edit." Before Natasha could reply, Devon had flounced toward Tyrell to help him deliver the drinks.

Natasha hadn't said a word as Stephanie slipped off and disappeared within the massive bowels of the hotel. Without having to be told, she knew that Mike Quazar hadn't gotten on a plane yet. She was just glad that Devon had found a cute ship crew member to draw him back to the yacht. The irony of being left alone, as the den mother, to herd all the camera crew and contestants back to the boat, made her simply find a bar stool to rest upon.

From her peripheral vision she saw Jorgette. Camille had been long gone. The whole thing was outrageous.

Jorgette came up, ordered a frozen drink and leaned next to her, talking casually as though they'd just met.

"You like the show?"

Natasha smiled, feeling the effects of everything she'd ingested earlier, ginger ale notwithstanding. "Later, I'll ask *you*, before I wring your neck," she said, chuckling. "You guys are messing with my job."

"Only trying to help," Jorgette said without looking at her.

"Mmm-hmmm. And when did you meet the friend of the guy who we will not name?"

"As he was getting on the boat," Jorgette said calmly, accepting her drink and paying for it. "Bernard fell out over Camille, and then he introduced me to Jermaine."

Natasha shook her head and chuckled. "When did you guys cook up this scheme?"

"Don't ask, don't tell, is the policy. Camille said the less you know, the better. That way you ain't in it, directly." Jorgette sighed and took a long sip of her drink through the straw. "We're going upstairs, now. Enjoy the islands."

She watched her girlfriend sashay away, and then slip into an easy embrace with a very fine vocalist named Jermaine. Natasha stood and sighed hard as a pang of loneliness hit her. Morning would come too soon, and it was time to call the limousines, get a very juiced group of contestants back to the ship in one piece, and then crash.

The problem was, as she scanned the group, not all of them were there. Annoyance ripped through her. They'd been given expressed instructions about what time they needed to convene in the lobby for transport back to the yacht. This was like taking a group of fifth graders on a school field trip. In her head she heard a teacher's firm, but singsong voice: *Now, everybody be sure to have a partner, stay with the group, and when we get back on the bus, everyone count off their number and sit in the same seat.* Man!

She signaled for the cameramen to wrap it up. One came to her side to shadow her as she tried to marshal order. She approached Linda, Nelson, and Joe, first. "Anybody see Anthony and Kimberly?"

Joe briefly glanced up from the table. "Lucky bastard won ten large, sis. Ain't seen him since he cashed in his chips."

Nelson was so focused that she dared not question him. But she leaned into Linda and whispered her question. "Where's Kim?"

In an unusual display of discretion, Linda kept her voice low and even as she watched the table and waited for the cameraman to move toward Joe's activities. "I don't like her, but I ain't mad at her. Can only speculate, but she was with Adams the whole time, watching him win . . . seeing that type of thing can do something to a sister, feel me?" Linda winked at her, nodded toward Nelson, and let out a slow breath. "Girl, you need to get us all back on the ship, pronto."

Natasha nodded, knowing exactly what Linda was talking about. "That's what I'm trying to do, sis. Tell the guys five minutes and we meet in the lobby. Anybody not there when the limos come is on his or her own to get back to the boat tonight. Anybody not on the boat tonight, has to deal with the group in the morning. Don't let anybody straggle. We up anchor and head for Jamaica first light." The two exchanged a knowing glance and Natasha was off to find the next group.

She located Sam and Lillian next. They were by the slots, but Natasha took her time approaching them. Sam stood behind Lillian, who sat on a padded stool. He seemed transfixed as he dropped coins in her cup, nuzzled her neck, and made her giggle. It was so openly private a moment that she felt like she had no right to intrude, but had to. Sucking in a deep breath to steady her nerves, Natasha went up to the happy couple and pasted on her brightest smile.

"Five minutes till the caravan pulls out," Natasha announced in an upbeat tone, trying to ignore the cameraman and act like he wasn't there.

"Oh, wow, where did the time go?" Lillian said,

laughing and pulling the huge slot machine lever, then leaning back against Sam.

Sam hadn't even glanced at Natasha and seemed oblivious to the camera; his hands were on Lillian's shoulders, caressing them as she worked the slots, his eyes half closed.

"We'll be there in a little bit. Five minutes," he said, practically breathing out the response.

"Cool," Natasha said quickly, walking away fast with a cameraman on her heels. Colorado was in deep. The man was almost panting as he stood behind Lillian, pressed to her back—dang!

She walked for what felt like miles, her cameraman scanning the scene, both of them searching high and low for the rest of the teams. They stumbled upon Tony and Vera alone in an alcove by the rest rooms and telephones. Tony's neck was bent, his voice low; Vera was pressed up against the wall, giggling as he negotiated something in her ear.

"Hi, guys," Natasha said, seeming oblivious. "All this champagne is sending a sister to the ladies' room. But, guys, we have five minutes to all meet up in the lobby to get the limos back to the yacht." From some reservoir of propriety, suddenly she wanted to protect their intimate moment from the camera's probing eye. She'd tried to lighten things with a little joke, to no avail. The tension between those two was palpable. Even if the cameraman had shut his lens, she was sure that the hot vibrations would still be cooking on the tape.

Vera's eyes widened as she tried to extricate herself from Tony's hold. He placed a hand on either side of her head and flat-palmed the wall, looking down at Vera as he answered Natasha with a one-word response.

"Cool," he murmured, then pushed off the wall, his expression pained. He smoothed the front of his suit jacket, gave Vera a long glance, and walked toward the lobby with his back so straight it seemed as though it would snap.

The heat that radiated within the space he'd vacated almost made Natasha fan her face. Okay, boyfriend was done—just stick a fork in him. She peered at Vera, not sure what to say. But she didn't have to say a word. Vera had closed her eyes and was holding onto the wall.

"Five minutes," Vera whispered. "I just need to put some water on my face, and I'll see you in the lobby."

The cameraman let out a long, silent whistle. Natasha was out. This was obscene. People should be allowed to organically connect, she thought, half laughing at her own foolishness for concocting the show and half ready to cry. But when she rounded the corner and found Jason Fulbright hugged up with Michelle in the far corner of the lobby near the piano bar, she almost stopped her cameraman from coming with her.

"Want me to get a telephoto of that?" the cameraman asked, zooming in on the couple before Natasha could respond. "Me and the fellas are placing odds that Michelle or Vera go down first."

"Let 'em be, for just a moment," Natasha said, closing her eyes briefly as guilt stabbed her.

"Which one do you think is going down tonight?"

"Paul, please, I don't know," she said in a weary tone, and then took a deep breath and walked forward.

As she approached she knew she'd be interrupting a very personal, deep, conversation—one that

Jason and Michelle both seemed to desperately need and deserve. She could tell by the way Michelle's eyes searched Jason's, and how he held her hands, caressing them gently, speaking in a soft tone. This man was opening up, and that was a rare moment that didn't need to be caught on tape. It was like opening a confessional, and barging in with bright lights. Something about having to do that made Natasha sad.

"Guys," Natasha said, her tone apologetic. "In five minutes the limos will be here and we have to go. You all having a good time?" She'd asked the question to give them some face-saving recovery time. But she was not prepared for the response.

Jason kept his eyes on Michelle, and held her hands tightly when she tried to play it off and go back into her shell. "No, don't," he murmured. "I've never experienced anything like this, and I'm not ashamed."

Michelle looked away, her face flushed. "I'm having the time of my life," she said softly. "I wish this night didn't have to end."

Natasha swallowed hard when Michelle looked up at her, tears brimming in her wide, hazel gaze. "Thank you so much, Natasha . . . for inviting me to be on your show. No matter what happens, I've won. I'll never forget you for this."

What was there to say? Natasha made the signal for Paul to kill his camera. She looked at the couple, her voice a mere murmur. "Five minutes, okay? You have to get back on the boat."

Jason nodded. "Yeah. We do, don't we."

Natasha used her chin to motion for Paul to follow her. With his camera slung low, he trudged behind her like a dejected pup.

"That was deep," he said, quietly. "You know, 'Tash, what we do for a living isn't all that bad. We're not really vultures or carpetbaggers, are we?"

"I don't know the answer to that, Paul," she said in all honesty, her gaze raking the environment, futilely searching for Anthony and Kimberly. "Just do me a favor, okay?" she asked, looking at him with a plea in her eyes. "You guys kill the bets. These are people . . . and . . ."

"I know," he said with a sigh. "Bad form. No taste. It's just that we have to do something to stay detached and to be able to do what we've gotta do."

She gave her best cameraman a quick hug and patted his cheek. "Let's go find out where Floyd and Tyrell are, okay?"

He nodded and followed her with much less enthusiasm than before. She could tell that her cameraman was exhausted, too—and it wasn't just the fatigue of constant filming. The show was wearing out his spirit, just like it was eating away at hers.

She spied Floyd sitting alone at a table in the hotel club. Music was thumping, drinks were all around, and Floyd was nursing something that seemed very strong from a short rocks glass. Natasha approached him with gentleness. The man seemed wounded, and even her cameraman seemed to sense it. Paul had taken the slow advance of a documentary filmmaker, versus the fast rush of sensationalist TV.

"Hey, Floyd," Natasha said as cheerfully as possible. "Five minutes and we're out. Everybody is headed for the lobby. You having fun?"

He looked up and smiled sadly. "Lost all my money. Guess that means I'm off the ship."

"Yo, man," the cameraman said. "It ain't over till it's over. Buck up, champ."

Natasha looked at Paul for a moment. Even the camera crew's boundaries were crumbling.

"Yeah," she added, putting a hand on Floyd's shoulder. "That's the whole thing. We can't even begin to predict what will happen."

"Everybody's paired off," Floyd said with a resigned sigh, and stood. "Those guys will remain, I'll go. Some things are inevitable. I just thought I'd make it to Jamaica . . . but, hey."

"Tyrell isn't paired up, so you guys have an even—"

"Oh, that's what you think," Floyd said, cutting Natasha off and weaving as he stood.

Her head snapped up in reflex to stare at Floyd hard. Where was Tyrell? He'd been AWOL for the better part of an hour. He'd hooked up? Grief and anger and disappointment claimed her. She could barely hide it as she tried to smile, but failed.

"We have to meet everyone in the lobby," Natasha said flatly. "Five minutes," she said, moving away from Floyd as she felt the blood rush to her cheeks. Her stomach was doing flip-flops. She couldn't breathe. But what had she expected? There were no promises.

"Hey, wait up," Floyd said, catching up to Natasha and Paul. He held her arm and then glanced at Paul. "Do her a favor and kill the camera."

A new surge of panic swept through Natasha as Paul complied. It was out of character for him to stop rolling tape upon the request of a show subject, but she was glad that he did.

"Even a blind man can see who he really likes. But Ramsey is old-fashioned, like me. Has a lot of respect, regardless of all his flash. It's wearing him out, sis . . . he went by the pool to get some air. If you want, I'll go find him and tell him we all leave in five. Okay?"

"Thanks," she said quietly, unable to look at Floyd or Paul as she left them both to go to the lobby. Relief had restarted her heart and made it possible to breathe, but feeling totally exposed was locking the muscles in her shoulders, back, and abdomen. The bustle and anonymity of the lobby seemed like a perfect refuge at the moment. She had to get there, without a camera on her, to savor the news and to also regroup from having her cover blown.

From a very distant place in her mind she watched the contestants straggle back to the lobby, couple by couple. She kept her gaze averted, not wanting to pry into their lives any more. When Floyd neared her with Paul in tow, she bristled.

"Listen," Paul said. "You might have to go talk some sense into Tyrell. Floyd couldn't get him to budge. He wouldn't say a word as Floyd tried to make him feel better about Kimberly being AWOL with Adams."

Natasha looked up at both men and blinked twice, not sure she was hearing them correctly. She almost bit her lip to keep from smiling.

"I tried, Natasha," Floyd said, his voice low and soft. "Dude apparently had it bad for the chick, and you know he and Adams were the top two contenders. I guess when Adams won all that loot at the table, and Kimberly went off to a room with him, Tyrell threw in the towel."

"I'm going to leave a message at the front desk for Kimberly and Anthony. I do hope you're wrong about them checking into this hotel." She stared at Floyd, who shook his head.

"I saw it with my own eyes. Hell, I'd lost my money, but sorta hung around to see if maybe she'd talk to me—but Adams had her all wrapped up. Tyrell was doing reconnaissance flybys every so often . . . then after a while he just went outside when Adams cashed in his chips, whispered in her ear, and she went to the ladies' room and never came back. Next thing you know, Adams was ghost. Put two and two together." Floyd let out a fatigued sigh. "Ramsey claimed, when me and your camera guy went out there, that he didn't care what Adams and Kim did, but he needed some space . . . said it was a very long night, his nerves were fried, and to back off. Now doesn't that sound like a man who's been jilted?"

Natasha swallowed another smile, and said a silent prayer of thanks that she hadn't been busted.

"What do you want to do, boss lady?" Paul asked, hoisting his camera up with a yawn. "You want me to get some footage of you talking him off the ledge?"

"No," Natasha said. "Let me leave a message at the concierge's desk to locate our missing couple, and I'll also check with hotel registration to see if they were actually crazy enough to check in. Then I'll go try to talk to Tyrell. You guys get shots of our weary contestants getting back into the limos to reboard the yacht. Hit me on my two-way when you're ready to pull off. If the three of them don't come, then, what can I say? They've self-selected off the yacht. For them, game over."

Chapter 16

Natasha had given the concierge the note, but stood at the front desk in disbelief. Neither Anthony Adams nor Kimberly Gibson had checked in? This was really bad. Instinctively she knew what had happened as she walked out to the pool area. They had stolen away to another hotel; that was the only explanation. But as she spied Tyrell, watching him stare at the horizon with his back toward her, could she blame them? Not at all. However, the consequences in the morning would be awful. That's what she had to keep before her and remind herself as she approached Tyrell.

"Hi," she said gently, coming by his side. "Heard you weren't coming to get in the limos with us."

"Naw, you heard wrong. Floyd is drunk. I said I wasn't ready to move from where I was standing and needed a moment. I wasn't bailing." Tyrell tilted his head to the side, his smile warm and inviting. "Why do you always think I'm ready to just leave you and be out?"

Natasha shrugged, not sure she wanted to answer the question. "I don't know. Maybe because that's what always happens to me, I guess."

"Then, those brothers were crazy," he said, shaking his head. He started to reach out to touch her, but upon her warning glance, shoved his hands in his pockets. He chuckled, closed his eyes, and then stared up at the moon. "That's why I came out here, finally. I had to do something to keep my mind off of doing that."

His statement warmed her and released the butterflies within her stomach again. "Floyd said you were upset about Kimberly," Natasha said with a sigh.

"It's better that way," Tyrell said, still staring at the moon. "Don't need our business in the street and those two are toast, anyway."

"Oh, Tyrell, where'd they go?" Natasha held her forehead, lamenting the couple's fate. "We never even made it to Jamaica."

Tyrell chuckled. "Nope. But every man has an Achilles' heel," he said, turning to look at her, forcing her gaze to meet his. "All of us have an aphrodisiac that just messes us around. Adams, knew it when I met him, has a weak spot for winning . . . power and money. Brother wiped the tables at blackjack and stood up trembling. I knew he was done, then."

Natasha covered her mouth and laughed. "Oh, Lord. I didn't know it worked like that."

"Yep," Tyrell said with a sigh. "Take Colorado, for instance. He's gonna kick all our behinds on the sports challenge, I know it. But the question is, after he has that adrenaline spike, will his big, Hulk ass break down and go for broke—you know Lillian has his nose open."

Natasha laughed harder. "Yeah, you're right. Lillian has him weak in the knees. Gambling didn't do a thing for him."

"My point exactly, which is why Floyd is so messed up. That brother prides himself on brainpower, and if it's an intellectual pursuit, who knows who he'd have targeted as his lady? When he couldn't beat the house on statistical odds tonight, he was crying in his scotch. Just like I figured out that Campanelli's button was the wining and dining thing—that's why he flipped and went off. Quazar lost it on the beach, his thing obviously being the natural elements. I think our boy from St. Louis is all about the Benjamin's—making it to the end to win the prize pot will keep him in the race for the long haul, if the ladies don't put him off the boat for being a cheap, stingy SOB."

They both laughed hard, and Natasha folded her arms over her chest. "You just have this all figured out, don't you?"

"Pretty much," Tyrell said with confidence. "Like, I know for a fact that, Rodriguez gets messed up by a VIP party, Jason . . . hmmm," he said, one finger to his lips for a moment. "Soft voice, candlelight, solid conversation. Michelle is blowing his mind. Those two keep talking, and our boy is history. Nelson, shoot. Give that man a good drink, some laughs, good friends—like an old-fashioned barbeque—and he's messed up. I like him, though, just like me and Rodriguez are cool . . . so I can't tell all their secrets," he added, laughing harder.

"I noticed that you missed a name to dissect, Mr. Ramsey," Natasha said, teasing him.

Tyrell smiled and winked at her. "Guess it?"

"Man, stop playing and come on and get in the limo."

"No, seriously," he said, coming closer to her than was probably appropriate, but leaving enough space between their bodies to also seem platonic.

Natasha sighed hard, but kept her arms folded. She had to. It was important that if anyone spied them that she'd appear to simply be talking a reluctant contestant back onto the ship. "You like to party," she said with a widening grin.

"I do, but it doesn't rock me," Tyrell said, shaking his head no.

"Brother, you like to eat—I've witnessed that."

"Yep. Love me some good home cooking . . . but I can recover from that."

She laughed. "You like socializing, orchestrating things, and—"

"Woman, you are going from warm to cool to cold. Yeah, I can do that, and can read people, love people, but that ain't what blows me away."

She stared into his eyes, curiosity having a chokehold on her. His smile was warm, affectionate, and she loved his good-natured way. "You're a great conversationalist."

His smile waned as desire flickered in his eyes. "You're very warm, close, but haven't hit my hot spot yet."

She glanced away flustered, the reference almost too intimate. "Well, since you walked away with a pocket of money . . ."

"Cold, woman; iceberg freeze."

She chuckled, but had noticed his voice had dipped. If there was anything frozen on her, it had melted some time ago. "Oh, man . . . I don't know."

"Yes, you do," he said quietly, closing the gap between them. "Want me to tell you the reasons?"

She gasped. "Music . . . of course. Your business . . . That was so obvious. Dang!"

Pleased with herself that she finally got it, she laughed. But the mirth ebbed away like a quietly receding tide as she stared at his serious expression.

"You understand why I had to walk away and keep moving when we left the penthouse suite?" he murmured. "Couldn't take my eyes off you, and was afraid I wouldn't be able to keep my hands off you."

"We should go rejoin the others," she said softly, feeling the instant heat flare up and capture every inch of her.

"When you came up on the deck, poured into that gold dress, looking fantastic . . . and then Jerm started doing Barry White, Sade, Norman, and polished it off with EWF . . . I'm thinking, tonight's the night I get voted off the ship, start a scandal, and help me, Father, I don't care . . . because all I could do was watch you."

She could feel her cell phone vibrating, but it took a moment to discern the tremor of the telephone and the one running through her body. "Each of us has a weakness, too," she murmured. "Care to guess mine?"

"I already know it," he said, his voice becoming huskier. "Slow, deep, private . . ." He inhaled and let his breath out slowly when she sucked in a sharp inhale and closed her eyes. " . . . Meaningful conversation."

She opened her eyes, but could only seem to get them to respond to half-mast.

"What else did you think I was going to say?" He asked, a mischievous smile playing about his lush mouth.

"Something totally inappropriate," she said, her voice almost lost within her throat.

"Glad I wasn't wrong about that, either, then," he said, totally sealing the space between them.

"You have got to stop talking junk," she said, trying to laugh as she stepped back to get the phone out of her purse. "They're calling us to get in the limos, and . . . and . . ."

"Why do you think I keep talking to you, being honest, telling you everything that's on my mind?"

Natasha smirked, but didn't answer the telephone.

"I want to open up your head like you've opened up mine," he said, no pretense in his tone, no amusement on his face. "Your voice runs through me like an old standard, like a ballad, and every time I get a chance to listen to a private serenade, it does something to me . . . especially out here in the tropics."

"I have to answer the phone," she said, closing her eyes.

"Tell them you've finally talked me into coming back, but need five more minutes so I can get myself together."

He stepped closer without holding her until his belly brushed hers, allowing her to feel the truth in his statement. It was the most profoundly erotic thing a man had ever done to her, and feeling the hard length of him graze her thigh, all the while knowing that it had to stop there, made her want to slide against him and take his mouth hard. Instead, she nodded and flipped open her phone, repeating to her cameraman what Tyrell had offered as an excuse, verbatim, then flipped the unit shut.

"Now do you understand why I couldn't dance

with you all night?' he asked, not moving against her, just tensing the muscles in his thighs and abs as he spoke.

She could feel herself swell and moisten till she feared that the thong she wore beneath her dress might fail her dignity. "That was probably best," she murmured and opened her eyes.

He glanced at the beach. "What time does the ship sail in the morning?"

She smiled and shook her head no, stepping back.

"I'm really distraught," he offered, his smile waning as a new wave of desire hit him hard.

"They'll want to catch that on tape, Ty . . . you know that."

He raked his fingers through his hair. "Your roommate gone?"

"Ty . . . be serious."

He stared at her. "I'm as serious as a heart attack."

She smiled and stepped back farther. "No."

"What if you go back to the ship, and then say you're going to look for her . . . and, uh, I could say I'm leaving to search for Adams?"

"They'll send a crew with both of us," she said laughing, but flattered beyond his comprehension.

Crestfallen, he hung his head and blew out a long, frustrated breath. "This is such a waste," he said, talking to his shoes. "The woman of my dreams, paradise, the beach . . . music, Lawd."

"I know," she said, her voice gentle with despair. "But it's not forever . . . just for nine more weeks."

They both stared at each other knowing that nine seconds, nine minutes, nine hours, let alone nine days, or weeks, was asking a force of nature to be too patient.

"We should get back to the limos," he said as she touched his arm. He looked at her hand as though it were burning him where it fell. "You have no idea how close I am to just saying screw it, and throwing caution to the wind."

She slowly removed her hand from his arm and tucked her cell phone away in her purse. "Oh, yes, I do, Ty. That's what you just don't know."

By the time she got everyone back on the boat and had safely made it to her room, she practically had tears in her eyes. She needed to be with that man so badly, she could barely strip off her clothes. Her body ached for him so bad, the surface of her skin hurt. Every part of it was alive with pain. Frustration was driving needles into her breasts, stabbing her between her thighs, making her wince.

Being alone in the bedroom on the ship, with Tyrell not far away, wasn't helping one bit. Knowing that he, too, had a private room now, also didn't help at all. But his room was bugged, cameras stashed—just like the walls had eyes and ears everywhere.

She found her pale pink silk nightgown and slid it on over her head. The caress of the fabric made her shiver so hard that she had to hold onto the dresser. She covered her breasts with her palms, a slight moan escaping her lips, and then hugged herself. No, that would make it worse. If she slipped beneath the sheets, closed her eyes, and fantasized about him, pretended he was there, while touching away the ache, it would only make it worse when she saw him in the morning.

Her hand slid down her torso and rested on her belly, trembling. No. She had to remember that there was so much at risk. Two contestants had gone AWOL. There was too much going on to give in to this feeling. The knock at the door made her stomach do flip-flops. Her heartbeat skipped as her pressure spiked. She was only human. The answer was yes. *Please, Tyrell, make good on your word . . . long, deep, and slow . . .* Natasha went to the door and opened it, holding her breath.

"Love, listen, I have to apologize to you . . . for a minor indiscretion," Devon said, breezing into the room and looking five ways, his voice dipping with conspiracy. "I know you're probably freaked out and angry right now, but things just got carried away, and I don't want Captain Russell to have his nose out of joint if he found out that, well . . . you know, sweetie, everyone is not as open and evolved."

Natasha held up her hand, unable to process that the wrong man had just entered her room. "I completely understand," she said quietly. "The environment, the pressure . . ."

"Exactly!" Devon said, his eyes darting around the room. "It is impossible to bear all this—everything is so perfectly designed for an interlude."

Natasha leaned against the wall, holding onto the edge of the dresser. "I know. Get some rest. I'm not angry—"

"Disappointed?"

"No," she said, her eyes shut tightly as she shook her head. "Not at all."

"You have a headache?" He stared at her. "Oh,

love, I forgot, you weren't feeling well. Do you want me to get you something?"

"No, no, I'm fine," she said, feeling too exposed. "I, uh, just need to lie down and rest."

Devon came to her, hugged her, and then led her to the bedside. He pulled back the sheets and helped her into the bed, tucking her in like a mother hen. "I so love you, 'Tash," he whispered and kissed her damp forehead. "You're so good to people and you care so much. I hope something truly wonderful happens for you, too, out of all of this."

She touched Devon's cheek and cupped it. "I love you, too. And go easy on Steph. She found somebody really nice—so please don't pull off without our girl, 'kay?"

"Wouldn't dream of it," Devon said with a wink as he clicked off the light. "Like she could hide that monster hickey from me. Pullease."

They both laughed as he turned to leave.

"By the way, 'Tash, do you girls have any concealer?"

A cold shower wouldn't help. He knew that as he stripped off his jacket, shirt, and then kicked off his shoes. There was only one cure, and she was down the hall. The other option wasn't even a possibility, not with damned cameras everywhere. He was pretty sure that the show would use some discretion, but he had his pride—*that* was not going on tape anywhere—*eva*.

Tyrell flopped on the bed facedown, kept his pants on, and would hope they'd simply pass it off as a guy having had too much to drink all night. The real problem was going to be getting to sleep.

Everything beneath him became her. The soft mattress and comforter, in his mind, were becoming her skin. With his eyes shut tightly, he ran his hands over the satiny textures of the spread and froze. No, he was messing himself up. Had to shake it off, forget about it. Tomorrow was another day. But the throb in his groin was insistent, angry, and very irritable at the moment.

He turned his mental attention to playing the game, figuring out a new strategy that could be employed for another day. But each time he thought about who was still left standing, he'd envision couples pairing off, the music melting down their resistance, and his with it. There was only one way to kick this desire that had him in its grip.

Tyrell pushed up hard and shot out of bed, found his headphones and a gangsta rap CD. As the music blared at an eardrum splitting decibel he sighed, sank back down on the bed, and closed his eyes.

Stephanie greeted her on the stairs leading from the top deck, bleary-eyed and pleasant, as each contestant straggled into the dining room one by one. Natasha mumbled a grumpy good morning. Devon gave her a cheerful salute.

"Is everybody here?" Natasha asked without looking at the teams.

Stephanie and Devon nodded their heads.

Natasha sighed. "Let me guess. Anthony and Kimberly made it back before dawn."

"Yeah, I guess so," Devon said sheepishly. "I, uh, really can't vouch for the time factor."

Stephanie shrugged and poured a cup of coffee, smiling. "Me, neither."

"Well, since everyone is present and accounted for, I guess we should tell the captain to weigh anchor?" Natasha slurped her coffee and swallowed it, closing her eyes. Nine weeks was boring a hole in her brain.

"They have to vote, first, love," Devon said, quietly. "Remember?"

"Yeah, yeah," Natasha said, feeling testy. "Let them have a cup of damned coffee and then let the women vote so we can move out." She walked away from Devon and Stephanie and snatched a muffin from the buffet, then found a seat in the far corner of the room.

"Wow . . ." Devon said. "Her cramps must be really wicked this morning."

Stephanie chuckled. "Uh, yeah, kicking her butt."

Tyrell looked at the buffet, and headed straight for the coffee. Every male on the show was keeping his distance from the other, being sure not to bump anybody, tease anyone, or say more than a muttered greeting, if that. Nerves were wound tight, and with the frustration level on high, getting punched in the face for an accidental shove was highly probable.

No one really seemed interested in eating, and when Stephanie came to gather the female contestants away for the vote, every man just sat staring into his mug. This, to him, was the second worst part of the show—the waiting for the vote. The cameras were always poised for the close-ups, to see how the fallen died on the game, and to see how those left standing would react. The thing of it was, though, no matter who got booted off today, he couldn't imagine there being a happy response. Try as he might, he couldn't stay mad at Adams. Hell, the man got lucky, how could he blame him? And poor Floyd, putting him off the yacht might be putting that brother out of his misery. At this juncture, he was too tired and evil to care. He just wanted it to be over so they could get moving. No sleep, Natasha out of arm's reach, having to sleep with his pants on because he was so horny his body wouldn't chill . . . they could even put him off the boat and he wouldn't have cared at all.

"The rules clearly state that, if any woman has an unfair advantage and sleeps with one of the contestants, Kimberly, her behind is history." Linda folded her arms over her chest and leaned back in her chair.

"That's not fair! You don't know for a fact that we slept together!" Kimberly shrieked. "We talked all night, and it's not like you have any DNA evidence!"

"Maybe we're jumping to conclusions," Michelle said quietly. "I know what it's like to sit up all night and just talk . . . it doesn't always have to consummate physically, right then, Linda."

"That's true," Vera said, her voice unusually soft. "But, on the other hand, how is it fair that she got to go off with him, have her private moment, when the rest of us had to come back, under scrutiny . . . I mean, just deal with the cameras—when we *all* wanted to be alone with someone last night."

"This is my point," Linda said, backing Vera's comment. "Whether you did or not, is not so much the issue. The fact is, you two left the group, had time alone to bond—"

"Oh, like each one of you doesn't have your favorite?" Kimberly said, her voice shrill and defensive. "If you each can say you don't have your favorite guy already in your minds, then put me off the ship."

The group fell silent. Trumped, not a woman said a word. Victory within her grasp, Kimberly pressed on as the cameras rolled.

"I'm voting for Anthony, because the objective of this challenge, as I understood it, was to see how a man spent and used his money. Am I wrong?"

No one answered Kimberly, the women's gazes remaining steadfast on their coffee.

"Right," Kimberly said, answering her rhetorical question. "Therefore, examine the facts." Using her fingers, she began counting off Anthony Adams's good traits. "He has been respectful of all women on this ship. He's well educated, handsome, has a great enterprise, and is athletic. Last night he showed risk taking balanced with patience and resolve, skills necessary to come away from the blackjack table with ten thousand dollars—and from what I understand, Nelson only won five hundred, after losing two hundred—which is a net gain of three hundred. Floyd lost all his money, Joe went down by a thousand, Sam spent it on the slots for Lillian—not the group—and Rodriguez blew most of his at the bar with Vera." She looked at Michelle until Michelle glanced away. "And after Jason lost two thirds of his, he spent the rest on yet another private dinner, for only one female contestant."

It was all Natasha could do not to speak up for Tyrell, who'd spent his money evenly and fairly across the teams. The fact that his name wasn't even in the discussion made her grip her coffee mug hard with anticipation. If these heifers put him off the boat . . .

it was only as the thought began to take on its own life that she realized she'd gotten too involved in the dispute, and she eased back in her chair. Oh, no, she was not going there—so she watched on in silence.

Linda was on her feet in a sudden storm. "You know what?" she yelled, her head bobbing as she spoke. "Tyrell is really the only brother who spent his money across the board fairly and evenly. So, let's start there," she said, slamming her palm on the table, and making all the coffee mugs and juice glasses slosh. "Number one, Miss Thang, they are *all* fine, educated, and have businesses, or good jobs. But Joe Scott is a stingy sucker, so he can go. Floyd is whiny and pitiful—he can go. Sam doesn't do jack but go with the flow, he sets no tone—the white boy can go. But Tyrell hooked us up with the party of our lives, and then brother spent his money on all of us all night. So, how you gonna put some Anthony Adams up as *the one*? Pullease!"

When Kimberly simply folded her arms over her chest and looked out the window, Linda's gaze went to each woman and lingered until she got a re-action. "Be honest, y'all. We all have found some-body to be sweet on—but facts being what they are, and we're supposed to be judging on who's being the fairest to us all . . . hey. No brainer."

"That's true," Michelle said softly. "I'm willing to put my personal feelings aside on that one, although I admit to having my personal favorite . . . that just sort of developed out of nowhere."

"All I'ma say is, Tyrell deserves to stay and he's all that—but if you put Tony Rodriquez off this ship, I'm out. He's funny, parties with everybody, and is sexy as hell. I'm not that evolved, as you would say,

Michelle." Vera looked at Linda. "I'm being real, and not playing."

Linda pointed at Vera. "Now, see, I can respect that. The sister is honest. We all know Rodriguez has her falling out every time he passes her, and she just flat-out admitted it. So, I'm cool with that, just like I don't mind telling you that before it's all over, I'll probably get put off for doing that wild brother from Philly." She laughed as nervous laughter followed her. "Heeeey . . . what can I say."

Vera and Linda exchanged a high five, but Lillian pushed away from the table with such a fierce look in her eyes, no one moved.

"Yes. Tyrell should stay, and we all appreciate what he did. But if you go after Sam, just because he's white, I'm out. He doesn't deserve that."

Linda covered her mouth and sat down. "Go, Colorado," she whispered. "My bad."

"That's right, your bad, Linda," Lillian shrieked, veins standing in her neck as she leaned across the table. "Do you hear yourself? How prejudiced is that—the white boy can go? Oh, my God! He's funny, talented, nice, is gregarious, gets along with everybody, is fair, and is the glue on the male team—and always, like Tony and Nelson, gets Tyrell's back!"

"You're right, you're right," Linda said, her tone apologetic.

"For real, Lillian," Vera said in a soothing tone. "We're not gonna vote him off just because he's the lone white guy standing."

Lillian sat back, wiping her eyes with trembling fingers. "I just want you all to be fair," she said, sniffing. "Damn, I can't take this this morning."

Natasha stood and brought Lillian a tissue. She

could totally understand where girlfriend was coming from. She was right there with them, only her battle for her man was silent and not captured on tape. She knew what it was like to want to be with someone so badly you thought you'd lose your mind, but couldn't. Knew what that morning after was like, having frustrations settle in your bones and make your nerves wire-taut. Knew the feeling of wanting your guy to be the one to win—not for the money, just to see him happy, claim his prize, and for once come out on top. Her heart bled with them through all the pathos as tears filled eyes, women slumped from the emotional fatigue, and wrangled with an impossible decision. Perhaps she was the most dishonest one in the group, even Kimberly was exposed.

"All right," Linda finally said, trying to wrest back the group's focus. "We have to make a decision. Tyrell stays."

Heads nodded.

"We don't want to seem prejudiced . . . so, by default or whatever, Sam gets another round."

Lillian sighed and put her forehead on the table. Natasha kept her gaze fastened forward. When Tyrell got the thumps-up, her internal reactions was the same as Lillian's had been.

"I wanna see what Tony is going to do next, myself," Linda said, chuckling. "We keep that live Latino brother from L.A., for some spice—cool?"

Loosening up, laughter filtered throughout the group.

"Now, Jason is a little snobby for me, but if the psychologist says he's cool . . ."

All eyes went to Michelle. "He's such a nice man," she said, her voice gentle and appreciative. "It's a façade because of his upbringing. But he's deeply committed to his community."

Linda looked at her and winked. "Only 'cause we love you, girlfriend. But next couple of rounds, after Floyd and Joe get ditched, brotherman is gonna have to step up . . . or . . ."

"I know," Michelle murmured. "Thank you."

"Well it's left up to Mr. Adams. We let this transgression go, or what?" Linda looked at the female team as Kimberly's gaze narrowed on her.

"I just don't like the man," Vera said. "Let's say if Kim wasn't even on the boat."

"Kimberly," she corrected. "My name is Kimberly, not Kim."

"You are not helping your own 'cause," Linda said, shaking her head and sighing. "Go, 'head, Vera."

"As I was saying," Vera said, her tone acidic. "He looks down his nose at all the women, except *Kim.* He's coolly civil, as though he somewhat tolerates our presence. Unlike Tyrell, who jokes with us, has fun with everybody. But Anthony is sooo distant. And, if he did win ten thousand dollars, he should have said, hey y'all, a round of drinks, on me. But he didn't even do that. What he did was hustle girlfriend off somewhere and hoard his money. If we're voting on how a man deals with his cash, then at least Floyd played, and lost, so he had an excuse for not being able to buy more than a round. And, even Joe played *with* Nelson and hung out with Linda—but Anthony is a loner, and that makes me nervous."

"Oh, so since when does having single focus concentration on a game like blackjack make you a

loner or a bad person?" Kimberly sucked her teeth
and folded her arms over her chest.

"I think that's the point, Kimberly," Michelle said,
her tone even. "These other guys played with the
women they were escorting. Sam was feeding the
slots for Lillian, engaging her. Tony was teasing and
laughing with Vera the whole time, and talking trash
to the other men, as Vera put good luck on his number choice at roulette . . . he engaged others in
his playtime and shared his money, buying drinks for
whoever was around. Nelson and Joe also did that.
We've discussed Tyrell, who is simply a social butterfly. Then Jason, I think others can vouch, got put off
the tables, nearly because he was trying to teach me
to play cards—something I never learned . . . and he
gave up something he enjoyed to put me in an environment I preferred by the piano bar. Poor Floyd
tried to engage you and Anthony in blackjack, but he
got shut out. That, I saw with my own eyes."

Linda shrugged. Lillian nodded and looked
away. Michelle nervously toyed with her cup. Vera
played with a spoon.

"I know you are not going to allow a dud like
Floyd, or a practical pimp, like Joe, stay on this ship
over *Anthony*?" Kimberly was on her feet leaning
across the table toward Linda. "Have you all gone
mad? I know what this is all about. You all are doing
this just because you're jealous of me! You want me
out of this competition, just so you'll have better
odds at getting picked in the end—because you
know that's most likely what will happen, no matter
which man is on the yacht at the end of the show!"

"Tell her to get out of my face," Linda said so quietly that Vera and Lillian backed up.

"Or, what, Linda—you'll beat me down?" Kimberly

spat, goading Linda into a fight. "Raise one finger against me and not only will your big, ugly ass be off this ship but you'll have a civil suit on your hands!"

Michelle placed a palm on Linda's arm and looked at Linda hard. "I think it's time to vote," Michelle said coolly.

Linda nodded.

"Yep," Vera said, calmly, folding her hands in her lap. "Your politics just screwed you, girlfriend. Regardless of our reasons, Adams is gone."

"What!" Kimberly was a blur of motion. She'd reached across the table and throttled Vera. It took security and the rest of the contestants to break it up. Natasha, Stephanie, and Devon had also gotten in the fray, trying to avoid scratches, bites, punches, and kicks. None of them realized how strong Kimberly actually was. Girlfriend was fit, and it was probably best that Lillian and Michelle had dragged Linda away from the fight's epicenter. Male contestants had entered the dining room, despite the rules that they stay out. A good portion of the ship's crew had as well.

Two sides were formed: crew, security, Kimberly and Anthony were on one side, with the rest of the ship's visitors on the other—cameramen in between. Show staff was shouting for people to calm down. Tears were flying on either side of the line, confused faces, women hiccup crying, contestants were rubbing backs, wringing their hands, everyone trying to gain clarity in the chaos.

"I'll kill that bitch," Kimberly shrieked as Anthony held her in his arms. "It's not fair! It's just not fair!"

"You put her off because of last night?" Anthony

bellowed. "Just because she spent the night with me! That's bullshit! No matter what, she—"

"Wait, you slept with her?" Linda shouted, making the other female contestants release guttural sounds of disbelief.

"Oh, no, she didn't try to lie and say y'all sat up and talked all night!" Vera screamed, still shaken from the fight. "That's why we busted her!"

"Damn, man, what can we say?" Rodriguez said. "You know the rules, and we was all trying to be cool and keep your business on the DL, but the cat's out the bag now—you know the rules."

"Shut up, Rodriguez!" Anthony shouted, moving forward and making the security team hold him. "Mind your business, and last I checked, the men don't vote—or does your punk ass need to go over there and stand in for the women?"

Tyrell grabbed the back of Rodriguez's shirt, ripping it to keep him from barreling into Adams as they two men squared off.

"You're both off the ship," Linda yelled over the din. "Two for the price of one for fraternizing. Period! The truth always comes out."

"Done," Lillian hollered.

"Gone," Vera shouted.

"This was so ugly," Michelle said in a quiet voice, walking away.

Natasha walked away with Michelle, needing space, wholeheartedly agreeing. She didn't want to listen to Kimberly's wails, or see Anthony's dejected spirit. She didn't want to see the leaving-the-boat-footage or the cameo aftermath of the booted contestants' last words or last digs. She wanted to find a quiet corner and curl up into a little ball.

Chapter 17

It took nearly an hour for the dust to settle and for Kimberly and Anthony to calm down enough to collect their gear and leave. And the camera crew couldn't get back on the boat until they got the last controversial statements of the couple as the cab pulled up to take them to Nassau's airport. The entire time, Natasha sat in one spot on the deck, her head leaned back, her eyes closed, willing peace. She felt a presence beside her, but had not expected the voice. It made her finally open her eyes and stare at the person near her.

"I can't do this," Michelle said, her eyes searching for answers within her drawn, tense face. "I don't want this conversation on tape, but I feel so terribly responsible for this outcome . . . they didn't do anything worse than the rest of us nearly did, and . . ." Michelle covered her face and began to sob. "Kimberly has issues, but this was unnecessary."

Natasha rubbed Michelle's back for a while and then lifted her chin, swinging her body off the chaise longue to sit before Michelle with both feet firmly planted on the deck as she held Michelle's face. "I heard the conversation, too. Remember?"

Natasha said, trying to stem Michelle's tears. "You explained how he's acted toward every woman, and the decision was based on how he hung himself with the others—you just stated the facts."

"But they were already predisposed . . ."

"Why?" Natasha asked, and then answered her own question before Michelle could. "Because Kimberly sashayed in here arrogant and selfish, and so did Adams. They alienated the group from the door, and you and I both know that a woman will tolerate even a boring guy who's got a good heart over a syndicated SOB like Adams. Tell me I'm wrong."

Michelle sniffed and nodded, then let out a weary breath. "I just don't want to be a hypocrite," she said, her voice so quiet that Natasha had to strain to hear her.

"How are you a hypocrite, Michelle?" Natasha asked, smoothing back her mussed hair. "You told these ladies how you saw things—which I happen to agree with. You tried to keep them fair and honest, and not let them rule him, or any other man, out for trivial reasons. You stated why Adams had some profound behavior flaws that—"

"They ultimately put her off because they found out she slept with him, and were jealous of her," Michelle said on a hard swallow, new tears filling her eyes. "And I don't want to be a hypocrite," she said again, her gaze holding Natasha's as two large tears formed and fell down her pretty cheeks.

Natasha's hand slowly went to her mouth as her instinct revived. "Oh, my, God, Michelle . . . when?"

"Last night," Michelle said in a garbled whisper. "Top deck . . . the stars were out, I, we couldn't . . . I can't even breathe, if this was caught on tape.

Please, I'll forfeit now, I'll pack, just don't put that on television . . . my parents can't be humiliated like that . . ."

Earnest sobs wracked Michelle's body as Natasha held her.

"Listen to me," Natasha said, her heart not consulting her brain as she spoke. "There are no cameras on the top deck, no hidden ones. The cameramen sweep that area with handhelds." She shook Michelle to force her to look at her. "Do not panic. I have a mother, too."

"But Kimberly's mother is probably having a stroke, and she and Anthony did no more than Jason and—"

"Shush," Natasha said, covering Michelle's mouth briefly until she calmed down and stopped babbling. "I have a heart, even though I'm in TV, although you may not believe it." She wiped Michelle's tears and let out a long sigh. "The camera guys had probably turned in for the night, after everyone went to their own room. I'll check the tapes. But there's no hidden footage up there."

Natasha glanced around, already knowing that every aspect of her so-called professional distance was in shreds. There was so much favoritism going on till none of it would hold up in court. But how could she just throw a woman like Michelle to the wolves?

"Take a couple of deep breaths and wipe your face," Natasha ordered. "You are upset because of the fight—that's it. Understood?"

Michelle nodded and drew in a shuddering breath.

"The only reason you and I are having this conversation is because you and Jason are nice people," Natasha said, holding Michelle's hand. "You treated others on the boat with kindness and respect, and you're always the peacemaker. Kimberly dug her own grave by just being so obnoxious. Jason is a little shy, but isn't haughty, like Adams. And the bottom line is, you came clean, didn't front, you told me."

New tears again filled Michelle's eyes as she stared at Natasha. "I know what Jason will say, I think," she whispered. "You're such a nice sister, and we're just glad not to have our business splashed across the screen, that maybe, in Jamaica, we should just say that we want to be together and we've self-selected out."

"You don't have to do that, if you don't want to," Natasha said, meaning it. "I never heard any of this . . . people should fall in love and be together under romantic conditions. *That's natural*. This show is flawed—just like the whole dating scene is flawed and unnatural. When I pitched the concept, I was in a whole different mindset, a different place entirely. Since you guys have boarded the boat, I've learned, seen things . . . oh, girl, I am so sorry I've created so much pain for you guys." It was Natasha's turn to hold back a flood of tears. She made herself laugh. "See, now you've got me going. Good thing one of us is a licensed psychologist, huh?"

They both laughed and sniffed and hugged.

"We do not want to see a rising star like you, a sister with a heart, whom we are so proud of, blow her job over our . . . situation," Michelle said. "You heard the women. Jason wasn't going to make it past the next few rounds, anyway. He doesn't have the personality for this, any more than I do. So, why go through this? At the end of the game, neither he nor I will get chosen, so what's the point? We've gotten the best we can out of this situation—each other."

"But you *don't know* that," Natasha argued. "Things have been going in wild directions. Who's to say—"

"We could mess up your job if anyone found out that you subwayed information on our behalf. Think about it, Natasha. You don't even know us, and you'll be risking your career." Michelle sighed and sniffed hard, wiping her cheeks with both hands. "We couldn't live with ourselves if we did that. After it's all said and done, Jason goes back to his very cushy job on Capitol Hill, and I have my practice. Who knows, I might write a book about post reality show stress syndrome."

Even though they both laughed, Natasha held Michelle's hand tightly, as much to give support as to receive it.

"And I can't live with myself if I think two people who deserve—"

"Stop," Michelle said, smiling through her tears. "Breathe deeply and let it out slowly." She waited as Natasha complied. "You gave us all a chance to find out what was or wasn't important in our lives. I guess, in a very odd way, Anthony and Kimberly learned something valuable in all this, as did Campanelli . . . about treating people nicely. Isn't that the basis of business, people forming relationships and doing extra favors or using their power when it counts for those they like and have allegiances with?"

Natasha sat back, not having considered that.

"I'm from D.C., hon," Michelle said with a chuckle. "Adams should know that's how politics work, and he and Kim," she said with mischief in her voice, "got slammed because their politics were wrong, even though they didn't do anything really worse than the rest of us playing this crazy game."

"Wow," Natasha murmured.

"Yeah. Wow," Michelle said calmly. "And Quazar left to do whatever he had to do, his priorities got reset to family on this show. So, even though it's not all neat and tidy, you've given people a lot through this vehicle." Michelle sighed and stood. "I told you last night that I'd never forget you. After this conversation, I really mean that and consider you a friend. And as a friend, we're going to do the right thing by you. We can't allow you to give us this level of favoritism, which could get found out and one day come back to bite you in the butt."

Natasha stood facing Michelle, watching new strength enter that very shy woman. It was awe-inspiring to watch the subtle transformation. "Are you going to speak to him?"

Michelle nodded. "If you can let us ride with you guys to Jamaica, we'll make the announcement before the next round. That way, we can put a little distance between the incident that just happened with Anthony and Kimberly, and our bombshell. I'm still not comfortable with our parents knowing exactly what led to the decision. The only thing people need to know is that we fell in love."

"I can respect that," Natasha said, giving Michelle a quick hug. "I wish you two all the best in life, lady."

"You, too," Michelle said, pulling away. "I'll always be rooting for you."

* * *

The whole thing was crazy, and he still wasn't sure how he felt about anything. Tyrell just stared at the endless blue ocean, the sun coating him with perspiration. The teams were in total disarray. Everyone seemed shook that a female contestant had actually gotten put off the boat for sleeping with a guy she was crazy about, even though no one liked Kimberly or Adams. Still, it was the principle of it.

The female contestants were very quiet and removed, probably rethinking the haste and anger that led to Kimberly's ousting, regardless of how much she got on their nerves. The male team was so morose that no jokes passed, no one said a word. It was as though each man was quietly contemplating his own endurance. Nine weeks was a very long time, and after the night before, every one of them knew they could have easily been the one to get the axe . . . all it would have taken was a simple, "Yes, baby." One tiny slip, one too improper action caught on tape. One false move, one piña colada too many, with the music being a little too right, and the vibe way too strong, and an incident could go down to get a brother put off . . . and not just him, but the lady he cared deeply for. It wasn't right.

But it so reminded him of all the jobs he'd had. Any office improprieties, and you were history. It was twisted, this culture, of putting people together without time to date outside the workplace, but thrust them onto teams and work cells where they'd get to know each other as individuals, under intense conditions, and then not expect natural affinities to occur. And, why were those natural affinities gossiped about, he wondered? If two people hit it off, became involved, then, so what?

Tyrell stood and stretched, needing space to think. But even with all the room on the nearly vacant top deck, there was no way to figure any of this out. What he was sure of, though, Natasha felt lousy about the outcome this morning. It was written all over her face. Her plan, and the show's concept, was brilliant. It mirrored life, even down to the rules of workforce propriety—but what she obviously wasn't ready to deal with was the fallout. Were any of them? In all truth, was anybody?

He began walking around the edge of the deck, just watching the waves, staring at the beauty of nothingness. That was the whole issue. All of this was abut everything and nothing. All this drama in the world, for what? He could feel himself going down a very pointlessly philosophical path as the lunch announcement sounded. He closed his eyes and silently groaned. At lunch the next challenge would be presented.

"Okay, teams, listen up," Devon said, brandishing the microphone as the contestants slowly took their seats. "Get a hearty meal under your belts. After this morning's fiasco, nobody really ate. But when we get to Jamaica, everyone, especially the guys, will need their strength."

The male contestants let out weary exhales and nodded.

"Well, don't all seem so excited at once," Devon teased, but even his voice held a hint of fatigued reservation within it. "When we get to that island, we'll debark. Wear your exercise gear, because, gentlemen, you'll be going over heavy terrain."

Devon glanced at Stephanie and Natasha. Tyrell

noticed that 'Tash's focus was beyond the window, just seeming as though she were lost deep in thought.

"You'll each be given a mountain bike, water, a waterproof watch, a map, a backpack with some energy bars, a first aid kit, a two-way cell phone—in case you get in trouble—and a compass. The goal is one of endurance. Your objective will be to cross the Duns River falls in Ocho Rios, make your way up the mountain to the designated group location by nightfall, where we'll be camping out, rustically. We want to see how you fellas handle the physical endurance. And, ladies, while they are on an endurance challenge, you'll have one of your own."

Every woman looked at Devon, worry etched across her face.

"It's time for a little bonding, or not," Devon said, thrusting his chin up. "You all will have a group project, and must handle the challenge as a group to form cohesion. While the guys are cycling uphill, like salmon swimming upstream, on this primal nature challenge, your task will be to take a limited amount of funds, pool it, and go with our SUV drivers to the local outdoor markets. You'll have to scour the marketplace for food, bring it back up the mountain, and use only the rudiments of nature to cook it and to create the homecoming celebration for the men by the time they reach camp."

"Are you crazy?" Linda muttered.

Michelle just closed her eyes.

"Will there be water, at least?" Vera asked, sounding like a lost child.

"This will either make us, or break us," Lillian grumbled, sighing.

"Precisely." Devon tossed his head toward the lavish buffet. "The ranks are thinning out, and you ladies have shown the male contestants how you behave under the best of circumstances. But the winning male also has to make a choice at the end of the game. He'll need to see how each of you function for better, for worse, for richer, or for poorer. Get the picture?"

"Yeah, we got it, we got it," Linda said in a sullen tone. "You all are evil."

"That's my job," Devon said with a bright smile. "That's why there will be no fancy serving dishes, gourmet pans, knives and forks, and any of the accoutrements of fine dining. But we'll see what each of you are made of and how well you can burn on an open flame that you'll have to literally start from scratch. Hope somebody in the group used to be a Girl Scout."

The women slumped and held their heads in their hands. The men sighed and sprawled out in their chairs.

"You got this, Colorado," Tyrell said. "Make us proud."

"No lie," Rodriguez said. "Endurance? Gimme a break. We've already passed a couple of endurance tests, man. So have the ladies."

Joe and Nelson pounded Rodriguez's fist. Tyrell shook his head and gave Tony a high five. Nelson and Floyd didn't comment, but their expressions said it all. Jason just hung his head and let out his breath in a quiet stream.

It was hot as blazes in Jamaica, waiting on the side of a dusty road for the gear to come. Tyrell paced over to a tree and leaned against it, watching

Michelle and Jason go over to the show staff. His line of vision remained keen, as he watched handshakes pass, and hugs get shared. He slowly made his way back toward the all-male team. "Yo, y'all. Check it out. Something's up. Does it look like they're saying good-bye, or am I imagining things?"

Instant consensus was reached as the men gathered together in a huddle and approached the show staff. Female contestants were laughing and crying and hugging Michelle. Confusion tore through their ranks and hovered as each male picked up bits of conversation.

"We talked about it on the way over here," Jason said, his gaze softening as he pulled Michelle close. "I adore her," he said without fanfare. "I want to be with her, and although it's probably financially foolish for both of us to throw in the towel, there's no need to act like I'd pick anyone but her, if I were lucky enough to make it to the end. So, I need to self-select out of the group."

The male team stood quietly stunned, and one by one each man went up to Jason and shook his hand.

"Damn, man," Rodriguez said. "I respect that . . . we'll miss you, brother."

The two exchanged a bear hug and then laughed.

"I'll miss you guys, too," Jason said with a wry smile. "But the thought of doing five hours up the mountain when me and my lady can go over to the hotels and watch this on TV in a week . . . uh, somehow I can't find it in me to be all that upset."

Everyone laughed, even the camera crew. The entire show staff had misty eyes. They hugged Jason and Michelle, slapped backs, wished the couple well. The ladies were all teary, but laughter rang out in their small huddle of friendship.

"Dag, girl, you just gonna up and leave us to the mosquitoes and tents, huh? How you seem?" Linda said, laughing and bawling. "You are such cool people, girl. We love you, hear? The voice of reason—stay in touch, but be happy."

Vera was sobbing so hard that all Lillian could do was hold her. "Oh, she can't leave," Vera wailed. "That's my girl!"

"Michelle," Lillian said, her voice cracking with every word as she held Vera, "you are such a sweetie—what'll we do without you?"

Even Stephanie and Natasha were crying as they pulled Michelle into warm hugs. Devon was holding and patting Michelle like a doll before he kissed her cheek hard and released her so someone else could get a turn. But Michelle nearly became hysterical as Natasha held her close.

"You are the nicest, fairest, *kindest* human being I know," Michelle said into Natasha's hair. "Thank you for allowing me to do this my way."

Natasha just nodded and turned away, waving off the camera. Tyrell could see her shoulders shake and he watched her back slowly expand and contract with heavy breaths.

"Oh, damn, man," Rodriguez said, looking up at the sky, fighting back tears. "This is too emotional, too over the top," he confided to Tyrell. "And we ain't supposed to go over to our ladies and hug them and whatnot, so they stop crying hard?" He wiped his face as his gaze went to Vera. "Look at her, man," he said, leaving Tyrell's side.

"I can't focus on a damned race, now," Floyd said, dropping his helmet to go stand off for some space.

Nelson walked away from the group to gather Linda up in his arms. Joe retreated to the bikes and sat on a tree stump, his eyes closed. Sam raked his fingers through his hair and went over to Lillian, who barreled into his arms. Tyrell gripped his helmet and began adjusting the strap. He could not walk over to Natasha, out in the open like that. There was only one thing to do: go get his map and then ride.

Chapter 18

Tyrell stood with the male team receiving last minute safety instructions as the female team climbed in open Jeeps headed away from the site. Each man would have a camera on him, following his path in a nearby SUV. But as they all unfurled their maps, it became apparent that each man had been given a different trail.

"We all have to spilt up during this bull?" Joe said, clearly indignant.

"I thought we all did this thing together," Tony said, glancing around the group.

Before anyone even got on a bike, an argument had broken out between the nature trail specialists and the male team.

"Let's everybody keep their heads," Sam implored. "Listen, guys, we can do this."

"You can do this," Floyd argued. "Look, I'm from Detroit and didn't grow up in Colorado, skiing Vale."

"Word," Tony said, walking away and shaking his head. "Outdoors to me is a street party. This is complete bull. Five hours, uphill, in the freakin' Jamaican sun—after being out all night drinking, with no sleep? You must be nuts!"

"Yo, man," Nelson said, going to Tony Rodriguez to bring him back to the group. "I used to work outside on construction crews, then overseeing them all day, with my old man. You just have to pace yourself, look alive, follow the safety standards to the letter, and suck it up, man. Stop whining."

"I ain't whining," Tony said, offended. "All I'm saying is that if we had known, last night, everybody might have gotten some real rest, you feel me? Tell me you go out partying like we did before you have to climb a skyscraper?"

Nelson slapped Tony on the back, but returned him to the group. "There have been nights . . . and when we get up the hill, remind me to tell you how I almost fell off some scaffolding from hanging out too late with this fine honey."

Nelson's good humor made everyone, even Tony, chuckle. Tyrell was watching it all from a very remote place in his psyche. The wheels in his mind were turning a mile a minute, flipping gears so hard and fast he thought his head would explode. It wasn't about getting up the mountain all ripped up, beat up, and broken down. This was over the top. But with no options before him, he reluctantly conceded.

Tyrell let his breath out hard, looked at the instructors, and motioned toward the bikes. "Let me get this right," he said. "If we pass out, get injured, or otherwise don't have the stamina to make it up the mountain to base camp, we lose this round—but we're still in the game, right?"

All eyes were on the instructors, and each male contestant listened intently to the response as a towering, ruddy Jamaican stood tall, biceps flexing, muscles in his chest rippling while he spoke, using his hands to emphasize his point.

"If you get in one of our rescue vehicles, that will also be carrying the cameraman, then we take you down the mountain to spend the night on the ship. You'll be separated from the group, and will have lost a night at your disposal to allow the female contestants to get to better know you. Your decision."

Natasha rode in the front passenger's seat, looking at the beautiful countryside that yielded a profusion of lush foliage, naturally growing hibiscus, and fruit trees. Yet the poverty of the backcountry also struck her. It was a visual conflict just seeing the ravages of economic turmoil that tourists normally didn't see off the beaten trail. That is what she had wanted to show the teams, just how fortunate they were by world standards. Interspersed between the simple lean-to homes and shacks, there would be a sprawling estate that heralded back to plantation days.

"Get that," she murmured to Paul, urging the cameraman to get backdrop shots that could make a point.

Paul nodded. "Your old documentary urges coming out, huh, lady?"

"Yeah, something like that," she said quietly, wondering if the female contestants who had been complaining nonstop, saw what she saw.

They got on her nerves, complaining about the air-conditioning, the insects, the condition of the roads, and their challenge. In her heart Natasha knew they would freak out when they got to a real market, one not neat and tidy with bright lights and sanitized, shrink-wrapped and packed meats. There would be flies, and vendors hawking wares, and limited options, unlike an urban supermarket in the States. But that was the goal: to bring out each woman's best and worst under the circumstances presented. Part of her was sad that Kimberly hadn't made it to this part. The television audience needed to see just how spoiled and pampered their urban lifestyle truly was.

She sighed hard as the vehicles came to a stop in a clearing, churning up red-orange plumes of dust and making the contestants frown and squint as they exited their transportation.

"Okay, ladies," Stephanie said. "You have two hundred dollars to feed everybody and show crew."

"Two hundred dollars?" Vera said, shocked. "To feed *all* those people?"

"Make good buying decisions," Devon said, unfazed.

Linda put her hands on her hips, wiping the sweat from her palms onto her jeans. "Aw'ight, y'all. Stop whining. It is what it is. This is just like buying from the produce trucks or going down to the docks."

A new level of respect dawned within Natasha as she watched Linda gather the female contestants around and give them a pep talk.

"These brothers will have a dawg of a time coming up that steep-assed mountain we just drove down, and thank Gawd we don't have to walk this mess we're gonna buy back up it. They'll be tired, hungry, pissed off, whatever. So, since we have limited funds, we know we need to get some fruits and vegetables—that we can serve without burning."

Heads nodded and disgruntled agreement filtered throughout the group.

"You've gotta go food shopping with a strategy," Linda said. "When you have a limited budget, but have a lotta mouths to feed, you have to have a plan. I say, we get chicken, since everybody eats yard bird, then do some yams and corn—because you can barbeque those and they fill a hole in the belly. Add some fruits, because I know they have to have bananas, pineapples, and mangoes here, cheap. Plus that puts potassium back in your system after you've been exercising. Forget greens or a salad—too messy and too labor intensive. But bread, yeah, starch and meat, feel me?"

"If we scrimp enough," Lillian offered, "we could get some paper plates, forks, and some of the cooking things we'll need."

Linda nodded.

"Yeah, like some damned lighter fluid and matches."

The group laughed as Linda slapped Vera high five.

"What about something to drink," Lillian asked. "I know they'll want a beer and—"

"Too expensive," Linda said firmly. "Buy some lemons, again, what do the people have here, cheap?" Vindicated when all heads nodded, Linda relaxed. "They make sugar here, right? The crew is providing free water. We make lemonade." She chuckled. "Plus, if your hands are sticky and nasty and you stink from cleaning chickens and grilling, save the old lemon rinds and use that to freshen up."

"Damn, girl," Vera said, slinging an arm over

Linda's shoulder. "Glad you're on our side. You used to do all this outdoors stuff?"

Linda laughed. "Naw, girl. I was just broke as a dawg for most of my natural born life." She nodded to the shacks nearby. "A lot of this right here ain't no different from Brooklyn."

Natasha and Linda's eyes met as the female team trudged toward the market. One of them got it, she thought, remembering her own childhood. Peace settled into Natasha's spirit for the first time since this adventure began. Instead of feeling tense as the women tried to be polite and not turn their noses up to the available meats and produce, she found it amusing in her new, relaxed state. Linda tickled her so much as she haggled with the older, female Jamaican vendors like a pro. It was so odd. She'd met so many different men and women from so many different walks of life. Each had his or her own culture, way of seeing the world, a fresh perspective that she could appreciate.

She'd never expected to wind up helping Michelle, or crying when she left the show. She never knew how really tight she was with Stephanie and Devon, each being an angel in his or her own right. She didn't know how blessed she was by having dear sister-friends like Camille and Jorgette. Nor did she truly understand how similar people were regardless of race or creed.

Any of the men who had been on the show could have been a life partner. There were profoundly positive things about each guy's attributes and the way he handled himself in the world. She'd meant to send a quiet message with this portion of the show, had meant to open people's eyes and minds, and wound up learning quite a bit herself. Tyrell jumped into her consciousness as she patiently waited for the shopping mission to conclude.

She just wondered how a street savvy brother would handle this endurance test. She just hoped he would be at the top of the mountain when it was all said and done.

His back and his thighs were on fire. Dust and grit made his eyes sting and water, and the thick, heavy Jamaican heat was insufferable. Unlike the beaches that had trade winds and surf to give one a false sense of coolness, on the open, rocky road, going uphill for two hours, he wasn't sure he could make it.

Tyrell stopped. His red T-shirt was now a burgundy, wet wrap of cotton pressed to him like a second skin. His khaki shorts felt like they were strangling his groin, waist, and buttocks. He had tiny pebbles in his sneakers. How they got there, was anybody's guess.

He dropped his backpack with a thud when he dismounted, and found bottled water that was now sun temperature. He leaned against a large boulder, looking down the slope of the mountain at the crystal blue sea, wondering if he'd be able to hit the turquoise patch if he just jumped.

Spraying his face with his water, he stretched and pulled out his map. From this point he'd have to give the Jeep driver his bike, and hike on foot through a densely thicketed trail to a waterfall. He'd have to cross that, meet the Jeep on the other side, and continue the steep ascent. Insane.

Without a word to the anxiously awaiting crew, he

ditched his bike, snatched up his backpack, and began walking. This made no sense.

Passing little shacks, children in yards, beat up and broken down cars, slowly a sense of peace overcame him. This was like back home. Georgia came into his mind. The real roots of where he'd been from. Atlanta was a new addition to his family's resume. But his mom, grandmom, his people, they were from Savannah.

The dogs in the front yards were not off-putting or vicious. He remembered how to stare a dog down and make it stay on its property line, yeah. These weren't street-crazy pit bulls, these were yard dogs. He smiled at curious children as he passed them. Studied the faces of old men and women who sat on wobbly chairs to catch a breeze as he made his way. It was much cooler in the thicket; trees and greenery had created a canopy from the sun. He could hear insects and birds, and the stir of people just trying to live their lives.

It suddenly dawned upon him as he walked that he felt lighter. He could do this. He came from people like this who had to walk miles to segregated schools, had to shop at small, locally owned stores . . . every neighbor knew the other's business. Tyrell chuckled. That's what had made him an astute judge of character and an entrepreneur. All one had to go on was one's reputation, and all transactions were done with a man's word as his bond. You *had* to know people. Everything was a character loan. What was a bank? Nobody had money, but they had resources. He remembered his mother doing hair for a favor, or cleaning a house to get a bathroom sink fixed. People *traded* and made a way out of no way.

The rules said if he got in *the television show's* rescue Jeep, he'd have to be taken to the boat. But what if he made a way out of no way, he wondered. What if they *all* got a lift, so no man was left behind?

Tyrell stopped and looked at a woman hanging clothes on a line. "Excuse me, ma'am," he said in his most polite, southern genteel voice. "I left my bike on the road and need a ride up the mountain. You know anybody around here who can give me and my buddies a lift? We got separated on a bike trail; each went a different way and were supposed to meet up in the middle. They're probably as tired and turned around as I am."

The woman stopped working, her eyes scanning him for danger. She wiped her hands on her purple shift, and tightened the dingy floral scarf on her head. She looked him up and down and then finally called into the house. A young man about nineteen years old came out, seeming prepared to defend his home. Tyrell could dig it. These people didn't know him from a can of paint. He could be a robber, a foreigner trafficking drugs, whatever. So he waited, taking off his bike helmet and putting it under his arm with one, easy, nonthreatening motion. He dropped his backpack to show that it was unimportant to him and mopped the trickle of sweat from his brow.

"You a biker?" the young man asked, his bare chest glistening and his jeans fitting baggy against his narrow, trim waist. "You on the trail for de falls, mon?"

Tyrell nodded. "Yeah, got messed up, turned around, and the Jeep that dropped me and my buddies off is supposed to meet us on the other side, up the mountain. They took my bike already."

The young man's shoulders sagged as his mother looked on with several neighbors. In that instant, Tyrell knew the kid wanted the bike as a trade for the favor. What had changed in a hundred years of evolution?

"I don't have much on me," he said, carefully reaching for his backpack. Tyrell made a quick visual sweep of the young man before him. Hair corn-rowed, like Allen Iverson, a pair of old Nike sneakers, jeans—maybe he'd take fly U.S. gear versus cash. "But I have a cool waterproof watch, some bottled water, a two-way cell phone, a—"

"You got a two-way and a watch?" the kid said, considerably brightening. "Plus a backpack, *and* a helmet?"

Tyrell laughed and outstretched his arm with the red and black racer's helmet. He watched the young guy come over, study it with deep appreciation, and smile.

"Dis all right, mon. We might know some people who can get you and your posse up de way."

"Cool," Tyrell said, pounding the young man's fist.

"You got CDs?"

Tyrell laughed. "I wish, man. This is all I've got on me. But, for a ride, I know my boys will give up their gear, too."

The one thing he knew, patience was a virtue. Living down South had taught him that. In the islands it required exponential levels of grace. Nobody moved fast. So he sat in the front yard, watching the boy's mother eye him with a little less suspicion, but it was obvious that she still wasn't comfortable with his presence. She gave him a wide berth, walking around him out of arm's reach, but was polite.

He could see straight through the house from the front yard. It was nothing more than corrugated tin roofing seemingly slapped on top of four half wood, half cinder block walls. It had to be a virtual oven in there. The widows were open, not a pane of glass or screen in them. He doubted indoor plumbing existed for her, and yet knew that somehow, she probably worked down the mountain in the plush tourist area.

Again a profound awareness awakened within him. She reminded him so much of his mother—going into the wealthier areas to clean for other people. Every one of the people who'd waited upon the show teams and staff most likely came home to what was so much less than where they worked. Yet, he also knew that no matter how humble, home was always a sanctuary away from the prying eyes of people who ordered you about, judged you, and tried to run your life.

Just sitting there, waiting, thinking, he renewed his mission. He didn't want his woman to ever have to come down the mountain, or down from the projects, into the rich, decadent valley of the spoiled and unappreciative to work like a dog. He didn't want her to have to figure out how to make rice and beans fill the bellies of his children, or to press her pretty nose against the glass of some fancy store, wishing, just once, she could have a dress she saw that wasn't on sale. Looking at this boy's mother made it all so very real in the context of the artificial game show world he'd been dealing with for weeks. This was the point.

Tyrell briefly shut his eyes. Natasha Ward was a genius. She definitely had a lot to say; her voice was screaming this message so loud and clear on videotape—but if one weren't tuned in with a frame of reference, they'd miss it.

"You all right?" the older woman asked, peeking through the clothesline at Tyrell. "Heat down here is different den where you from. You need to drink water."

"Thank you, ma'am. I'm fine," Tyrell said, giving her a nod of respect. "I really appreciate your son helping me and my buddies."

"He's a good boy," she said, proudly. "I do the best I can, with my husband gwan died. Just don't want no trouble." She sighed and wiped her hands on her apron. "You want some ginger tea?"

He knew it was a deep gesture of hospitality, and dared not overstep his bounds. "Ma'am, I thank you so much. But I cannot ask you to fix for me on your day off."

She smiled and waved her hand at him. "I never have a day off. You lucky to catch me home when you did. I don't mind. Today is my home chore day. Cooking, cleaning, fixing up—no trouble. Have to do it anyway."

He watched her enter the little shack, her breathing labored as she huffed up the two high steps past him. He waited for what seemed like a long time for her to return, but when she did, she brought out a cool glass of ginger tea. She presented it to him with a smile, studying him hard as she then waited for his response.

It was so sweet and tangy that he nearly squinted, but his momma had taught him better than that.

"This is good," he said, taking a deep swig in

order to get it down fast. "I'm lucky I came your way. My buddies are out there, somewhere, lost in the bushes."

She found it hilarious that men would get lost on a trail she most likely knew in her sleep. She laughed hard, slapping her legs. Just watching her laugh made him chuckle, too. Her joy was so earnest as she straightened and wiped her eyes.

"Whooo-boy!" she said, shaking her head and adjusting the straps on her purple sundress about her plump form. She pointed to her dirty white flip-flops. "Almost make me lose my shoes laughing wit you, mon." She put her hands on her hips and appraised him. "You somebody's son, and seem like a nice young man. You be careful out here. You and your friends should eat and stay near the hotels, understand what I say?"

"Yes, ma'am," Tyrell said, hearing her loud and clear. "We're going to meet our entire team up the hill, cook out—"

"You cooking?" She seemed so shocked that she leaned back and covered her heart.

"No, no no, the ladies—"

"Oh, good. You hired people—"

"No, no, they're like . . . friends."

She smiled. "Oh. Girlfriends." She nodded and gave him a curious wink. "Dey nice?"

Tyrell chuckled. Just like a mother to ask. "Very nice, ma'am."

"Can they cook?"

He laughed hard as he watched the older woman place her hands on her hips and furrow her brow.

"Truthfully, ma'am, I don't know. They ain't got pot nor pan the first."

His laughter went into belly laughing spasms as she screamed and fussed.

"Wha?" she exclaimed, her thick accent making it difficult for Tyrell to understand her. "Dey up in de mountains, nooo pan, *no pot*, no knife, no nutting, gwan cook for men who been biking up a trail? Young girls dese days jus' make my head pop off!"

Tyrell was waving his hand for her to relent her humorous tirade. Oh, yeah, this lady was definitely like his mom.

"Lawd, I'd pay you to teach 'em, ma'am, for real, but I know—"

"Huh! I teach 'em. Take me best girlfriends right up dere and bring our own pots and pans, don't talk crazy, mon. I'll make food to make your girlfriends mad at you for life."

Tyrell straightened up. He'd heard an offer, and he genuinely hadn't been angling for a barter. But it was in the way the woman waited with an expectant smile on her face.

"Really?" he asked, shocked. "You'd come all the way up there and cook outside. They ain't got no stove up there, ma'am, no grills . . ."

She waved her hand and scoffed. "For a right price, on me time off, on a day when I have to cook, anyway. Humph."

His smile widened. "I have five hundred on me right now." He stood up, and pulled the wad of bills out of his pocket and handed it to her. He then yanked his shorts pockets inside out to show her that what he'd offered was all he had, and they both laughed.

She clutched the bills tightly, her eyes wide open with amazement. "You don' even know me," she said quietly. "You gwan jus' give *me* money *like dat* to cook *one meal* . . . no references, before I do da job for you?"

Her amazement hurt his soul, because in his mind it meant that this hardworking woman had never been just offered a break. Tyrell looked at her squarely, his voice gentle with respect and appreciation. "Ma'am, I can tell you're good people. You remind me of my own momma. I know you can cook if you say so—your word's good enough for me. Plus, your boy is helping me get up that mountain, and is helping me round up my friends . . . where I'm from, that means something."

She nodded and stashed the knot of bills in her bosom without counting them. Still seeming puzzled, she moved toward the house. "I'ma go fetch my girlfriends to help. We have to get the food . . . how many is it?"

"About twenty, thirty people. If that's too many, it's okay, just do what you—"

"No problem," she said fast, cutting him off. "But, can I ask a question?"

"Of course, ma'am."

"You not from America, right? But I thought sure I heard your accent."

Tyrell laughed. "I'm from the States, just down South. We do things a little different, ma'am, that's all."

Chapter 19

Natasha couldn't believe her ears as she pressed the two-way cell unit to her skull. "He did what!"

Devon and Stephanie were hanging on Natasha's every word, making hand signals to her to explain the situation as she closed her eyes. Ignoring them, she kept talking to one of the Jeep drivers, trying to get clarity.

"No, there's nothing in the rules, per se, that said they couldn't get there using their own creative resources—the contest issue was, *they couldn't use ours.*" Natasha raked her scalp as she walked in a circle clutching the telephone. "Yeah, yeah, I know. But, where are the—" Natasha stopped short, leaned over, and laughed as the driver cut her off and filled her in. "All of them? He got a hook-up for all of them? Oh, this is priceless. Did you guys get it all on tape? Do not, hear me, do *not* miss any of it!"

Sam was the last team member they found. He'd made it the farthest, was covered with mud from the falls, and almost seemed disappointed that he wasn't going to be able to put a pick axe in the side of a cliff to dangle off it. But even he had to concede when the open pickup truck loaded with men and teenagers rolled up and Tyrell and Rodriguez jumped out, brandishing a cold beer as a lure.

They'd beaten the odds, a celebration was in order, good food was on the way, and all of them had chipped in whatever they'd had in their pockets to throw the bash. Reggae music was going to lumber up the hill soon, probably in a smoking truck like the one they were riding in; another brother was bringing a generator and some old Christmas tree lights, just so he could get twenty bucks and could hang out with the bunch. They were bringing the party with them, up a narrow incline, driving on what they considered to be the wrong side of the road . . . dirty, grimy, laughing, and content.

The camp team hadn't even gotten the tents pitched yet. Food was being sorted on a rickety aluminum table, and the women gave the stream a spurious glance. Devon agreed with both Natasha and Linda, and even admitted that using the water truck might be best, citing the potential gastric dangers of ingesting possible parasites and larvae in a natural stream.

Slowly but surely, a sense of order and unity befell the camp group. Tents were near a hillside that offered a spectacular view of the surf below. A fire site had been established in the clearing. Food was off to one side. The ladies were making chicken and vegetable shish kabobs. Corn on the cob was being husked, yams washed and wrapped in foil, then speared with small sticks, while lemonade got made.

Laughter rang out as the women swatted small insects and bees and gabbed. Camaraderie filled the air. Natasha found a quiet place in the shade to sip bottled water and watch the magic unfold. This was like family. It was like an old-fashioned family reunion, the kind of gathering she'd missed so dearly. It was hot, grubby, frenetic, and fun. She found herself smiling for no reason at all, just from the sheer joy of being.

When a smoking, backfiring truck groaned up the road in the distance and the engine stopped, everyone dropped what they were doing and ran toward the sound.

Cheers and laughter from contestants and show staff echoed through the trees, as the men jumped out of the truck, beers raised, victorious.

A hundred questions barraged the male team amid the cheers while teenagers in the truck watched it all unfold with excitement glittering in their eyes, laughing. Each man regaled anyone who would listen, explaining his solo trek with vast embellishment that no one seemed to mind. But there was a united front when it came to telling what Tyrell did.

"Yo," Rodriguez exclaimed. "Dude came through, man. We was on our last leg, and *hombre* pulls up with a truck and says, 'Jump in.' I was like, sho' you right!"

"I ain't neva been so glad to see a brother in all my life," Joe said, laughing hard. "Maaan, I live the smooth life. I don't do this mountain climbing mess, not a brother from St. Louis."

Floyd saluted Tyrell with a beer. "Tell me about it.

I do computer work, video games, not the great outdoors."

"All I know is," Nelson added, laughing, "brother-erman had the brews, is all I'm saying."

"A cold beer never tasted so good," Sam said, taking a deep swig. "Plus, Tyrell is the master hook-up artist. Dude got a party on the way."

"What!" Linda said, laughing. "Tyrell, for real, tell me *where on earth* did you find a party out *here?*"

"Aw, girl," Tyrell teased. "Wasn't nuthin' to it." He glanced at the food table and then winked at Nelson. "They gonna be mad. You tell 'em. We might not have gotten here in time."

"Our boy met this older sister," Nelson said with a respectful nod to the beaming teenager in the truck. "His mom, we're told, can *burn*, girl."

"Yeah," Tony said, winking at Vera. "You ladies shouldn't have to be out here cooking and what-not. That's why we got us a band and—"

"A band?" Natasha couldn't help herself and Stephanie doubled over with laughter while Devon slapped his forehead.

"We had money left over from the casino and put it in a pot. It stretched a long way," Sam said with pride.

"My momma can cook good," the teenager said, standing taller as his friends slapped his back. "She'll bring you a whole pig, fried plantains, callaloo, johnnycakes, jerk chicken, kingfish, home made ginger beer, *key lime pie*," he added with emphasis. "Made from home, no store, mon. She makes it fresh. Conch fritters . . . yeah, mon. No worries. And, me olda brodder, he plays reggae. His posse comin' up here with de lights and music, so you can jam wit de ladies, righteous."

"Daaaayum," Linda exclaimed, shaking her head. "You go, boyie!"

Linda slapped Tyrell a high five so hard she almost fell. Even the cameramen followed suit.

Although it was hard to get next to Tyrell alone, Natasha was determined to steal a moment with him for herself. He was buzzing around the camp, joking, and helping out, teasing people, making the ladies squeal and throw lemon peels at him. It was like watching a seasoned politician work a crowd, and at the same time, it was like watching a man who was of generous spirit and used to down home family. In her core she knew it was his way to just do what came natural. He didn't have to share his hook-up. He could have come up the mountainside alone, taken all the credit for himself, and left the others to struggle and find their way. He could have entered the camp the victor of the day, with a reggae band and food in tow, and made the other men look and feel worthless.

But he didn't. That was the point.

It was grace beyond measure, to her way of thinking. It told her all that she'd ever need to know about this man. Her gaze wandered to him and lingered. There was no need to hide her glances now. Everybody watched Tyrell and enjoyed soaking in whatever antics he was up to. The ladies watched him. The men watched him, waiting for his next adventure. The cameras ate him up. The show staff loved him. She did, too.

And that he'd managed to convince some older woman, out in the bush, that he was honorable enough to go alone with her son, and a band of what could have been highway robbers . . . and got the lady to cook for almost thirty people? Natasha laughed out loud and sighed. God, that man was a gift. She just wished she could unwrap the package.

Natasha pushed away from the tree as Stephanie neared her. The band was setting up, the smell of good food was filtering through the foliage, laughter was everywhere along with the crickets. Amplifiers made the forest come alive even more, as the pulse of reggae made people slow down, unconsciously walk with the beat, and chill.

"Isn't this fabulous?" Stephanie said, her face awash with sheer joy. "Look," she said, nodding toward Devon. "They have him playing MC, and he loves every minute of it."

"I couldn't have dreamt this up," Natasha said, laughing quietly as her gaze remained on Tyrell. "He is such a trip."

Stephanie shook her head. "The skinny dipping thing was wild. Nathan is gonna bust a blood vessel laughing when he sees Tyrell streaking over to the stream to get washed up, with all the other guys jumping in behind him. I thought we'd have to revive Devon. Then the ladies actually jumped in like that, too—even Linda?" Stephanie whooped with laughter. "Only three weeks together and the teams have clicked like that? Kiddo, we have enough tape for eight to ten episodes, now. By the time we all get to St. Lucia for the romantic trail portion . . ." Stephanie stopped rambling on and laughing. "'Tash, hon, what's wrong?"

Natasha looked away from the group and into the darkening wooded area. "That's just it. I don't want another soul to be cut from the roster. I don't want those folks to have to eliminate anyone." Her gaze went back to the active campground. "I want them all to leave the show like they are tonight—happy, laughing, friends." She searched Stephanie's face. "Does that make sense?"

"Yeah. Totally," Stephanie said. "What if we did a spin-off show, or a reunion show? Mike is simply devastated that he's missing the fun. It's not the money, just the adventure and the teams, you know?"

Natasha nodded. "You have enough tape to stretch for eight to ten episodes?"

"Definitely."

"What if we say, because we've had such early eliminations, that they won't have to do a vote until we get to St. Lucia . . . let's give these folks a mental break, even if for a little while."

"Agreed," Stephanie said on a long exhale. "We can tell Nathan that we have hot stuff to stretch the episodes, but we had to slow down on cutting contestants because quirky things had happened and we've already sustained heavier losses than anticipated."

"Sounds like a plan," Natasha said, much relieved. "We should definitely design a reunion show, inviting everybody back who made the boat."

"Feel better now?" Stephanie asked, offering her a sheepish, sideways glance.

"Much," Natasha said, her smile widening.

"You gonna finally get up the nerve to, uh . . . not worry about—"

Natasha held up her hand and chuckled. "One day at a time, girl. Let's go get some homemade grub."

* * *

The mood was so relaxed that it was hard to tell who was show staff or a contestant. People lounged, leaned on one another, talked in natural groupings, no one seeming to care about the invisible dotted line. When Tyrell plopped down between her and Stephanie with a humongous plate, they all laughed.

"How can you eat like that and not have an ounce of excess body fat? It's not fair," Stephanie lamented.

"High metabolism," Tyrell said, his jaw working overtime as he shoveled plantains in his mouth and offering Stephanie a piece of roast pork. "Girl, you'd better stop eating like a bird and act like you know. That boy's momma can burn, no lie."

"You are making that look so good," Stephanie admitted, leaning over and taking a pinch off Tyrell's plate. "Maybe I'll just mosey on over and get a little bit."

"Better hurry before me and the fellas go back over there. Key lime pie is almost gone, too."

Stephanie was on her feet in seconds. "Now, we will battle. If they wolfed down all the pie that nice lady made, and if I didn't get a slice, it's on."

Natasha dropped back on her elbows and laughed, too full to care. "Brother, you definitely have wooden leg. I don't know where you put it all."

"Don't start a conversation you can't finish, girl," Tyrell teased, totally misconstruing her statement.

Natasha shook her head. "You're a mess and need to stop."

He simply winked at her and kept eating as they sat quietly, listening to the chatter and laughter around them. They were not far away from the others, just pulled back enough from the fire so they could enjoy it without the immediate heat. On the other side of it, couples lounged against one another, Floyd and Joe debated some unknown topic, and the reggae seemed to thread everything together. Devon had found a comfortable spot and was gabbing away with the cooks, pestering them for recipes as they giggled and refused to hand over family secrets. The cameramen looked sated and exhausted, their movements slow, just like the beat of the music. Weary staff members stretched out and snoozed on the blankets, their cell phones on vibrate, ready for the call to respond to any crises, but smart enough to know that a five-minute catnap could work wonders.

From a deep place in his chest, Tyrell sighed, finally put his plate down, and sucked the spices off his fingers. "You having fun?" he asked, dropping back on his elbows to stare up at the open sky.

"Now, I am," Natasha said. "You did this, created this fantastic atmosphere and vibe. Everything before that was forced, unnatural, contrived. But, this . . ."

She sighed, stretched out on her side, and bent her elbow, lifting her head to rest on her palm. "This was pure magic, Tyrell. Thank you."

He dropped down on his side and leaned on his elbow, his eyes roving her face as though it were taking a slow camera pan to capture every facet of it. "No, thank *you*," he said quietly. "I wouldn't have known that this was what I needed, if I hadn't been those other places, first. You've given me perspective, 'Tash."

She picked at a blade of grass, studying it to keep herself from reaching out to touch his face. "I've gained so much perspective around you, till it isn't even funny," she said just above a whisper. "And I keep asking myself, how did that happen . . . when did that happen? How had I gotten so offtrack?"

"Well, you aren't alone in wondering that," he murmured, picking at a blade of grass very close to her hand. "Every day that has gone by, and with every crazy challenge or situation presented, I've been asking myself, why hadn't I seen this before? How could I have been so blind . . . so numb, to what was really important in life?"

They lay there quietly, saying nothing, allowing the chatter and music to blanket them. When their gazes met and locked, it felt as though the dull heat from the faraway fire had crept up the small patch of grass between them and lingered.

"I'll wait the rest of the weeks," he said softly, finding a new blade of grass to torment. "You're so worth the wait, and I've already been waiting my whole life to find someone like you. What's a few more weeks?"

"A very long time," she whispered, needing to tell him the truth.

He nodded and she could see his fingers tremble as he toyed with a blade of grass between them. "Yeah," he said quietly. "But having gotten to know you, and what's important to you . . . and seeing what your brand of magic does to people, I'm not trying to mess that up."

She had to look away and find a new blade of grass to pull from the earth. His words had made her hands shake with the repressed need to touch him. "Maybe my priorities have been screwed up," she said, the heat between them feeling as though it had caught fire to her tank top.

He stared at her, watching her breasts rise and fall beneath the semi-sheer white tank top. Her

skin was covered with a sheen that the fire bronzed
deep red golden orange. Her tiny coffee colored
nipples pouted as she sipped shallow breaths, and
as his gaze traveled down her torso, he watched
her stomach clench at the visual undressing. He
saw the muscles in her thighs contract ever so
slightly, her jeans unable to hide the depth of how
she felt. He returned his gaze to her face slowly,
studying the hard swallow that moved within her
throat. Her lush, barely parted lips breathed out
a stream of sweet, key lime flavored air. Her nostrils flared at the very edges, just a hint of move-
ment. Her gorgeous eyes were nearly shut, her
expression that of desire produced delirium.
Gooseflesh had risen on her arms, making him
know and understand where she was. Lying there,
less than an arm's length from her, the music stoking the ache to touch her sent the jones through
his system.

"Your priorities haven't been screwed up," he finally said, his breathing staggered. "You wanted it
right, by someone who would treat you right—the
whole package. Nothing wrong with wanting what
you deserve."

She stared at him, listening to the way his breathing was now labored. His eyes were almost closed,
his lips remaining parted after he spoke. She allowed herself to indulge in a slow, molten glance
down his body and watched his stomach tense beneath his light blue T-shirt until his thighs con-
tracted when her gaze swept his laden groin. His
hand was flat against the carpet of grass, his fingers
no longer pulling out blades. His palm offered the
earth a slow caress that she could oddly feel as she
watched his hand slowly move back and forth. She

saw the thick muscles in his forearm work beneath his dark skin, the shadows playing havoc with her imagination as he patted the grass, his gaze burning her, not saying a word by saying everything with silent communication.

"Let me give you the whole package, Natasha," he finally murmured. "Everything."

"When?" was all she could say. It came out more as a plea than a question, upon a hoarse whisper. Were it not for a fully loaded camp and people on her job . . .

"You tell me," he said, barely breathing as he spoke. "I don't care about the show, getting busted . . . this is your gig. I'll land on my feet."

Unconsciously, her hand had begun to trace the same lazy pattern on the grass that his was. She watched him study her movements and then give in to closing his eyes.

"I want you so bad right now that it doesn't even make sense."

She allowed her fingers to graze the edges of his and nearly gasped when his hot palm covered hers and then slid away. "I think I'm ready to lose my job tonight," she said, as a shiver of want claimed her.

He opened his eyes, watching her chest rise and fall so fast it almost seemed like she was hyperventilating. It did something to him, to have her react that way without him even touching her. His finger found the soft inside of her bent arm, and he traced the inside of it in a lazy, steady path back and forth. He watched a slight shudder claim her, and watched her nipples strain harder against the fabric. His mouth went dry and he licked his lips in reflex, but couldn't stop touching her. His finger kept the steady rhythm as her partially closed eyes glistened with unshed tears. Even when her hand made a fist against the grass, he couldn't bring himself to part with the butter-smooth skin. Tiny beads of perspiration had formed on her brow, and he'd wanted to kiss away the offending moisture, but her hand covered his, breaking the sensory invasion.

"You have to stop out here," she said.

Her voice was so low, and gravelly, and sexy that it sent a depth charge through his groin.

"I'm sorry," he whispered. "You're right, but . . ."

She shook her head and stared at him, her pretty eyes glittering in the moonlight and firelight. "I haven't made love in years, and there are so many people around, and . . ."

He nodded and withdrew his hand. "I'ma say this one time. Okay?"

She nodded and closed her eyes.

"When those boys go down the hill, I'ma be in that truck. My excuse is gonna be, I had to be hospitable and pay them in full for going over the top with this gig—and I think that'll suffice. I need a two-way and your cell number. I'ma get a room at the closest, most direct hotel, motel, or whatever I can find. You can tell your staff whatever you like, just be there, before we both lose our minds."

She watched him sit up slowly with effort, stare at the fire for a moment, his profile sculpted by the light of it. He stood in one deft motion, went to the coolers and got a beer, downed it, then began walking toward the band. It was written all over his face. The man was on a mission. Stephanie was by a tree engaged in conversation, her gaze discreetly averted. The need to break camp and run shot adrenaline through her. She got up fast, found paper and a pen and jotted down her cell number.

There was a sense of urgency propelling her forward as she walked up to Stephanie, and pulled her away from her discussion.

"I need your cell for a little while," Natasha said, nearly out of breath.

"Okay . . . everything all right?" Stephanie asked, walking away from the group with Natasha.

Natasha shook her head no. "I'm going into town for a while, and need your cell." Her gaze went to Tyrell, and returned to Stephanie's smile without shame. "I have to get out of here, you understand? I need to be out on the DL, and—"

"Done," Stephanie said. "You have to go make arrangements for our debark tomorrow down on the ship, and with all the passenger changes in this era of heightened security, you can't wait to review the manifests, or something like that." Stephanie handed her the cell phone that had been clipped to her waistband. "Good choice, have fun, and I'll see ya in the morning."

Chapter 20

She wasn't sure if it was the silent, CIA secret-level-type cell phone and number hand-off, or driving down pitch-black roads on the wrong side of the street, that was making her heart almost thud out of her chest. Perhaps it was the incredibly exhilarating aspect of stepping by prone staff members who hadn't a clue as the band played on, or watching Tyrell from afar as he casually made up a ruse, got everyone to buy it, and begged off any need for a team member to ride shotgun with him. Or maybe it was just the prospect of being with this man that she wanted so bad that had her scared to death.

She pulled up to the small motel and sighed. Instead of mission-accomplished calm relaxing her, however, a second wave of panic shot through her. She stared at the place Tyrell had discovered, becoming both excited and intrigued by the range of his resourcefulness. Pink and whitewashed walls that were covered with vines and fragrant flowers greeted her. If she'd been in trouble, she couldn't have told a soul where the heck she was. All she knew was that she had to park her vehicle and knock on the right door.

* * *

What had he been thinking to allow her to venture out in no-man's-land, in a foreign country known for roadside dangers, on a crazy mission like this? Tyrell slapped his forehead and groaned. God forgive him, he'd been focused on one thing, and if anything happened to this woman . . .

He snatched the cell phone she'd given him from his waist and punched in the number he already knew by heart. The wait for her had seemed like an eternity. Please, God, let her be all right. He didn't even have a way to go get her, didn't know the way back to camp; this was raggedy as all get out. Two rings, c'mon, baby, pick up the phone.

When he heard Natasha's voice, he slumped against the wall.

"Thought I'd changed my mind?"

He laughed, but it wasn't funny. "Naw, I was worried about you, girl. The roads are crazy, it's dark . . . I should've—"

"Yeah, I thought about that as I was driving on the wrong side of the road in pitch-blackness."

"You made the right decision to turn back. You safe?" Total disappointment fused with relief that she was all right made him close his eyes.

"Yeah, I'm safe, and I think I made the right decision."

"Okay," he said, glancing around the room at the queen-size bed in despair. "In the morning, I'll hop a ride to the boat in time to make it. If I get jammed up, I'll say the truck broke down and the young boy ditched me at a local motel. Cool?"

She laughed. He wanted her so bad it was as though he could hear her voice in stereo.

"How about if I drive you?"

"Too risky. Attempting this was crazy, as it was."

"Open the door, man."

He sighed. "Baby, my emotions are open, I'm not blocking you out or playing games. Damn, I wish you were here."

"Then open the door."

He sat down hard in the chair by the dresser, his voice pleading with her. "I don't know what you're asking me right now," he said, his voice escalating with frustration. "I'm as wide open as a man can get—I'm sitting here, no ID on me, no money, in freakin' Jamaica with a pocket of condoms . . . in a room by myself, strung out like a junky, waiting on a woman I'm crazy about to come, who can't now, and—"

"Tyrell, would you just open up and let me in, I'm serious."

"Open what!" he shouted, unable to contain himself. He was definitely losing his mind. He was hearing her laughter in stereo for sure. He shot out of the chair and began pacing. He hadn't meant to yell, but his nerves had frayed and snapped. "Natasha," he said, forcing himself to stop walking and calm down. "Baby, explain it to me, I'm sorry, c'mon. This situation is jacked and stressing us both out."

"Open the motel door, please," she said, giggling.

He froze, and then bolted for the door, clumsily managing the locks on the flimsy structure. It took a second for his brain to sync up with his vision. But she was truly standing there, a cell phone pressed to her ear, a wide smile on her face. He watched her close the cell phone with a contented sigh and shove it into her pocket. He backed away from the door to allow her to come in and he closed it without looking at it, watching her glance around the environment. So much tension had twisted around his spinal column that his shoulder blades hurt.

"This okay?" he asked, not sure how to read her bemused expression.

"Less than an hour ago, the grass outside would have been fine. What do you think?"

Her warm smile wiped away all his apprehension as she filled his arms and took his mouth, her tongue prodding, seeking, finding his. He'd had it in his mind to take things slowly, if he ever got this far with her. Had it all planed out, had run it through his mind in fantasy so many times. But the separation, and having to wait, now having to sneak, made the gentle embrace become frenetic. The only thing that absolved his conscience was that she was stripping off her clothes as fast as he was shedding his.

When she fused against him like hot wax, he couldn't hold back the moan.

"Put one on, right now," she gasped, sweeping his pants off the floor and shoving them toward him. "Let's not even play with this."

She didn't have to tell him twice.

She'd thought she'd wanted a slow dissolve of her senses. But her body had other plans. She couldn't touch enough of him fast enough, hard enough, or pull him into her quickly enough. She heard her voice bounce off the walls as he lifted her up and her legs encircled his waist, and it became shrill as he entered her while walking her toward the bed. She didn't care that they'd fallen hard and lopsided, or that she sounded like a woman being murdered. Anonymity was a gift; she didn't know a soul in this sleepy, hideaway refuge. All she knew was that this man was killing her hard, and long, and fast, till tears streamed down the sides of her face.

Years stripped away as he stripped a gear within her. Time was of no consequence, even though it was immediately of the essence. Sweat rolled down his back and her hand followed it like it was chasing the tide. Her palm found the deep valley of his spine, coaxing his repeated return to her with all the forces of nature he could bring. His voice thundered against the side of her neck, sending shockwaves through her core. She could feel herself drowning in pleasure so profound that she called out his name for help, the syllables of it becoming strangled, broken by gasps, a stuttering wail, the snap jerk of her head, and the seizure that took her under.

It was when she'd called out his name that he'd lost all perspective. It was right then and there that he knew it was all over. Everything he'd ever needed and wanted was moving beneath him with the force of the sea . . . wet, deep, dark and mysterious, more powerful than anything manmade. He couldn't get enough air to enter his lungs, nor could he slow his climb on the tidal wave she'd produced within. Out of nowhere it rose, spiked, crested and plundered him. He lay broken against her soft, damp shore, rivulets of sweat coursing down his face, mixing with tears, the salt stinging his nose.

Panting from the exertion, he tried to push up from her and give her room to breathe. But his arms trembled as he tried to shift his weight. He just hoped that she wouldn't be angry.

She didn't even have to open her eyes to know he

was staring at her. She couldn't even speak as small riptides of pleasure still swirled inside her womb. All she could do was pat his hot face and breathe through her mouth. Why were men so silly, she wondered.

"'Tash, listen," he murmured, kissing her forehead. "I—"

She blindly put her finger to his lips, savoring just hearing him breathe. "Oh, my God . . ."

She felt him instantly relax and sink against her, his breathing beginning to normalize as his pulse slowed. "Have you any idea . . ."

She felt him chuckle before she heard his deep, warm voice push past his lips.

"Have you any idea?" he asked on a slow drawl.

She shook her head, no, and smiled with her eyes still closed.

"I was supposed to give you the whole package . . . I think you mighta got gypped, girl."

"Gypped?' she said, chuckling low and softly. "Are you crazy?"

"Yeah," he murmured, kissing her neck, "about you."

"If I got cheated, shoot, I'm sckurred of the whole package."

He laughed slow and easy, his voice reverberating through her bones, slowly making her body come alive again.

"I was supposed to do this long, and slow," he whispered, brushing her mouth with a kiss and allowing his mouth to slide down her chest to capture a nipple.

The sensation made her shiver and produced a pang that made her arch. "You've been doing this long and slow," she said on a gasp. "Weeks of foreplay," she murmured as his hands slid under her hip and caressed it. "Sending me to bed every night aching for you till I couldn't sleep."

"For real?" he whispered, the tone of his voice telling her that the confession had pleased him as well as turned him on.

She nodded and slid her hand between their bellies, allowing it to inch down her torso and stop where he was lodged. "A couple of nights," she sighed, "especially that time when we almost did . . . I needed to feel you so badly I almost gave in to a poor substitute."

Her truth was so volatile and so real that it sent a shudder through him. He could just imagine it, and also remembered the encounter clear as day, as her hand worked against his base, sliding back and forth along her swollen, slick surface.

"You should have called me," he said, his voice husky with rekindled desire. "Any time it gets like that," he said, his body responding, moving with her hand, "you call me, hear?"

"I couldn't at the time," she murmured, her hand cupping her breast. "Remember?"

"Yeah . . . how could I forget?"

He stared down at her, as she opened her eyes and they drank him in. He was moving against what felt like satin, and knew he had to stop and change the barrier between them. But he couldn't get up as her finger traced a dark brown nipple and her eyes slid closed. He'd never been with a woman who was so open in his life. It was a gift that he made a vow not to squander as he replaced her finger within his lips. When she arched into the suckle, he took his time, learning her hot spots. He wanted to get each one imprinted in his brain, just so long as he could make her respond like this.

When he withdrew from her, she squeezed her thighs together, agony in her gorgeous eyes. He nodded and truly understood, cupping the ache, massaging it slowly, whispering his promise to make it stop hurting in a little while.

"If I had some ice, I'd numb it," he said, chuckling softly, kissing her as his fingers delighted in exploring her terrain. He loved the expression on her face as he slowly discovered her. "It's been years for me, too. Out there on the grass . . . We have a lot to try together."

Her hand stopped his words; it burned white-hot where it landed.

"I wanted you to get on top of me right then," she said, sending a warm shard of air into his ear. "But I guess we have to be patient, we have time."

"On the beach . . ."

"Yeah," she murmured. "Then, too . . . and just looking at you had made me wet."

He nodded; speaking becoming impossible.

"Why don't you go put another one on?"

He complied without comment, beyond words.

The plan seemed like it had gone off without a hitch. Very early in the morning, it was hard to separate, but finally they had to give in or get busted. Although neither of them was sure that they really cared, they'd decided to try to at least keep up appearances for the moment. It was so simple. She'd drive him into town; he'd hop a cab, and return to the yacht like that. She'd drive up before him and get her hips on the boat before the teams returned.

This way, no matter who was looking, they weren't coming back to the ship together.

Natasha glanced at her cell phone and the one Stephanie had given Tyrell. Devon had called ten times that morning, if once. She'd just chalk it up to low batteries, sleeping heavily, whatever. At the moment she was too tired and happy to care.

"Okay," Tyrell said, giving her a long, slow kiss as he hopped out of her vehicle. "Stay cool, just stroll in there like everything is everything. Don't worry about the messages. I'll tell Stephanie the truth—I didn't have her code, couldn't check her phone for Devon's calls, and shouldn't be doing that anyway, which is why I turned it off and went to sleep."

"Roger that," Natasha said, giggling as she gave him a thumbs-up. She blew him a kiss. "Be safe. I'll see you on the ship in a little while."

Her life was changing, pure joy filtered through her. She was in paradise, and had almost missed all that the good Lord had to offer! She kept her eyes on the road, merrily humming to herself, and being extremely cautious not to have a collision. The only thing that calmed her about driving in Jamaica was that it was still so early that there wasn't a lot of traffic on the road.

She giggled as she thought about the motel clerk's expression when Tyrell checked out. Ty had said the man raised one eyebrow, his voice serious and laden with a bit of British accent colored with Jamaican, and asked, "We take it you enjoyed your stay, sir?"

Natasha covered her mouth with one hand and laughed. Too crazy!

As she neared the docks, panic made her drive faster than was advisable. The full team with cameras was assembled in front of the ship she was supposed to already be on. Ooops. But she knew the itinerary by heart!

Bringing the Jeep to a screeching halt, she jumped out of it, immediately aware that she had the same clothes on as she did the night before. So, even if she was gonna lie and say she'd been on the boat but had left to run an errand, the story was flawed.

Devon immediately rushed toward her, as did Stephanie. Natasha froze.

"We have a real crisis," Devon said, his voice strained. "Where the hell have you been!"

"'Tash, we have a double drop out," Stephanie said, pulling her farther away from the crowd and trying to body block Devon. "We can worry about that later—"

"But I've called her twenty times, your phone, her phone, trying to—"

"Devon, not now!" Stephanie shouted, holding Natasha's arm.

"Talk to me, people. Somebody explain what's—"

"They were in the hammock, oh, my God," Devon wailed. "The poor kids—"

"Who died?" Natasha gasped, ready to fail. "An accident in the hammock—too much booze, the physical exertion, a heart attack, oh, Jesus!"

"No, boo," Devon said, shaking Natasha like a madman. "Rodriguez and Vera lost their minds and were in a hammock—Paul was up early, panning the after party devastation, he wasn't trying to get it on tape! Paul has that much of a heart, you can tell those two are destiny, but—"

"Oh, no . . . not them . . . they're so nice!"

Natasha closed her eyes, willing herself not to run from the docks shrieking.

"But there's more," Stephanie said. "Boss, I wish you were sitting down."

Natasha's eyes flew open and Devon covered his.

"Joe, from St. Louis, got tight with the boys in the band . . . and he's screwed. Good thing he's an entrepreneur, but it could hurt his business."

"What happened? He's been abducted and held ransom for his winnings? Talk to me!" Natasha yelled, her ears ringing.

"Worse," Devon said on a dramatic gasp. "He's high as a freaking kite—was smoking ganja, mon! Smoking Jamaican trees, pot, weed, whatever, and with the food, heat, exertion, liquor, his dumb ass is in the hospital!"

Natasha stared at Devon and Stephanie, unable to speak.

"He'll be all right, boss lady, but needless to say, one of the clauses in the show is that the contestants must remain drug free. It's in our insurance riders, and with the liability we have for their health and safety . . ."

Natasha closed her eyes and waved her hand. "Nathan will have a coronary. I know."

"Oh, but there's more," Devon said, one hand on his hip and the back of the other pressed to his forehead. "I cannot even speak. Stephanie, I'm so upset, I cannot even speak!"

"Oh, God . . ." Natasha looked at Stephanie, wondering if she were being sentenced for her crimes against humanity by the powers of heaven. This was her show, and all the pain she'd inflicted by her crazy rules had erupted in one night—the one night she, herself, was embroiled in her own scandal.

"Samuel Hartman just proposed on air to Lillian Reed," Stephanie said flatly. "Apparently, after the bike race, with the music, whatever," she said, her tone blasé and nasal as she stated the facts without theatrics, "they escaped into the woods with a roll blanket, yada, yada, yada, the rest is history. They don't care about the money, just wanna plan their wedding—besides, her period never came on."

"What . . ." Natasha asked on a slow, steady breath.

"Those two had a hot, stand up encounter in the ladies' room at the casino. Camera guys let it ride when they saw dude coming out of the wrong door red-faced . . . figured he, like them, was three sheets to the wind and had gone in there by accident." Stephanie sighed. "It's always the quiet ones."

Stephanie and Natasha shared a knowing glance.

"The show is ruined," Devon lamented. "We don't have a show! We only have Tyrell, Nelson, and Linda left! We have five more episodes to go . . . even with creative editing, stretching—"

"Air it," Natasha said flatly, and began walking away.

Devon ran behind her, Stephanie on his heels.

"Are you insane! Air it?" Incredulous, he stopped walking, looked at Stephanie, and began skip running behind Natasha again.

"Controversy sells, ask, Nathan. According to the faxes and E-mail we've received, this is the number one summer show. Stretch out the segments until Nelson and Linda are the last ones standing. That's all. I have to—"

"But what about Tyrell?" Devon screeched. "Why

are you talking as though he isn't still in this game?"
Devon stretched out his hands toward Stephanie.
"He's our show franchise. What're you thinking!"

"She's not," Stephanie said quickly, giving Devon
the nonverbal *kill it* signal by running her hand
horizontally across her throat. "She's having a nervous breakdown, but will recover as soon as her car
note and rent come to mind," Stephanie shouted,
grabbing Natasha by the arm to keep her from
walking away further.

"I have to talk to him," Natasha said quietly. "This
is a travesty."

"He doesn't have to drop this bomb on them
today, and there's a way to do this very discreetly."

Guilt stabbed Natasha in her heart. She had to
get to Tyrell. He had to come clean, even if that
meant her career was in the toilet. There was no
way that she could live with herself knowing that
Mike Quazar, Kimberly and Anthony, Michelle and
Jason, now Vera and Tony, or Lillian and Sam had
been forced off or self-selected off the show for
doing what had happened to her. They fell in love,
and had paid the dear price of having their intimate encounter. If she had to pay, too, so be it. For
it was far better for this to all come out as a clean
self-confession, than to live her life worrying about
the possibility of a little old man in a Jamaican bun-
galow somewhere, one day turning and selling hidden videos or outrageous audiotapes of her and
Tyrell to a tabloid. Never happen.

Natasha shook her head. "We'll save the execs
money by stopping the show with a default winning
couple. The locations we'd burn crew and location
expenses with, might help keep some of the staff,
which would normally go down with the ship when

a show cancels, employed. We'll pitch the love blew everybody's mind, angle, let the ratings go through the roof, and let the chips fall where they may." She stared at Stephanie and then gently moved a stray wisp of hair away from her damp forehead. "You don't have to be exposed. I'm just telling you what I know I have to do."

Stephanie sighed and hugged Natasha. "All for one and one for all." She pulled back and sniffed hard, her gaze tender. "'Tash, if this ship sinks, we're with you captain. It was a wild ride."

Natasha smiled. "Think about it, first." She nodded toward an approaching cab. "Gotta go. Keep Devon from jumping into the marina."

He knew the moment he spotted Natasha and the commotion at the docks that something had gone terribly wrong. Natasha's normally vibrant complexion was ashen, and that was definitely not the way he'd left her. She walked toward him so lifelessly, as though with each step she was carrying an anvil on her shoulders. He paid the cabbie fast, and jumped out, trying to be rational and not run in her direction.

"Everything cool?" he asked as soon as he was within her earshot.

She shook her head no, sighed, and then calmly told him what he could hardly believe. Numb, it took a moment for all that she'd said to register. Her question was simple, and he saw that she made no demands, but in his soul he knew that if he chose unwisely, she'd walk—and that would be the end of his real dream come true.

"What do you want to do?" She looked at the boats and not at him.

He pulled her into his arms and kissed her long and slow, and hard, praying the cameras were on them. "Tell the truth," he murmured. "What the heck? We'd never make it to St. Lucia without getting busted, anyway."

She could feel her body being pushed and shoved as paparazzi crushed them, microphones nudged her, but she kept kissing her prize. When she looked up she saw Nelson and Linda hugging and crying, but it wasn't a joyful occasion for them. Elbowing through the mayhem, Linda found her and barreled into her arms.

"Oh, girl, you ain't hafta go out like that!" Linda wailed.

Nelson gave Tyrell a bear hug. "Man, I ain't wanna win like this."

"It's cool," Tyrell said as a hundred flashbulbs went off. "I won, big time. I'm unemployed, true, but hey—I always land on my feet."

"We couldn't hang," Natasha said, laughing through the tears, hugging Linda harder. "You deserve it, lady. Kiss that hard knock life drama goodbye!"

Stephanie tapped Linda on the shoulder. "Yeah, she did, that's why me and Mike Quazar are coming out of the closet." She held up her cell phone to the cameras. "I'm getting married!"

Everybody laughed as a once crestfallen Tony and Vera joined the huddle.

"Yo, dawg, damn, you went out with style," Rodriguez said, laughing. "My thing was a little raggedy, but hey—"

"But it was goood, baby," Vera said, snuggling against him.

"You should do a show after this one gets torched off the air and then do a couples reunion show," Devon yelled over the crowd, making the cameras follow him like a school of sharks.

"My phone is vibrating," Natasha said.

"It's Nathan," Stephanie yelled over the hubbub.

"Tell him she's unemployed, too," Tyrell hollered, laughing. "Tell him she's been signed to a permanent contract with a hot, new record label out of Atlanta."

They both laughed as the cameras rushed them again, setting off a new round of shutters. He kissed her again, slowly, making the reporters wait.

"Did you just propose to me, or am I reading too much into the word contract?"

"You heard me, right, girl. I'm just keepin' it real."

Epilogue

One month later, in St. Lucia . . .

"Camille, how many times do I have to tell you, I don't want to work for Nathan Greenberg anymore? I'm not even sure I want to deal with network television again."

Camille sat across the table from Tyrell and Natasha, her glance going to the other couples lounging on the deck, for support. "He wants you to do the reunion show, you've got four networks bidding on both you guys as a package deal. You'd be on-air talent, which is real different than producing behind the scenes." She looked at Tyrell. "I know your label is hot right now, the group who did the casino show is off the charts, as is that reggae group you signed in Jamaica, but you guys could make a fortune."

"Think about it, 'Tash," Stephanie said, glancing at her fiancé.

"Money is money, as long as you guys get to travel together," Quazar said with a shrug. "And as long as you're happy in the process."

"That's what I'm afraid of," Natasha murmured.

"I don't want to start chasing the brass ring again and ever lose perspective. Finding this balance and happiness was too hard-won."

"Think about it," Devon urged. "As hot on-air talent, Nathan actually has to kiss your butt." He paused, stood and bent over, making them laugh. "The Internet polls and votes went through the roof during the show. The calls almost shut down the telephone systems. The hot romances that came out of a simple game show have created a tidal wave of copycat shows for the fall. That gives you bargaining power, love. You're bankable as an audience draw." Devon extended his arms and pretended to be surfing. "Ride the wave while it's hot, then let your career coast into the shore."

"Dude," Sam said, giving Lillian a sly smile as he stood up next to Devon and also mimicked riding an invisible wave on the villa deck, "ride in style— righteous."

"Tell her," Lillian said, raising a ginger ale. "Surf's up!"

They laughed as Linda buzzed around the kitchen of her newly acquired summer home to produce another tray of fresh fruit for the group to nosh on while waiting on dinner. "Me and Nelson are in for the reunion, whatever you decide. Six months here, six months on the East Coast, both our businesses booming . . . hey, a life-changing event makes you think differently."

"Whatever you wanna do, baby," Tyrell said. "You know me, I land on my feet."

"That's because you go with the flow, *hombre*," Rodriguez said, jumping up to ride the invisible wave with Sam and Devon.

"My baby can ride, too, trust me," Vera said, making everyone burst out laughing again.

Jorgette sucked her teeth with a smile, "Jermaine, tell 'Tash to stop trippin'. My girl has been like that since the beginning of time—takes forever to make a decision with her crazy Libra self." Jorgette shook her head. "Tyrell, I don't know how you stand it."

Tyrell winked at Natasha, watching her begin to get defensive. "Yeah, y'all . . . she takes a looong time to make a decision . . . strings a brother out, makes him lose his mind, then blows his game on national TV. So, I'ma chill and wait for her to get comfortable with the concept of riding the wave." He dropped his voice low and sexy, playing around. "Any time you wanna ride, it, lemme know, hear?"

Natasha swatted him away as everyone laughed. "Bernard, tell your boy not to be putting all our business in the street!"

"My name's bennit and I ain't in-it," Bernard said, laughing as he came to the table with two pitchers of frozen strawberry daiquiris.

"Uh, I hate to be the one to point out that your business is beyond the street, 'Tash," Jason said with a chuckle. "I think it circled the globe on satellite a couple of times, already."

"Fear is over," Michelle said with a bright smile. "'Tash, your career is rising with the bullet—you don't have to think about the long climb up, or falling. You guys can send money home, help your parents, do whatever, but keep the naysayers at a distance. You don't have to keep hearing those old nagging voices planted there or doubts that tell you about what you can't do—just because their lives didn't offer the same opportunities. Banish those voices. *You can.* And it's all right to know that you can."

Natasha looked at the wonderful group that had formed their own bond and impromptu reunion. Out of what had seemed like a disaster, the silver lining was as magnificent as the many rings around Saturn. It took a therapist, the shy and reserved Michelle, to make it all sink in. Her gaze went to Tyrell, a man patient beyond measure, and she smiled.

"Let's go for it," she said to him quietly.

He glanced around sheepishly and leaned in toward her. "Now, right here?"

The deck erupted with a roar of mirth.

She pushed him away with a kiss and laughed. "The shows!"

"Oh, see, I was still stuck on riding the wave . . . you have to get specific and let a brother really know what's on your mind."

Look For These Other
Dafina Novels